W9-BXT-156

British Manor Murder

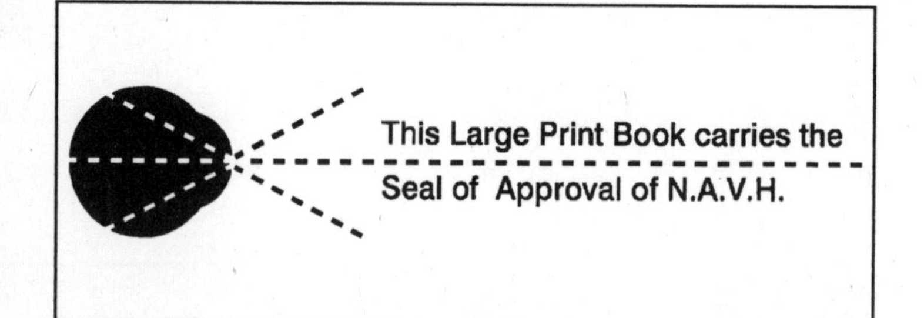
This Large Print Book carries the
Seal of Approval of N.A.V.H.

A LUCY STONE MYSTERY

BRITISH MANOR MURDER

LESLIE MEIER

THORNDIKE PRESS
A part of Gale, Cengage Learning

Farmington Hills, Mich • San Francisco • New York • Waterville, Maine
Meriden, Conn • Mason, Ohio • Chicago

GALE
CENGAGE Learning

Thorndike Press® Large Print Mystery.
The text of this Large Print edition is unabridged.
Other aspects of the book may vary from the original edition.
Set in 16 pt. Plantin.

LIBRARY OF CONGRESS CATALOGING-IN-PUBLICATION DATA

Names: Meier, Leslie, author.
Title: British Manor murder / Leslie Meier.
Description: Large print edition. | Waterville, Maine : Thorndike Press, 2016. | Series: A Lucy Stone mystery | Series: Thorndike Press large print mystery
Identifiers: LCCN 2016036050 | ISBN 9781410492456 (hardback) | ISBN 1410492451 (hardcover)
Subjects: LCSH: Stone, Lucy (Fictitious character)—Fiction. | Women detectives—Fiction. | Murder—Investigation—Fiction. | Large type books. | BISAC: FICTION / Mystery & Detective / Women Sleuths. | GSAFD: Mystery fiction.
Classification: LCC PS3563.E3455 B75 2016 | DDC 813/.54—dc23
LC record available at https://lccn.loc.gov/2016036050

Published in 2016 by arrangement with Kensington Books, an imprint of Kensington Publishing Corp.

Printed in Mexico
1 2 3 4 5 6 7 20 19 18 17 16

For Stella Rose

Chapter One

"If only they'd send a ransom note," wailed Lucy Stone, pulling her old gray cardigan tighter across her chest. "Then at least we'd have a chance of getting Patrick back."

Looking out the kitchen window this early March morning she saw the same wintry scene she'd been staring at since Christmas: an endless expanse of snow several feet deep, punctuated here and there with bare black branches. There was a complete absence of color, just like her life since her five-year-old grandson Patrick had been snatched away from her.

"He wasn't kidnapped, Lucy," reminded her husband Bill. "He's with his parents."

"In Alaska," replied Lucy, making it sound as if Alaska was located on the moon.

Actually, she thought to herself, the moon might be closer to the little Maine town of Tinker's Cove than Alaska, which seemed impossibly far away.

"Toby's building his career," said Bill, referring to his son, Patrick's father. "He has to go where there's work and this was too good to pass up — a full-time government job in fisheries management . . . with excellent benefits."

Lucy gazed at Bill, her husband of more than twenty years. He looked the same as always, tall and fit, dressed in the working man's winter uniform of plaid flannel shirt, lined jeans, and sturdy work boots, but now his beard was frosted with gray. As usual, he was being entirely reasonable.

"I know," she admitted, "but I don't see why they had to take Patrick. They left him with us when they went to Haiti," she said, getting to the crux of the problem. Patrick had lived with his grandparents for nearly four months before Christmas, while his parents, Toby and Molly, had gone to Haiti where Toby completed a graduate-level study of fish farming practices. Lucy had adored spending time with her only grandchild, reliving the days when she was a young mother herself.

"Alaska is not Haiti," said Bill.

"It's practically the frontier," grumbled Lucy. "And all this moving around is very disruptive for a child. Kids need stability. They need to be in one place."

"He's in the right place. With his parents."

Lucy did not like hearing this, even if it was the truth, and was quick to retaliate. "They're not Patriots fans in Alaska," she said, naming New England's beloved football team. "Patrick's probably a Seahawks fan by now."

Bill looked stunned, hearing this heresy spoken. "Toby would never let that happen."

Lucy raised her eyebrows. "It's hard to resist group pressure. He's probably already got a Seahawks hat or jersey." She paused, then went for the jugular. Invoking the name of the Patriots' quarterback, she said, "He probably doesn't even remember Tom Brady."

This didn't get the reaction from Bill that Lucy expected. Instead of fussing and fuming, he sat down opposite her at the round golden oak table. "I know you're joking, Lucy, but the truth is you really haven't been yourself since Patrick left." He reached across the table and took her hands in his. "This can't go on, Lucy. You've got to pull yourself together. You've got to think of Sara and Zoe," he said, naming their two daughters who were still at home. Their oldest daughter, Elizabeth, like her brother Toby, had already flown the nest; she was living in

Paris and working at the tony Cavendish Hotel there.

Lucy thought guiltily of Zoe, who was in her senior year of high school, and was waiting anxiously for the college acceptance — or rejection — letters that should arrive any day now. Zoe prided herself on being independent and had written the essays all by herself, refusing help from her parents, but Lucy wondered uneasily if she should have insisted on getting more involved. The truth was that she took Zoe at her word that it was all under control, simply because she hadn't felt like arguing after working all day as a reporter for the local weekly newspaper, the *Pennysaver.*

As for Sara, who was a student at nearby Winchester College, well, Lucy had to admit she didn't even know what courses Sara was taking this term or if she was still dating Hank, someone she had met at the college dive club. She was rarely home these days. Lucy assumed she was deeply involved in college life, but she hadn't taken the trouble to find that out, either.

Lucy was uneasily aware that she hadn't been much of a mother lately or even much of a wife, and the worst of it was that she didn't care. She was operating on automatic. She dragged herself out of bed in the morning when the alarm rang, drank her coffee, and ate her oatmeal. Then she drove to work, where she dutifully put in her time but found the work she used to enjoy so much as a part-time reporter and feature writer had become merely tedious. The worst part of the day came later, after she went home and cooked supper, cleaned up the kitchen, and sat herself down in front of the TV. The shows came and went, but she couldn't say what she was watching. She was only waiting until it was time to go to bed, and bedtime seemed to come a bit earlier every night.

"I'm sorry," she said, brushing away a tear. "I'm just so sad. I miss Patrick."

"Don't cry," said Bill. "There's been enough crying. Too much crying."

"I'm sorry," sobbed Lucy as he slid the tissue box across the table to her. She pulled out a handful and wiped her face, giving him a weak smile. "I'm going to try harder. I really am."

"Good," said Bill, exhaling a big sigh and standing up. "Don't forget. It's coffee-klatch Thursday."

Lucy propped her chin on her hand. "I don't know . . ." she began, thinking that she'd have to comb her hair and get dressed and put on some lipstick. Then there were the boots and jacket and scarf and hat and gloves she'd have to wear. And she'd have to brush the two or three inches of new snow that had fallen during the night off the car. It all seemed so hard. She had the morning off because Thursday was the day the *Pennysaver* came out. Since she wasn't needed at the office she could go back to bed, which was what she was planning to do as soon as Bill left for work.

"C'mon, Lucy. You promised to try harder," he said, reading her mind. "I'm not leaving until I see you washed and dressed and in the car. You better hurry or you'll be late," he added, glancing at the clock. "I'll clear the snow off your car while you get ready. Is that a deal?"

Lucy glowered at him, then pressed her hands on the table and stood up. "Deal," she muttered, narrowing her eyes.

Lucy was late but only by a few minutes when she got to Jake's Donut Shack and found her three friends already seated at their usual table. They had first met as young mothers, bumping into each other frequently at school and sports events, but as their kids grew older and those encounters became fewer, they agreed to meet every Thursday for breakfast. They'd kept up the tradition for years, celebrating the good times and supporting each other through the bad.

"Hi, Lucy," said Pam Stillings, welcoming her. Pam had not only retained the ponytail and colorful poncho she'd worn as a teen, but she'd also retained the enthusiasm and positive outlook she'd exhibited as a college cheerleader. It was her unshakable optimism that helped explain her success as the wife of a small town newspaper editor in a time of rising expenses, dwindling subscribers, and increased competition for advertisers. Her husband Ted was Lucy's boss.

"How are you doing?" asked Rachel Goodman as Lucy sat down but neglected to remove her parka. Rachel's dark eyes were full of concern as she put one hand on Lucy's shoulder and with the other gave Lucy's zipper a tug; she was a psych major in college and never got over it. Her husband Bob had a busy law practice in town.

Taking the hint, Lucy unzipped her parka and removed her hat and gloves, dropping them on the table.

"They're still having winter clearance sales at the outlet mall," said Sue Finch, eyeing Lucy's tired winter gear. "I saw some cute hats and scarves at fifty percent off in that ski shop." Sue was the group's fashionista, always smartly turned out despite her occasional stints as a substitute teacher at Little Prodigies, the childcare center she owned in partnership with Chris Cashman. Sue's husband Sid owned a custom closet company, which he claimed he'd had to do just to keep up with Sue's ever-expanding wardrobe.

"I'm doing okay," said Lucy. "We Skyped last night and Patrick was so cute. He said —" She stopped abruptly, choking up.

"What did he say?" asked Rachel as the three friends exchanged concerned glances.

Lucy sniffed. Taking the tissue Sue offered, she wiped her eyes. "He said he missed reading stories with me."

"Skype is so amazing," said Pam. "You could read stories to him on it."

"It's not the same without the physical contact," said Lucy. "I really miss snuggling with him. Who knows? Next time I see him he may be too big for cuddles. They grow up so fast."

"Let's order," said Sue, waving over Norine, the waitress. "I'm beginning to get the shakes."

"What do you mean? The shakes? You never eat anything," said Pam.

"I need more coffee," said Sue, indicating her empty mug.

"The usual for everybody?" inquired Norine, filling their mugs. "Black coffee for Sue, granola and yogurt for Pam, a sunshine muffin for Rachel, and hash and eggs for Lucy."

"Just coffee for me," said Lucy, reversing years of Thursday breakfast choices with a sigh. "I can't face a big plate of eggs this morning."

Norine cocked her head. "You sure?"

"Maybe some toast," said Lucy.

"Okay," said Norine, sounding rather doubtful.

When she'd gone, Rachel glanced at the others and, getting encouraging nods, plunged right in. "Lucy, we know how much you miss Patrick, but we really think you need to get some . . . um . . . help."

Somewhat stunned, Lucy realized this was something her friends had discussed and agreed upon.

"We think you're in danger of slipping into a serious depression," continued Rachel.

"Just because I don't want a greasy meal this morning doesn't mean I'm depressed," said Lucy, protesting. "Maybe I'm not hungry."

"You haven't been yourself lately," said Pam. "Even Ted has noticed."

"She's right," said Sue, chiming in. "When

was the last time you washed and styled your hair? Or put on a lick of lipstick?"

"I guess I forgot this morning," said Lucy. "I was tired. Really tired."

"Tiredness is a symptom of depression," said Rachel.

"Or of being busy," countered Lucy.

"You don't need to get defensive," said Rachel. "We want to help you."

"You can beat this," said Pam. "For one thing, you could try my yoga class. We work to realign our chakras and restore the proper mind-body-spirit connection. A lot of people find it very helpful and I have some openings in my six AM Monday-Wednesday-Friday class."

"I don't think so," said Lucy. "I'm not very coordinated."

"You don't have to be athletic to enjoy yoga," insisted Pam. "It's not competitive. That is not the point at all. The poses are very adaptable. I have quite a few students with physical handicaps. That's the great thing about yoga — you do what you're comfortable with. You get to know your body."

"My body likes to lie down," said Lucy, getting a chuckle from the group.

"We do that!" exclaimed Pam. "At the end of the session, there's breathing. Everybody lies on their mats and some people even fall asleep."

"I don't think I need a class to fall asleep," said Lucy with a big yawn. "I can do that all on my own."

"Yoga is definitely one approach you can use to combat depression," said Rachel, "but based on what you're saying, especially about being tired all the time and wanting to sleep so much, I think you could really do with some therapy."

"Therapy?" exclaimed Lucy. "You think I'm crazy?"

"Crazy is such a loaded word," said Rachel. "Think of mental health as a sort of spectrum. One end is bright and sunny and happy and the other end is dark and disorganized and troubled, with lots of various shades in between. We all travel back and forth along this spectrum during our lifetimes, depending on many factors. The teens, for example, tend to be rather a difficult time for most, and oddly enough, recent research seems to show that old age is actually a pretty happy time for most."

"So give me a few more years," said Lucy, looking up as Norine arrived with their orders.

"Normally, I'd say there's nothing wrong with Lucy that some shopping wouldn't cure," said Sue, taking a sip of coffee, "but this time I think something rather more drastic is called for."

"Not a makeover," said Lucy, frowning at the plate of buttery toast triangles that Norine had plopped down in front of her.

"They won't bite," said Norine, adding a big sniff for emphasis.

"Not a makeover," said Sue, giving her a once over. "But come to think of it, that's not a bad idea. No, I have something else in mind. A change of scene. Big time."

"Not Florida," said Lucy, naming the usual winter break destination. She picked up one of the toast triangles and took a small bite.

"Why not?" asked Pam. "Florida is great. It's warm and sunny and there are all those theme parks and spring training baseball games."

"One word," said Lucy. "Alligators."

"Ah, interesting," said Rachel, sounding like a comical impersonation of a Freudian analyst. "Alligators can summon up primal fears from the subconscious, reminding us of the monsters we feared in childhood."

"Except the monsters weren't real and alligators are," said Lucy, opening the little plastic packet of marmalade and spreading it on her toast.

"Well there are no alligators where I'm going," said Sue. "I've been invited by Perry —"

"That guy you met in London at the V and A?" asked Pam, recalling an incident that took place a few years earlier when the four friends had taken a trip together to England. "The one with the hats?"

"Righto," said Sue. "As you may remember, the Victoria and Albert Museum had a special exhibit of hats that year and that's where I met Perry and discovered a shared enthusiasm. He is the Earl of Wickham and has invited Sid and me to come visit him at his ancestral home, Moreton Manor. He's putting on a big exhibition of his hat collection and asked me to donate a few pieces. I inherited a couple of Lily Dache originals from my grandma, you know. So to make a long story short, he's invited me to bring my hats and my husband. Sid doesn't want to go so I asked his lordship if I could bring a friend and he said, 'Why ever not? We've got a hundred and twenty rooms.' So there it is, Lucy. You know how much you loved England when we went there a couple years ago."

"It's the opportunity of a lifetime," said Pam with a sigh. "Imagine staying in a stately home and hanging out with nobility."

"A change of scene can have a positive impact on the psyche," said Rachel. "New places, new people, new ideas — they can be very stimulating. However," she added, in a warning tone, "the effect can be quite short-lived. For real change, I still think Lucy needs to talk to a qualified therapist."

"Stuff and nonsense," snapped Sue. "There's nothing the matter with Lucy that a cream tea and a breath of spring won't cure. You know spring comes earlier in England than it does here. Remember the daffodils?"

Lucy took the last bite of her marmalade-covered toast and thought of the hundreds, maybe thousands, of naturalized daffodils with their nodding blooms she'd seen overrunning acres and acres of woodland at Hampton Court. "I'll go," she said, surprising her friends and even herself as the words flew out of her mouth, apparently of their own accord.

But that wasn't really true; deep down, she knew she'd been looking for something that would help her break out of this depression. She was ashamed that she was unhappy, even miserable, and she didn't want to go on like this. It wasn't fair to the kids who'd grown up hearing her repeat her mother's favorite adage that "you can find sympathy in the dictionary" all too often. Whenever she'd suspected they were feeling sorry for themselves, she had advised them to count their blessings, and though she'd tried to follow her own advice, it hadn't worked. Even worse, she felt that it wasn't fair to Bill to have a mopey wife who neglected him. But most of all, it wasn't fair to herself. This was her one life. It wasn't a dress rehearsal, it was showtime and she needed to take center stage. Maybe a trip, a change of scene, was just what she needed to perk herself up. "When do we leave?" she asked.

Chapter Two

"The show opens May eighth, but Perry wants us to have a nice visit, so he suggests we come a week or two before," said Sue as Norine stopped by their table to present their checks.

"Bluebells might be in bloom then," said Lucy, who remembered seeing a photograph of an English bluebell walk in a travel magazine she'd read in the dentist's waiting room. The photo showed a woodland where the ground was covered in a gorgeous carpet of blue blooms.

"Jo Malone's Bluebell was Princess Diana's favorite scent." Sue was an avid magazine reader and knew about such things.

"Wouldn't it be wonderful to smell bluebells," said Lucy, checking the tab and putting down a five dollar bill.

"Maybe we will." Sue stood up and was buttoning the luxurious shearling coat Sid had given her for Christmas.

"I'm sure there'll be bluebells," said Pam, digging into her enormous African basket purse in search of her wallet. "Be sure to take a photo and send it to us."

"We'll want to hear all about it," said Rachel, wrapping her plum-colored pashmina scarf around her neck.

"Do you think you'll meet royalty?" asked Pam as they made their way through the café to the door. "Maybe Perry is friends with Prince Charles or somebody."

"Oh!" exclaimed Lucy. Assailed by second thoughts, she stopped at the door. "I wouldn't know what to do!"

"I think you curtsey," said Pam, opening the door.

"I know you're not supposed to touch royalty unless they touch you first," said Rachel as they gathered in a little circle on the sidewalk. "Some basketball player got in trouble for hugging Princess Kate, didn't he? In Brooklyn."

"What was Princess Kate doing in Brooklyn?" asked Pam.

"Hanging out with Beyoncé and JayZ," said Rachel. "I read it in the *New York Times.*"

"Face it. They're the closest thing we Americans have to royalty," said Sue, adding a wistful sigh. "We're hardly in that category so I doubt very much that we'll be meeting any royals, but what if we do?" She smoothed her brown leather gloves. "They're just people and I'm sure our natural good manners will see us through. After all, we're Americans. We're not subjects and we don't have to bow and scrape and tug our forelocks. That was the whole point of that little revolution we had in 1776."

"I don't know," said Lucy as dark clouds of doubt started to build in her mind. "What if they dress for dinner like at *Downton Abbey,* and there's all those forks and knives and snooty footmen who sneer when you pick up the wrong utensil?" She shivered and stuffed her gloved hands into her pockets.

"*Downton Abbey* is a TV show and it all takes place a long time ago. They're in the roaring twenties now, which is almost a hundred years ago. The women are all wearing those awful chemises and ugly cloches, which I don't think flatter anybody," declared Sue, flipping up her fuzzy collar. "I think we can assume that a lot has changed since then."

"I wouldn't be so sure, if I were you," cautioned Rachel, fingering her car keys. "If

Perry has this big ancestral house, you have to assume he's rather well-off. I don't think they're going to be living like we do. You know, clipping detergent coupons and taking out the garbage."

Lucy knew she hadn't even had the energy to clip a coupon or take out the garbage lately.

"It's probably more like *Lifestyles of the Rich and Famous* than *Downton Abbey,*" said Pam, adjusting her hand-knit mittens and hoisting her bag over her shoulder. "I've got to run. I've got to teach a yoga class." Turning and hurrying off down the street, she passed the neat row of storefronts. "See you next week!" she called over her shoulder.

Rich and famous certainly didn't describe her lifestyle, thought Lucy, giving Pam a little wave and stamping her feet. She'd unthinkingly put on running shoes instead of winter boots, and her feet were beginning to freeze. "I don't know what to pack." She hated packing — all the worry about whether toothpaste could go in a carry-on bag or had to be carried separately in a clear baggie. She was sure she'd feel completely out of place in a stately home and thought it might be better to skip the trip altogether.

"I'm going to pack like I always do," said Sue, who prided herself on having the appropriate outfit for every occasion. "Mostly casual sportswear, comfortable shoes suitable for sightseeing, and one evening outfit. I have that long black skirt that I can dress up with a lacy top or a tuxedo shirt."

"I'll help you pack. I've got a TSA pamphlet at home," offered Rachel, sensing Lucy's hesitation and giving her a reassuring hug. "See you next Thursday, if not before." She tossed Sue a quick air kiss before crossing the sidewalk to her car and driving off.

"You've got those nice black pants. They will certainly do in candlelight," said Sue as they walked down the street. "Especially if you wear heels and something a little sparkly." They stopped by Sue's parked SUV, where she hesitated, then ventured a little joke. "And when I say sparkly, I don't mean your Christmas sweatshirt with the rhinestones and sequins."

At first, Lucy felt stung by the comment, but seeing Sue's suppressed smile she realized her friend was teasing her. "Darn! You must have read my mind," replied Lucy, revealing the first flash of humor her friend had seen in a long time.

"I think this trip is a good idea," said Sue, beaming at her and giving her a parting embrace before climbing into the enormous

Navigator. Settling herself behind the steering wheel, she lowered the window. "And don't forget to bring your good jewelry," she advised, before shifting into DRIVE and zooming off.

Seven weeks later, Lucy found herself following Sue in a straggling procession of freshly disembarked British Air passengers who were making their way through a maze of stainless steel and glass corridors at Heathrow, hoping eventually to reach Immigration and be admitted to the United Kingdom. As Sue had advised, she'd carefully packed a small leatherette case containing her good jewelry — a modest diamond and platinum lavaliere she'd inherited from her grandmother and a pair of cultured pearl earrings that Bill had given her — in her purse. She had disregarded the rest of Sue's advice, however, and had neglected to pack anything dressy in the carry-on sized roller suitcase she was towing behind herself. There hadn't been room after she'd thrown together a pile of comfortable jeans and favorite sweaters, plus a couple of guide books and a mystery novel or two.

Finally reaching the glass booths inhabited by immigration officers, Lucy patiently waited her turn, grateful for the rest from the rushed march through the terminal. She watched with amusement as Sue flirted with the rather good-looking young fellow who was smiling as he examined her passport. Sue could never resist a man in uniform.

Getting the nod from a rather less attractive officer whose neck rolls spilled over his tight collar, Lucy stepped forward and presented her passport along with the little slip of paper she'd been told to fill out on the airplane. It provided the details of her visit in England, including lodgings.

"Moreton Manor, eh?" he said, scowling at the paper. "Is that a hotel?"

"It's a house," said Lucy, smiling in what she hoped was a friendly manner.

"And what's your business there?" he demanded, fixing his rather small, pale blue eyes on her.

"I'm a houseguest," said Lucy.

"And who is your host?" he asked, turning to his computer screen.

"The Earl of Wickham," said Lucy, somehow feeling this wasn't going to work in her favor.

"And how exactly do you happen to know the earl?" The officer seemed to have developed a rather strong Cockney accent and was studying her bright pink all-weather jacket with some skepticism.

"My friend" — she nodded toward Sue, who was waiting for her beyond the barrier — "met the earl at a hat exhibit a few years ago. They both collect hats, you see, and there's going to be a show of the earl's hats at Moreton Manor. He invited Sue and her husband, but Sid didn't want to go, so I got invited." Lucy paused. "I've been a bit down in the dumps lately and everyone thought the trip would do me good."

The officer took a long look at her passport, then folded it closed and handed it to her. "I'm sure it will, luv, and be sure to give my regards to his lordship."

"Oh, I will," said Lucy, suspecting he was being rather sarcastic but not quite willing to risk joking with a person in authority.

"What was that all about?" asked Sue when Lucy finally joined her. "They couldn't have thought you were a terrorist or a smuggler, though that jacket does look like something a desperate refugee might wear."

"I like this jacket. It's bright and cheerful," said Lucy. "I saw someone wearing one just like it on the British version of *Antiques Roadshow.* I've been watching a lot of PBS, boning up for the trip." She nodded. "And I got it for practically nothing in a thrift shop."

"Why am I not surprised," said Sue with a resigned sigh. "We don't have anything to declare so we can skip customs, but we have to get the bag of hats. It's on to the baggage claim."

After collecting Sue's big roller case that contained her hats, they proceeded to the ARRIVALS hall, toting all the bags on a wheeled trolley. There, they joined a small group of travelers studying a large yellow sign with arrows pointing to various transport options.

"We're supposed to catch a bus to Oxford," said Sue, checking her smartphone for the instructions Perry had sent.

"That way," Lucy said, pointing in the direction indicated by the sign.

"It's still quite early in the morning. Do you want to stop for a coffee or something? I couldn't drink that stuff on the plane."

"Sounds good." Lucy could never sleep on a plane and was feeling even more tired than usual. "I need something to perk me up."

The two perched on stools at a little snack bar and ordered extra-large coffees. After a few reviving sips, Sue again consulted her smartphone. "The busses to Oxford run quite frequently. We can catch one in an hour."

"You've got the schedule?" asked Lucy, somewhat amazed.

"Perry sent it. And once we're on board, I'm supposed to call and he's going to have someone meet us."

"In a limo?" asked Lucy. "A Bentley or a Rolls Royce?"

Sue licked her lips and smiled. "I imagine so. Don't you?"

When the bus rolled into the Gloucester Green bus station in Oxford, a fortyish man in a dark green Barbour barn coat, green Wellies, and a tweed cap stepped forward and greeted them. "Mrs. Finch and Mrs. Stone?" he asked, tipping his hat.

"That's us," replied Sue with a big smile. "But I'm Sue and this is Lucy."

"Harold Quimby," he said, introducing himself. "Pleased to meet you ladies. Now if you'll just come this way . . ." He deftly relieved them of the giant bag and led the way past the busses' docking station to the parking lot where he stopped beside a huge and very muddy, very aged Land Rover. He opened the rear hatch and stowed their bags amid a collection of umbrellas, boots, blankets, flashlights, and assorted tools, including a small hatchet. "I hope you don't mind a few stops."

Lucy was doing her best to restrain a case of the giggles and not succeeding, despite a stern glance from Sue.

"Is it a long drive to the manor?" asked Sue.

"Not at all." Harold opened the rear door for them and removed a wire dog crate from the backseat. "I bet you were expecting a fancy car, weren't you?" he asked with an amused smile.

"We were," admitted Lucy.

"The Bentley's in the shop. Besides, I had to come this way anyway, so I said I'd meet you at the station."

"We're really very grateful," said Sue, climbing into the backseat and sliding over to make room for Lucy.

"We certainly are," agreed Lucy, joining her.

"I'll have you at the manor in two shakes of a lamb's tail," promised Harold, shutting the door. He went around to the rear of the car where he collapsed the crate and added it to the jumble in the rear, then slammed the hatch and hopped into the driver's seat on the wrong side of the car.

"It seems odd to have you sitting there on the right," said Lucy.

"I tried driving in the States once," said Harold, "and I kept slipping into the wrong lane. I even went around a roundabout the wrong way."

"Then I'm glad we're here, where you're used to the roads," said Sue.

"Aye, I could drive around here with my eyes closed," he said, turning to give them a wink. "But for your sake I won't."

Leaning back in the comfortable seat, Lucy gazed curiously out the window, watching as the densely packed, narrow streets of the old university town gave way to wider, more spacious modern roadways, dotted here and there with gas stations and shopping malls. Those eventually disappeared and they were in the countryside. Hedges lined the road, occasionally revealing thatched cottages and fields where sheep often grazed.

Reaching a small village where a pub and a few stores clustered together, Harold turned into a fenced yard filled with sheds, dog houses, mowers, and tractors. A sign on a large stone building announced in gold letters on a black ground that this establishment was GALBRAITH AND SONS, LTD. Beneath it, a smaller sign bore the words FARM STORE.

Harold hopped out and was greeted by a stout man wearing an apron, who clapped him on the back and led him inside. Lucy and Sue waited in the Land Rover. A couple of young assistants, also in aprons, barely acknowledged them as they began loading various and sundry products into the car. First, several bags of smelly fertilizer were tucked in next to Sue's suitcases. An enormous bag of chicken feed was arranged on top of Lucy's suitcase, and a huge bale of wood shavings wrapped in plastic was added to the pile. The final items were two boxes of adorable fuzzy yellow, chirping chicks, which Lucy and Sue were requested to hold in their laps.

"Everybody comfortable?" asked Harold, taking his seat behind the wheel.

"We're okay," said Lucy, uncomfortably aware of the bale of wood chips right behind her head.

"I meant the chicks," said Harold.

Sue lifted a flap, peered into the box, and studied the tiny balls of yellow fluff. "They seem to be all right," she said somewhat skeptically. "They've kind of hunkered down. I think they're sleeping."

"That's good," said Harold as the Land Rover lurched forward and crossed the yard to the gate. He suddenly slammed on the brakes when confronted with a delivery truck attempting to enter. The bale of wood chips slid forward, knocking Lucy in the head before bursting open and showering them all. The jolt wakened the chicks, who were all peeping frantically.

"The chicks!" exclaimed Harold, backing up to let the truck enter.

Lucy and Sue checked, discovering no harm had been done to the baby birds, who were flapping their tiny little winglets and settling themselves.

"They're fine," said Sue.

Lucy was tilting her head from side to side, stretching her neck to check for whiplash.

"No harm done, then," said Harold, shifting into drive and exiting through the gateway.

Lucy and Sue were still picking wood chips out of their hair when he turned through a pair of massive stone piers, each topped with a carved stone lion.

"Moreton Manor," announced Harold as they proceeded along a drive lined with leafy trees.

In the rather long grass beneath the trees, Lucy noticed dots of blue flowers. "Are those bluebells?"

"Indeed they are," said Harold. "Moreton is famous for its bluebells. People come from miles around."

"I can't wait to see them," said Lucy.

The Land Rover suddenly swerved round a bend, continued past a circular lawn with a fountain, and came to a halt in front of a massive stone building. "Welcome to Moreton," said Harold, hopping out.

Lucy gazed at the enormous stately home, which loomed high above them like a castle from a fairy tale. Dotted with ferocious gargoyles, the stone walls were punctuated with numerous arched and many-paned windows, including an ornate conservatory. In the morning sunlight, the stone walls took on a golden glow. The steep slate roof was topped with several pointed towers, each ending in a massive spike that threatened to pierce the clouds.

Lucy and Sue carefully set the boxes of chicks on the car seat, then stepped out of the car onto the graveled area in front of the stately home. They found themselves confronted with an impressive stone staircase that led to a rather forbidding set of double doors studded with black iron nail heads and strapped with elaborately curved hinges. Two crenellated towers stood on either side of the staircase.

While they stared in awe at the huge castle, Harold busied himself extracting their suitcases from beneath the heavy sacks of feed and fertilizer. Finally setting the baggage beside them, he said a quick farewell and drove off, leaving them wondering what to do. Should they climb the staircase to that forbidding door? Was there some other, more accessible entrance?

"I see only one doorway." Sue started up the steps, awkwardly pulling the oversized roller bag that contained her precious hats.

"There must be a doorbell or something up there," said Lucy. Pulling both of the smaller carry-on bags up the steps made her rather out of breath.

"I hope so," said Sue. "I wonder where Perry is."

"I'm down here!"

They turned and looked down to the bottom of the stairs where the earl was standing, hands on hips, looking up at them. He was dressed casually in a sweater and jeans, and his rather long hair was loosely combed behind his ears.

Taking in his slim build, rather like Mick Jagger's, Lucy thought of the adage that you couldn't be too rich or too thin.

"Come on down!" he yelled, grinning and sounding like a game-show host.

Getting down the stairs proved somewhat more difficult than going up, and Perry scampered up the stairs to help them with the suitcases. When they were all safe on the ground, he escorted them around the side of the staircase where a narrow opening led to a ground-level entrance beneath the stairs. "This is the easiest way in when you've got luggage," he explained.

When Lucy's eyes got used to the darkness, she noticed the entrance was dimly lit by an ancient filament lightbulb.

They followed Perry down a short ramp to a door, which he held open for them, allowing them to step inside. There, they found themselves in a narrow passage with a worn linoleum floor. The hallway was lined with doors and lit with a series of pendant fixtures that looked as if they were the latest technology in 1910.

"This is beneath the main house, which is open to the public," said Perry, doing a neat little dance in the tight space to get around them and their suitcases. "We live in an outbuilding we've had modernized. It's all connected by this underground tunnel. If I take this big boy, can you manage your cases and follow me?"

"No problem," said Lucy.

"I must apologize, but the staff these days are mostly involved with the visitors. My grandfather had a staff of eighty and never had to carry a suitcase or even get a cup of tea. We have over three hundred, but there's never anybody around when we need a hand."

"Lucy and I are used to fending for ourselves," said Sue as she trotted along behind Perry. "I do want to thank you for inviting us."

"Me, too," said Lucy. "This is a real treat."

"I do hope so," said Perry. "I'm so glad you could come."

"I wouldn't miss your hat show for the world," said Sue.

"I'm especially eager to see those Lily Dache hats you've brought —"

"Perry! Perry! The general's fallen!" called a woman, suddenly interrupting.

They all stopped in their tracks and turned around to face the woman who was running along the passage toward them, frantically hailing the earl.

"Is he hurt?" he asked as she drew closer.

"I'm afraid so," said the woman. "I think he may be beyond help."

Chapter Three

"Oh d-d-dear," stammered Perry, whose face had gone quite white. "Not the general. This is terrible, and what bad timing. . . ."

"I really need you to come," said the woman, who Lucy thought bore a strong resemblance to Perry. She was obviously upset and seemed to be physically struggling against the desire to grab Perry and drag him away.

"Of course, of course." Perry was once again doing his little dance around Lucy and Sue and the suitcases. "Duty calls," he told them, "but if you continue on just a little way, through that door, you'll find yourselves in the family kitchen. Sally should be there and she can show you to your rooms. I must apologize."

"No need," said Sue. "This is an emergency and you're needed elsewhere."

"I'll get back to you as soon as I can," he promised, before dashing away along the passage and following the woman.

"That sounded bad," said Lucy, fearing the worst as they resumed their trek. "I hope the general's all right."

"They did seem awfully upset," said Sue.

"I wonder if the general is a relative, perhaps an elderly uncle or something."

"Old people do tend to fall a lot."

"And they break their hips," added Lucy. "Wouldn't that be an awful beginning to our visit?"

"Definitely not optimal," agreed Sue as they reached the door at the end of the corridor. She reached for the knob, which turned easily, and opened it, blinking a bit at the bright sunshine that was a sudden contrast to the dimly lit hallway.

The two friends stepped inside and looked around, discovering a room that a shelter magazine would label a great room — a combination dream kitchen and cozy family room. The cabinets were obviously custom, the stainless steel refrigerator had double doors and was at least six-feet wide, the countertops were marble, the floor was stone, and a huge cream-colored Aga stove stood in a repurposed fireplace. Noticing the large pine dresser crammed with blue and white china, Lucy practically swooned.

Beyond the kitchen area was a comfortable seating area where two large sofas and several easy chairs covered in flowery chintz were arranged so that sitters could choose to view the fireplace, the flat-screen TV, or the paved terrace outside the large French doors. A number of throws and assorted pillows were arranged on the furniture, promising complete ease and relaxation. Two large labs, one black and one yellow, were sprawled on the sofas, taking full advantage of the arrangement.

"Wow," said Sue. "I didn't expect this."

"We're not at Downton Abbey, that's for sure," said Lucy. "Mrs. Patmore would kill for this kitchen."

"There's no Mrs. Patmore, and not even poor overworked little Daisy," said Sue. "Or Sally, for that matter."

Waking from their naps, the dogs yawned then set their eyes on the two intruders. Eager to pet them, Lucy approached the nearest, the yellow dog, but stopped in her tracks when the dog fixed his eyes on her and began growling.

"Not friendly," she said, retreating a few steps. When the black Lab also curled up its lip and growled, she decided discretion was the better part of valor and scurried over to the kitchen area where she joined Sue behind the large island. "What should we do?"

"Those dogs are making me nervous," said Sue, who was not an animal lover.

"I don't like the look of them, either. We can't stay here." Lucy was beginning to think the trip was a mistake.

"Maybe we can help Perry with the general," said Sue.

"What can we do? How can we help?" asked Lucy.

"Well, I just took a CPR course," said Sue.

"Good to know," muttered Lucy as they left the kitchen and retraced their steps along the passageway.

"I bet this was the downstairs where the servants toiled away," said Lucy, thinking how horrible it would be to work all day in the poorly-lit subterranean tunnel.

"Did you notice the bells in the kitchen?" asked Sue. "They were over the doorway. There were a bunch of them, all labeled. DRAWING ROOM, HIS LORDSHIP, HER LADYSHIP, NURSERY, and lots more." She stopped walking and squeezed Lucy's arm. "Can you believe it, Lucy? Here we are in an English country house, honored guests, for all the world like Lady Susan and Lady Lucy. It makes me wish for a big hat with plumes and a skirt with a bustle."

"I suspect that back then we'd be wearing black dresses and white aprons," said Lucy, glumly realistic. "And the plumes would be on our feather dusters instead of our hats."

"You're probably right," admitted Sue, resuming the hike along the passage. "But a girl can dream."

After passing through the door to the passage beneath the manor house, they continued on a short distance to a cellar where they encountered a utilitarian stone staircase with a plain black metal railing.

"Shall we?" asked Sue.

"Nothing ventured, nothing gained," grumbled Lucy, mounting the stairs.

Reaching the door at the top of the stairs, they paused to read the framed notice listing rules for servants, which were printed in black boldface on paper card that had yellowed with age.

KEEP OUTER DOOR LOCKED AT ALL TIMES.

ONLY THE BUTLER MAY ANSWER THE BELL.

BE PUNCTUAL.

NO GAMBLING OR OATHS OR ABUSIVE LANGAGE ALLOWED.

NO SERVANT IS TO RECEIVE VISITORS IN THE HOUSE.

ANY MAID FOUND FRATERNISING WITH A MEMBER OF THE OPPOSITE SEX WILL BE

DISMISSED IMMEDIATELY WITHOUT A HEARING.

THE HALL DOOR IS TO BE CLOSED AT HALF PAST TEN O'CLOCK EVERY NIGHT.

THE SERVANTS' HALL IS TO BE CLEARED AND CLOSED AT HALF PAST TEN O'CLOCK EVERY NIGHT.

ANY BREAKAGES OR DAMAGES TO THE HOUSE WILL BE DEDUCTED FROM WAGES.

"I imagine they've kept this as a sort of joke," said Sue.

"I hope so. Otherwise it would be very hard to retain staff these days," said Lucy, pushing open the door and revealing a space so large and grand that it caused them to gasp in awe. Craning their necks, they saw, high above them, a blue sky dotted with puffy clouds upon which perched numerous scantily clad pink-fleshed ladies and gentlemen of ample girth. Around them fluttered dozens of plump little cherubs, some playing musical instruments and others equipped with bows and arrows.

"I'd like to do something like this in my bathroom," quipped Sue, waving a hand toward the ceiling.

"I'm thinking of upgrading my back stairway," said Lucy, comparing the cramped little flight of wooden steps in her kitchen to the enormous marble staircase that dominated the magnificent hall. She continued to let her gaze wander around the huge room, which she decided must be the reception area approached by the massive flight of stone stairs they'd attempted to climb when they were dropped off outside the manor. This was the room that would greet visitors to the great house. Its grandiose size and luxurious furnishings were intended to impress. Huge bronze consoles with colorful marble tops stood on either side of the doorway and an assortment of polished white marble statues and busts were arranged along the paneled walls. Hanging behind the statues were many large, full-length portraits of gorgeously gowned women and bewigged men in satin knee breeches, often wearing crimson and ermine robes.

One of these portraits had fallen and was being examined by Perry and the woman who'd summoned him earlier. The painting was easily ten or more feet tall with a massive carved gilt frame, which was smashed to bits. The canvas was also torn, but the figure of a bewigged gentleman in a red coat astride a prancing white horse was undamaged.

"This is going to cost a mint," said the

woman, shaking her head and sounding very glum.

"That's the least of it. We've got to get this all cleared up before the house opens at ten," said Perry, scratching his chin. He looked up and caught sight of Lucy and Sue. "Oh, do forgive me," he exclaimed. "I've neglected you. Let me introduce you to my sister, Lady Philippa Maddox. These are my friends from New England, Sue Finch and Lucy Stone."

"We've been expecting you," said Lady Philippa. She looked like a smaller, feminine version of Perry, with frizzy blond hair and bright blue eyes. She was dressed in beige slacks, a much-washed blue cashmere sweater, and a string of pearls. On her feet, she was sporting a pair of bright neon-green running shoes. "Do call me Poppy. Everyone does."

"So this is the general?" asked Lucy.

"Yes," said Poppy. "Rather like Humpty Dumpty. He took a great fall and it's going to take an awful lot of money to put him together again."

"We were worried he was a person, perhaps even a relative," said Sue. "I took a CPR course and we thought perhaps we could help."

"Only if CPR is short for art restorer,"

said Perry.

"I'm afraid not," admitted Sue. "Who is he? An ancestor?"

"No, he was a gift, presented to the eighth earl by the subject himself, General Horatio Hoare," said Poppy.

"A horrible fellow, by all accounts. He was killed in Canada in the Seven Years War and they sent his body home in a barrel of rum," said Perry. "People at the time said he came home in much better spirits than he left."

"But he was terribly fond of the eighth earl," said Poppy.

"Extremely fond, they say," said Perry, with a raised eyebrow. "He promised that so long as his painting was on the wall no harm would come to Moreton Manor."

"Or you could say he jinxed the place," said Poppy. "Take down my picture and I'll make you sorry. Now that it's fallen, I guess we can expect a run of bad luck."

"That's just a lot of nonsense. An old wives' tale," said Perry.

"Remember what happened the last time it came down?" said Poppy gloomily.

"Never mind about that," replied Perry. "It was a long time ago."

"Well, I'd better make arrangements to have the staff tidy up. We can't have the visitors stepping over bits of frame." Poppy bit her lip. "I wish I could be as confident as you are," she said to Perry. "I have a rather bad feeling about this."

"What happened the last time the general fell down?" asked Lucy as they all retraced their steps on the long passage to the kitchen. The servants must have done this dozens of times every day, she thought, noticing the worn linoleum.

"The ninth earl's countess was found dead at the bottom of that big staircase in the hall," said Perry.

"That would be a terrible fall," said Lucy.

"It was never determined if it was an accident or suicide or foul play," said Perry. "There were lots of rumors, of course."

"The earl married his mistress in what was considered at the time to be indecent haste," said Poppy. "The king banned the earl from court for several years."

"But there was no trial or investigation?" asked Lucy.

"Not back then," scoffed Perry. "He was an earl and only the king had any power to touch him."

"Even the king had to be careful of upsetting the nobles," said Poppy. "Think of Magna Carta."

"And Charles I," volunteered Lucy.

"Point taken, but I think it was actually

Parliament that beheaded him, though to be fair, back in those days even the Commons was mostly titled gentlemen," said Perry. "His son Charles II stayed here for a night or two on his way to safe haven in the Scilly Islands, you know."

"It must be wonderful living in a house with so much history," said Sue.

"It's more like living in a museum now that the house is open to the public. We're the exhibits," said Perry. "Somewhat tarnished relics of England's glorious past, now on our last legs and forced to display our aristocratic heritage for ten pounds a head."

"Don't listen to him," advised Poppy. "The Heads Up! Hat Festival was his idea to attract more visitors to the house."

"Plagued by guilt, Poppy dear. You've been working so hard, managing this three-ring-circus."

"It's a business, Perry. Just a business like any other."

"And you do have a terrific head for business," said Perry as they finally reached the door to the kitchen. He opened the door and held it for them, adding a little bow and a flourish.

They entered, discovering Sally was in place, hanging towels on a wooden drying rack in front of the Aga stove. The rack was suspended on a system of ropes and pulleys and could be lowered for easy access, then raised up to the high ceiling where it would be out of the way.

"What is that fabulous thing?" asked Lucy, who wanted one for her kitchen.

"A Sheila-Maid." Sally had curly red hair and lots of freckles. She was not wearing a servant's uniform but was sporting a tight pair of jeans and an equally tight striped pullover with a scoop neck that revealed a rose tattoo on her left breast.

"I wonder if I can get a Sheila-Maid in the States," said Lucy.

"You can get just about anything on the Internet, but I inherited my hats from Gramma. Do you want to see them?" Sue asked, indicating her enormous suitcase, which she'd left beside the door.

"Oh, yes!" enthused Perry, bounding across the room.

She unzipped the case entirely filled with two hatboxes, one large and one small. She opened the smaller one first and lifted out a cloche entirely covered with pink silk flowers, green velvet leaves, and the occasional crystal dewdrop.

"Heaven!" exclaimed Perry, taking it carefully in his hands and admiring it. "Roaring Twenties?"

"No. The swinging sixties. It's one of Lily Dache's last designs. I have photos of Gramma wearing it to church on Easter Sunday, along with a stunning Givenchy-style suit she sewed herself from a Vogue pattern."

"What else have you got?" asked Perry, returning the hat.

"I guess this would be a fascinator," said Sue. From the same hatbox, she produced a black velvet headband topped with a black rose and a froth of veil. "The sort of thing women wore to church when times were changing and hats were no longer fashionable, but they weren't quite ready to give them up entirely."

"Heresy!" exclaimed Perry. "Hats not fashionable!"

"Not in the US," said Lucy.

"We've clung to them," said Poppy. "I wouldn't dream of going to a wedding without a hat."

"And the royal family are doing their part to maintain the tradition," said Lucy.

"Bless the dears," said Perry, peering into the suitcase curiously. "What do you have in the other hatbox?"

Sue reached into the second, larger hatbox and produced a creamy straw number with a small, rounded crown and a huge brim, at least eight inches wide all around. A length of matching chiffon was wound around the crown and ended in long streamers that tied beneath the chin. "Voilà!" she exclaimed proudly.

"Is that?" asked Perry, eyebrows raised.

"The very same," said Sue, presenting it to Perry. "Katharine Hepburn wore it in *The Philadelphia Story.*"

Perry held the hat reverently. "How did you ever?"

"It came up on eBay and I couldn't resist."

"It must have cost you a fortune."

"I wanted to wow you," said Sue.

"Well you certainly have," he said, returning the hat, which Sue carefully replaced in the box.

"Perry, I know how exciting this is for you, but don't you think you should let your guests settle in?" Poppy turned to Lucy and Sue. "You must be exhausted after the red-eye flight."

"I wouldn't mind freshening up," said Lucy.

"You've even got time for a little nap before lunch," said Poppy. "Sally will show you the way."

Sue left the hat box in Perry's care, then she and Lucy grabbed their bags and followed Sally out of the kitchen to another set of stairs, wooden and covered with a striped runner. They began climbing, continuing up one flight after another until they reached the former servants' quarters on the top floor.

"Don't worry," said Sally. "They've been fixed up. None of the old servants would recognize their rooms."

"At this point, I'd take a folding cot and an Army blanket," said Lucy, panting from the climb.

"That won't be necessary," said Sally, leading them down a spacious carpeted hallway to their rooms, which were joined by a shared bath.

Both guest rooms had sloping attic ceilings, and the walls were papered with Laura Ashley flowers. They each had a mirrored vanity table, a dresser, and a bench for their suitcases; the beds were covered with plump duvets that matched the wallpaper, as did the curtains on the casement windows.

"I'll leave you now," said Sally. "Don't be afraid to nap, if you want. I'll make sure you don't miss lunch."

"Thanks," said Lucy, closing the door behind her and joining Sue at the window, where she seemed transfixed.

"It's gorgeous," said Sue with a wave of her hand.

Looking into the distance, Lucy saw a seemingly endless expanse of rolling hills and fields that eventually met a series of distant bluish mountains. Somewhat closer to the house, a road wound its way through farmland, eventually turning through the gateway and the tree-lined drive. From this lofty vantage, they could see that a spur branched off from the main drive and led to an enormous parking lot already half-full of cars and busses. Hundreds of tiny little figures, mostly in pairs or small groups, were moving from the vehicles and making their way to a ticket booth. A long line of people were following a leader holding a closed umbrella aloft like a pennant.

"Moreton Manor is open for business," said Lucy. "Here come the hoi polloi, Lady Sue."

"Yes, Lady Lucy. It's the little people, here for a glimpse of the good life."

"From up here, they sure do look little," said Lucy, yawning. "I think I will retire to my chamber and rest my eyes."

"Just don't snore," said Sue, who was hoisting her suitcase onto the bench.

Once in her own room, Lucy discovered the view was quite different. Instead of the view across the park, all she saw out her window was a stone wall punctuated by windows. It was the manor, she realized. She was in a separate buildings connected to the main house by the underground corridor.

A charming framed watercolor on the wall beside the window gave the overview she needed, providing a bird's-eye view of the stately home separated from a smaller building on the right by a walled garden. Assuming the smaller building was the family's quarters, and comparing the view from the window to the painting, Lucy looked down and found the walled garden, a delightful square containing neat beds of plants centered by a sundial. What she couldn't see from the window but was pictured in the painting, was a row of outbuildings along the right side of the manor that created one side of a large walled area she surmised was originally a stable yard.

The whole arrangement was quite clever, she decided. The walled areas of garden and stable yard provided privacy for the family from the visiting public, which still had acres of manicured gardens and walking trails open to them.

Turning away from the window, she was drawn to the bed, with its puffy duvet and plump pillows. She slipped off her shoes and slid under the duvet. Feeling the hard case of her cellphone in her rear pocket, she decided she'd better call home before she fell asleep.

Bill answered on the first ring. "How was the flight? I saw it landed on time," he said, a slight note of reproach in his tone.

"I should have called sooner," she admitted. "It's been busy. Catching the bus, getting a ride to the manor —"

"Did they meet you in a Rolls?" he asked.

"Not quite," said Lucy, plucking a wood chip from her hair. "It was a Land Rover and there were baby chicks and fertilizer."

"Real country then. But I don't suppose the landed gentry actually get their hands dirty."

Lucy thought of Perry, with his enthusiastic love of hats, and doubted very much that he had anything to do with the farming aspect of the manor. "It's not like we expected. The manor is really a museum and the family live in a separate building. I guess it was once the kitchen and work area for the big house. The two are connected by a tunnel that's —"

"Like Monticello?" asked Bill, interrupting.

"Yeah, kind of," said Lucy, remembering a family vacation. "But this smaller house has been completely renovated. It's really like a McMansion. You wouldn't believe the kitchen. It's like something out of *House Beautiful.* The guest rooms used to be servant's quarters, but they've been fancied up."

"So you're feeling better and having a good time?" he asked, getting to the point.

The concern in his voice struck her and she felt tears filling her eyes. "So far, so good, but I am tired." She blinked furiously, quickly adding, "Jet lag. How's everybody?"

"Sara's studying for finals. Zoe's excited about the prom. . . ."

That was too much for Lucy, who was suddenly guilt-stricken. "Be sure to take pictures for me," she begged, sniffling.

"I will," he promised.

"Any news from Alaska?" she asked, feeling as if she was picking at a scab she really ought to leave alone if she wanted the wound to heal.

"No, but no news is good news, right?" He paused. "A guy stopped by, said he saw my truck, and asked about Toby. He said they were friends in college but lost touch. He wanted to know what Toby was up to."

"Did you get his name?" asked Lucy.

"Doug something. Fitzpatrick, maybe?"

"I don't remember Toby mentioning him."

"You know how it is. They have their own lives."

"I know," said Lucy, remembering how shocked she'd been when four-year-old Toby was greeted by a strange woman in the supermarket who turned out to be the mother of one of the kids in his preschool. All of a sudden she was thinking of Patrick and felt the familiar tug of sadness, which threatened to overwhelm her. No longer able to fight the tears, she said she was really tired.

Bill let her go. "Love you. Have a great time."

"I'm trying," she said, ending the call and reaching for the box of tissues on the night-stand.

Chapter Four

Putting the phone on the bedside table and pressing her face into the pillows, Lucy was afraid that she wouldn't be able to sleep. Oddly enough, even though she felt exhausted much of the time, when she got to bed, sleep would elude her and her mind would run in circles, imagining the dangers little Patrick faced in Alaska. She fretted about possible tragedies such as encounters with polar bears, falls into icy streams, and snowmobile accidents; knowing her fears were unfounded didn't matter and she would lie under the covers, wakeful and trembling with terror. That had been the usual scenario lately.

She was quite surprised when a knock on the door woke her up two hours later. "Mmmph?" was all she managed to say, feeling rather groggy.

It was enough for Sally, who poked her head around the door. "Perry sent me up to tell you and your friend that lunch is almost ready."

"Thank you," said Lucy, wishing she could sink back into the very comfortable pillows.

That wish must have become reality, because next thing she knew Sue was shaking her shoulder. "Rise and shine, sleeping beauty. Up and at 'em, onward and upward. You know the drill."

Lucy glared at her friend, who was impeccably turned out. Sue was always beautifully dressed. She was doing the country house look with a gray cashmere sweater, charcoal tweed slacks, the shiny new hunter green Wellies she'd worn on the plane, and a string of pearls. Her makeup had been freshly applied and her hair was shiny from brushing.

"How long have you been up?" inquired Lucy, suspecting she looked rather the worse for wear.

"About half an hour. Just since Sally called me." She gave Lucy a stern look. "You had better hurry or we'll miss lunch."

Lucy groaned and hauled herself out of bed with great effort. Once in the bathroom, a glance at the mirror over the sink proved her suspicion was correct — she looked awful. Her hair was sticking up every which way and a long, angry red pillow-crease crossed her face. She dampened a washcloth with cool water and used it to wipe her face, then quickly washed her hands and applied a quick slick of lipstick. Back in her room, she made a stab at taming her hair, which seemed hopeless until Sue grabbed her hairbrush and with a few deft swipes created order out of chaos.

"Thanks," said Lucy, studying her improved reflection with amazement.

"Is that what you're wearing?" asked Sue in a rather disapproving tone.

Lucy regarded her image in the mirror. She was wearing the same turtleneck sweater and jeans she'd worn on the plane, as well as her usual athletic shoes. "I just have more of the same in my suitcase." She got an eye roll from Sue.

"You can take the girl out of Maine, but you can't take the Maine out of the girl," complained Sue, opening the door.

Following an appetizing scent redolent of meat and herbs, they made their way together down the stairs to the family kitchen. There, they found Perry standing at the Aga stove stirring a bright red casserole with a wooden spoon. The two dogs were sitting on their haunches beside him, apparently hoping there might be a slip twixt the spoon and the lip as he raised the spoon for a taste.

"What is that? It smells delicious," exclaimed Sue.

"Venison stew. We try to live off the estate as much as we can," he said, putting the spoon down and adding a few grinds of pepper.

Discouraged, the dogs turned their attention to Lucy and Sue, approaching them with wagging tails.

"Ah, so now you like us," said Lucy, scratching the nearest Lab, which happened to be the black one, behind its ears. "I have a dog at home just like you."

"Did they bother you?" asked Poppy, entering through the doorway that led to the service corridor. She was carrying a couple needlepoint throw pillows and a somewhat dented silver ewer, all of which she dropped on a chair.

"They didn't seem to appreciate our presence earlier," said Sue, nervously eyeing the yellow Lab that was leaning its shoulder against her leg. "They were sleeping on the sofas and growled at us."

"They were just worried you'd make them give up their comfortable perches," said Poppy. "The trick with dogs is to be firm. Isn't that right, Monty?"

Hearing his name, the yellow Lab trotted

over to Poppy and sat down in front of her, one paw raised.

"Good boy." She pointed to one of the two dog beds that were arranged in a corner. "Now go lie down. You, too, Churchy."

The dogs obeyed, but not without reproachful glances and sighs.

"They're such actors," said Perry. "They could go on stage."

Poppy set a big bowl on the center island and began pulling salad greens out of the fridge, which prompted Lucy to offer to help.

"Thanks," said Poppy, handing her a head of lettuce.

After giving her hands a quick wash, Lucy began tearing the lettuce into bite-size pieces and adding them to the bowl. The butter lettuce was lovely, crisp and silky to her touch, much nicer than anything she had grown in her Maine garden, and she said so.

"That's one of the advantages of having professional gardeners on staff," said Poppy.

"Perry was saying most of your food comes from the estate," said Sue.

"We have quite a farm, and there's game, too," said Poppy as a rather stocky man dressed in Wellies and an aged Barbour jacket came in through the French doors. "Ah, here's my husband, Gerald. He manages the estate farm. Gerald, meet Perry's friends, Lucy and Sue. They've come for the hat show."

"Very good," he said, nodding affably as he removed his jacket and hung it on one of the hooks on the wall next to the door. Several other pieces of clothing were already hanging there, and a neat row of boots stood at attention beneath them. He paused for a moment, rubbing his hands and studying Sue and Lucy, almost as if he were sizing up a pair of fillies offered for sale at an agricultural show. Then he cocked an eyebrow and turned to his wife. "Since we have company, shall we open a bottle of wine?"

Lucy was quick to speak up. "None for me."

Gerald turned to Sue and, detecting a hint of interest, gave a chuckle. "I bet Sue here wouldn't mind a drop. Am I right?"

"I wouldn't mind, but don't open a bottle on my account."

"I'll have a glass," said Perry.

"And Gerald will have several," said Poppy with a disapproving expression.

"Just being sociable, m'dear." Gerald disappeared through a doorway, returning a few moments later with two dusty bottles.

"Not the Margaux, I hope," said Perry, casting a suspicious glance at the bottles.

"Just a nice old claret," said Gerald.

"I see I'm just in time. Dad's got the plonk out," said a young man, who had also come in through the French doors. He was smiling.

Lucy noticed he had an air of confidence and physical ease that seemed quite remarkable. With his blond hair, high cheekbones, and cleft chin, he could have been a model, she thought, or an actor. He was dressed stylishly in a dark pea coat and had a Burberry plaid scarf wrapped around his neck.

"Desi!" exclaimed Poppy. "You made good time!"

"Just sailed along on the M40," he replied, giving his mother a peck on the cheek.

Poppy introduced Lucy and Sue, explaining that Desi was her son and he was visiting, taking a break before taking up a position as a soloist at the Royal Ballet.

"Congratulations," said Sue, accepting a glass of wine from Gerald. "That's quite an achievement."

"Just luck," he said modestly as his father handed him a glass of wine. "I brought Flo with me, but she wanted to see the new chicks before coming in."

"Having a smoke, you mean," said Poppy.

"I hope she's not smoking in the chicken house," said Gerald.

"She wouldn't do that," said Desi. "She knows better."

"Who knows what she knows these days," grumbled Gerald. "I don't understand what's going on with that girl."

"That means we're seven for lunch," said Perry, counting out a stack of plates and handing them to Sue. "Would you mind setting the table?"

"Not at all," replied Sue.

"No sense setting a place for Flora. She won't eat anything," said Gerald.

"Don't be ridiculous," snapped Poppy, who had opened a drawer and was counting out cutlery.

"You know I'm right," insisted Gerald, refilling his glass. "Fine family we've got. Desi prancing about like Tinker Bell and Flora looking like she's come straight out of a concentration camp."

"Shhh! She's coming," cautioned Poppy as a faint shadow appeared at the French door.

Desi hurried to open the door, admitting the thinnest woman Lucy had ever seen. With enormous eyes and cheekbones that matched her brother's, Flora would have been pretty, but her dark hair was limp and lifeless, her skin dull and ashy.

She entered the room tentatively, as if entering a cage of wild animals. "I see you have company," she said, turning to go.

"Just some friends of Perry's," said Poppy, hurrying across the room to greet her daughter and giving her a big hug. "Come and meet Lucy and Sue."

Flora seemed to shrink, becoming even smaller under her mother's embrace.

Her mother quickly released her. "Give me your coat, dear," she said in a coaxing tone.

For a moment it seemed as if Flora would bolt and run out the door, then she seemed to settle and began unzipping her puffy black jacket. After the zipper was undone, she let her arms fall to her side and Poppy slipped off the jacket and hung it up.

"We're ready," said Perry, removing a fragrant loaf of bread from an oven and setting it on a round bread board he carried to the table.

Lucy brought the bowl of salad, Desi donned oven mitts to convey the heavy casserole from the Aga, and they all seated themselves at the large scrubbed pine table.

"I didn't know you were interested in cooking," said Sue as Perry began dishing up the stew.

"Necessity is the mother of invention," he replied. "Poppy runs the show, y'see. I do my best to earn my keep so she doesn't chuck me out."

"Nonsense," said Poppy, passing the salad bowl. "I'd never do that."

"You couldn't, even if you wanted to," said Gerald, busying himself opening the second bottle of wine. "He's the earl. The place belongs to him."

"Not exactly," said Perry, arranging the merest dab of stew on the last plate and passing it to Flora. "The corporation actually owns the trust. Poppy and I are officers, as are your children, Gerald."

"Fat lot of good it's ever going to do them," muttered Gerald, topping off his glass before sending the bottle around the table for everyone to serve themselves. Only Sue and Desi added more wine to their glasses.

"It's the family birthright," said Poppy. "It's a privilege and a responsibility. Lord knows, I've done my best to make them aware of their heritage." She paused. "Has everyone got salad?"

"I for one am very glad to be such a lucky boy," said Desi, accepting the bowl that his mother passed to him. "It's good to know I've got a job waiting for me when my legs give out."

"Can't be soon enough for me," grumbled Gerald.

"Oh, Dad," moaned Flora, "you're such a cliché. Ballet is tough. Desi works hard. I bet he's in better shape than those rugby players you admire so much."

Gerald set down his stemmed glass with a thud. "Rugby is a man's sport," he declared. "Ballet is for prissies."

Lucy and Sue shared a glance; it was a terribly embarrassing situation.

"Why do you have to be such a Neanderthal, Dad?" demanded Flora, who had leapt to her feet, leaving the food on her plate untouched.

"It's okay, Flo. He's just teasing," said Desi, tugging her hand. "Sit back down and eat some lunch."

Flora sat back down and even picked up her fork, using it to push the food around on her plate.

There was an uncomfortable silence.

Sue tactfully broke it by changing the subject. "How's the hat show going?" she asked, turning to Perry. "Is everything ready?"

"Almost," said Perry. "We're setting it up in the long gallery, and I'm pairing the hats with paintings and other artifacts from the house."

"That's a clever idea," said Lucy.

"Perhaps a bit too clever," admitted Perry with a rueful grin. "Sometimes I think I may have overreached. It's quite a lot of work."

"Whenever he takes something, we have to put up a notice, explaining its absence, or find something similar to put in its place," said Poppy. "It would be easier if things were properly catalogued. We've hired a curator, Winifred Wynn, but she's only about halfway through."

"Things are always so much more complicated than you expect," said Lucy.

"Damned nuisance, these English Heritage chaps," muttered Gerald, causing Desi to suppress a smile.

"Did you know the general fell?" Poppy was not so much asking as explaining the arrival of Harold Quimby, the driver who'd met Lucy and Sue at the bus station. He was standing outside the French door and Poppy waved him in.

"When did this happen?" asked Desi.

"Just this morning. The old fellow came down with a big crash," said Perry.

"What's the news?" asked Poppy. "Harold, you know everyone here, right?"

"Indeed I do," he answered with a nod to

Sue and Lucy. "I hope you ladies are enjoying your stay?"

"Very much. Thank you," said Lucy.

"How are the chicks?" asked Sue. "Are they settling in?"

"I presume so," said Harold. "I was only delivering them to the farm."

"Harold is our facilities manager. He's responsible for maintaining this old pile," said Poppy. "Have you had a chance to investigate the general's accident?"

Harold pulled out a chair and seated himself at the table. "I have and I'm afraid I have bad news."

"Have you eaten?" asked Perry with a nod at the stew.

"I have, thanks," replied Harold. "There's no easy way to say this. We've got dry rot. The general fell because the wall gave way. There's nothing but powder behind that paneling."

Poppy's face had gone white and she was wringing her hands. Perry was biting his bottom lip. Gerald poured himself some more wine, and Flora dropped her fork with a clatter.

Desi was the only one who spoke. "Can you give us an estimate of the cost?"

"Ruinous," moaned Poppy. "We'll have to hire experts to investigate and then we'll have to do the repairs, and that's just the wall. We also have to find an art expert to evaluate the damage to the painting."

"Don't forget the frame," said Flora, speaking in a quiet voice.

"She's absolutely right," said Harold. "The frame is every bit as important as the picture. Maybe even more so."

"Good to know she's learning something at university," grumbled Gerald. "Something besides texting and taking drugs."

"Right, Dad," said Flora, adding an eye roll. "You forgot bonking. That's what I do the most."

"Enough," said Poppy. "We need to focus on the current crisis. Harold, do you have any idea what this will cost?"

"Not at the moment, but I'm getting estimates. We should probably go with Titmarsh and Fox. They've done work here before and they're familiar with the property. As for the painting, I consulted with Winifred and she's got a call in to the National Gallery."

"Lord help us," said Poppy, raising her eyes to the ceiling.

"Well, you know how it is," said Harold. "There's never just a little dry rot."

"And how did it get this far?" demanded Gerald in an accusatory tone. "You're supposed to be on top of these things."

"Oh, believe me, I'll be on to the roofers about this," said Harold in a somber tone as the phone began ringing. "They didn't report any problems when they did that section a few years ago. We may be able to get some satisfaction from them or their insurance company."

"Very good then," said Gerald, nodding and humphing.

"I'll get it," said Desi, leaving the table and crossing the room to answer the phone.

"I told you," said Poppy with a resigned smile. "The general has cursed us and it's just beginning."

"Oh, you don't believe in that old tale," protested Gerald.

"Trouble always comes in threes," offered Flora, who was studying a piece of carrot she'd speared on her fork.

"It won't bite." Desi had finished the call and was returning to the table, where he sat down heavily.

"More bad news?" asked Perry.

"Afraid so," Desi replied with a sigh. "That was Aunt Millicent. She's coming for the hat show."

"Bugger," said Perry. "And when will the old bat arrive?"

"Tomorrow."
"Double bugger," said Perry.

Chapter Five

"Don't mind Perry," said Poppy with a smile. "He's actually quite fond of Aunt Millicent."

"I wouldn't go quite that far," protested Perry. "But this must all be horribly boring for you," he said, addressing Lucy and Sue. "Never fear, I have arranged for our resident historian, Maurice Willoughby, to give you a tour of the manor." He checked his watch. "He should be in the library about now, if that's all right with you?"

"Fine with me," said Sue. "Lead on."

Once again Lucy found herself following Perry through the subterranean passage and then climbing up yet another narrow, twisty staircase until they emerged into a spacious, carpeted hallway where a set of open double doors revealed an enormous library.

"Ah, you must be the Americans," said the only occupant, looking up from a rather cluttered desk.

"Let me introduce Maurice Willoughby," said Perry. "These are my friends Sue Finch and Lucy Stone."

Maurice quickly rose and came around the desk, where he clasped Lucy's and Sue's hands in turn with his rather pudgy, rather damp one. He had the soft, bottom-heavy build of a man who spent too much time sitting, and the doughy complexion that came from being indoors. His straight, black hair was slicked down and his smile revealed a mouth full of extremely crooked teeth.

"I'm terribly pleased to make your acquaintance," he said quickly in a dismissive tone as he sidled up to Perry. "If you have a moment, m'lord." He picked up an aged piece of parchment bedecked with wax seals and stained, crumpled red ribbons. "I have found some interesting information about the third earl."

"Later, I think, Maurice," said Perry, scratching his chin. "I was hoping you'd give the ladies a tour of the old pile. Poppy and I have all this dry rot business to deal with and, well, when you get right down to it, you know far more about the place than I ever will."

"Of course, m'lord," Maurice replied, clearly disappointed. "Your wish is my command," he added with a little giggle.

"Maurice, as you well know, there's no need for all this m'lord nonsense. Just call me Perry, okay?"

"Sorry. It's just these surroundings," said Maurice, waving his hand at the beautifully appointed room.

The walls were lined with wooden shelves holding hundreds, perhaps thousands of gilded, leather-bound volumes. A dozen large blue and white Chinese vases were lined up on top of the bookcases. Persian carpets covered the floor, numerous sofas and chairs were arranged in various comfortable groupings, and the ceiling boasted complicated plaster work that imitated twisting vines. The windows were made of old, wavy glass held in place by lead strips and set into stone casements. A peek outside revealed the moat below, the manicured lawns of the estate park, and the rolling countryside beyond.

"It's all so fabulously feudal, it can go to a fellow's head. Especially if that fellow went to a bricks and mortar university as I did." Maurice grinned.

Perry laughed. "Well, I can't say that Oxford did much for me," he admitted. "I didn't make it past my first term. And I may be the lord of the manor but we know who's really in charge, don't we? I better not keep

Poppy waiting . . . so I trust I'm leaving my friends in good hands?"

"Absolutely," promised Maurice with a nod that shook the loose skin beneath his chin. "I think we'll start with the hall. This way, ladies." He indicated the double doors with a little bow and a flourish.

Once in the corridor, he led them past a couple portraits of ancestors and then popped open a concealed jib door. "I'm afraid we'll have to deal with the madding crowd, the marauding masses, the hoi polloi," he said, indicating a narrow staircase, "but this will give us a bit of an advantage."

Lucy and Sue followed him down the twists and turns of the staircase, eventually emerging in the huge hall filled with visitors. Behind ropes, they were confined to a walkway of heavy-duty industrial carpet. The damaged portrait of the general was propped against one wall and the area was cordoned off with yellow caution tape.

"Rather like a crime scene," observed Lucy.

"I'm afraid this poor ancestor took a tumble," explained a guide, a pleasantly plump woman wearing an official green blazer with the Moreton Manor emblem embroidered in gold thread on the breast pocket.

"Not an ancestor at all," said Maurice, correcting her in a rather sharp tone as he unsnapped a segment of rope, allowing Lucy and Sue to join the throng of visitors gathered on the trail of carpet. "The victim of this rather unfortunate accident is General Horatio Hoare, a friend of the third earl, and you" — he paused to check the guide's name tag — "Marjorie, ought to know that. I suggest you review your Facts and Fancies of Moreton Manor this evening."

"Oh, yes, Mr. Willoughby, I will certainly do that," said Marjorie, clearly embarrassed by the scolding which took place in front of numerous visitors. "I do hope the curse is just an old wives' tale," she added in an effort to regain some credibility.

"The only curse I know of," said Maurice, giving her a baleful glance, "is the unemployment that befalls unprepared guides."

Lucy decided it was time to stop Maurice's bullying and tossed the poor woman a lifeline. "The curse is real enough. The earl mentioned it himself this morning, when they discovered the painting had fallen. It's supposed to keep the manor safe as long as it's on the wall. The last time it came down a countess had a fatal accident."

This declaration caused a little buzz

among the visitors, who were clearly impressed by this bit of inside information.

Maurice, however, reacted defensively. "Well, as it happens," he said, puffing himself up, "there are various viewpoints on that particular incident. Shall we continue?"

"Yes, please," said Sue. "Can you tell us who painted the ceiling?"

"Ah, yes. The ceiling was commissioned by the fifth earl after his grand tour of the continent, which was of course the custom of the time. Young gentlemen were expected to travel abroad to attain the refinement expected of the aristocracy. He hired an Italian by the name of Giardino, not well known, but I think we can agree he did a fine job."

Lucy and Sue, as well as the gathered visitors, gazed upward at the cavorting gods and goddesses perched on their sturdy clouds.

"Amazing," said one woman.

"Moving along," said Maurice, "I believe the next room is the salon, the manor's main reception room."

Lucy and Sue marched along, following him through one enormous room after another, all filled with tapestries and paintings and elaborately carved furniture.

The enormous dining table was set with

forty places for a formal dinner, complete with a massive silver centerpiece depicting Nelson's victory at Trafalgar. Maurice took great pleasure in demonstrating how the cannons on the silver battleships could actually be fired to produce a gentle popping sound and a puff of smoke. The conservatory they'd viewed from outside was filled with lush tropical foliage plants and gorgeous blooming orchids. The morning room, which Maurice explained was traditionally the bailiwick of the countess, contained charming French furniture upholstered with pale blue silk brocade. Continuing up the stairs, they passed through several richly appointed guest rooms and then came to the earl's and countess's bedrooms located on either side of a roomy hallway.

"Absolutely gorgeous," observed Sue, glancing at the huge four-poster bed with crewel hangings. Set on a raised platform, it dominated the countess's chamber. "I could get used to this," she added, glancing at the vanity table covered with a froth of lace that occupied the space in front of the bay window.

The earl's bedroom was even grander. Red brocade covered the walls and an enormous dressing stand encrusted with gilt and crystal fittings stood nearby. His bed was larger, the platform higher, the paintings more numerous.

"Hey, Perce, we could do with something like this, couldn't we? Plenty of room for a bit of slap and tickle," exclaimed one woman.

Perce winked at his companion. "We could even invite the neighbors in."

"Ooh, for shame, Perce," chided the woman, growing a bit flushed.

Hearing this exchange, Lucy gave Sue an amused smile, but her thoughts were rather different. She was thinking of her bedroom at home, where a handmade quilt she'd picked up at an estate sale covered the bed and the dresser tops were always filled with clutter — change and keys, photos and bits of jewelry, appointment cards — that they were too busy or too lazy to put away properly. And she thought of the cozy kitchen that was the center of Perry and Poppy's life. "I wonder if Perry and Poppy mind giving up all this grandeur for what seems to be a rather simple lifestyle," she wondered aloud.

"If you ask me," replied Maurice with a bit of a Cockney accent creeping into his tone, "they're just doing what their kind have always done, and that is taking advantage of those less fortunate. This place was built on the labor of mill workers and miners and tenant farmers and now they charge those same folk ten pounds a head to come and see what they did with all the money they sweated out of their grandparents. They've still got 'em coming and going, working up a bit of an appetite after touring the house, so they buy lunch or a cream tea in the café. And nobody goes home without a tea towel or a souvenir magnet."

"I disagree," said Sue. "I think most people come because they want to imagine being the lord and lady, if only for an hour or two."

"But what did they do with themselves all day, when they had all those servants to do everything for them?" asked Lucy. "It must have been a rather empty life, all for show. They didn't even bring up their own children. I'd rather do things for myself. I take satisfaction in cooking supper and digging the garden, I even enjoyed changing the kids' diapers."

"Different strokes for different folks," said Sue.

Maurice delivered them to the exit, which he was quick to point out conveniently led to the café and gift shop, as well as the garden.

"Thank you so much for the tour," said Sue. "I really enjoyed it."

"Me, too," added Lucy. "Can we visit the garden, too?"

"Absolutely," said Maurice. "Don't miss the maze.'

"I bet it's amazing," said Lucy, getting a groan from Sue.

He pointed the way and they parted, Maurice presumably returning to his work in the library and Lucy and Sue heading down the brick path to the walled garden.

Lucy gasped as they stepped through the gateway and discovered the wealth of blooms in the garden. Neat beds of flowering bulbs were defined by boxwood borders and filled with rows of bedding plants including petunias and geraniums as well as alliums and tulips. Arbors covered with climbing vines promised a profusion of roses in a few weeks, green shoots in the perennial borders were harbingers of the blooms to come. The two friends wandered along the winding paths, exclaiming over the rare forms and colors, and the sheer magnitude of the plantings.

"You know," admitted Lucy, "I buy ten of these and ten of those. Sometimes the packages — like alliums — contain only three or four bulbs. Look at all these. It's mind boggling."

"I'm beginning to think Maurice is on to something," said Sue. "This represents a lot of money."

"And a lot of digging," said Lucy.

"But I suppose" — Sue nodded nod at some of the visitors who were also admiring the garden — "if you're going to charge ten pounds a head, you've got to give them something to see."

"What's that?" asked Lucy, pointing to a small stone building perched on a distant knoll.

"A folly, I imagine," said Sue.

"Let's go take a look," urged Lucy. "I need to stretch my legs after sitting on that plane."

"This doesn't sound like you," said Sue. "You're supposed to be depressed."

"I'm feeling a lot better," admitted Lucy. "I want to breathe deeply and get my circulation going. Put some pink in my cheeks."

"That's what they invented blush for," complained Sue.

"Come on. It'll do you good. You'll sleep like a baby tonight."

"I'm pretty sure that won't be a problem," said Sue with a sigh. They stepped through an opening in the wall and found themselves following a winding path covered with wood chips that led through a small woodland. Coming to a fork in the path, they observed a neat sign with arrows pointing the way to DIANA'S TEMPLE, THE MAZE, MANOR VILLAGE, MORETON CARAVAN CAMPGROUND, and MORETON ESTATE FARM.

"The maze is one way, the folly another," observed Sue. "Which way shall we go?"

"We can't miss the maze," said Lucy. "It's famous."

"But the folly is closer," said Sue, starting up the path.

"I hope there's a good view at the top of this hill. Was I the one who wanted to stretch my legs?" complained Lucy, growing out of breath.

"You were, and there's no backing out now," insisted Sue, trudging up the incline and pointing out an ersatz Greek temple. "See! We're almost there."

The temple was a round structure with a domed roof and a porch entirely circled with columns. As they drew closer, they saw there was a round little room in the center of the temple, but it was completely enclosed apart from a single door and a pair of barred and shuttered windows.

"Wouldn't you think they'd want to enjoy

the view?" asked Lucy in a puzzled tone.

"Maybe it's just for storage," said Sue as the door suddenly opened and a tall, leggy blonde popped out.

"Hi!" exclaimed Lucy, somewhat surprised.

The blonde didn't reply, but merely tossed her long, professionally highlighted hair over her shoulder and hoisted a huge shoulder bag into place under her arm before striding off on her very high heels.

"Not exactly country clothes," observed Sue. "She was wearing Louboutins."

"Loulouwhats?" asked Lucy, seating herself on the stone steps of the folly and gazing into the distance.

"Louboutins. Very expensive shoes. I recognized the red soles," said Sue, sitting beside her.

"You're looking at shoes. I'm looking at the view. Have you ever seen anything lovelier?"

Sue nodded, admiring the nearby pasture dotted with cows, the neat fields enclosed by hedges, the fringe of woodland, and the blue hills beyond. "God must be an Englishman," she said.

"So I've heard," agreed Lucy, leaning her shoulder against a pillar. She was stretching her neck when a sudden "humph" startled her and she turned to see that Gerald was standing behind them.

"Marvelous view, eh?" he said, pocketing a set of keys.

"Absolutely," said Sue.

"We've just been admiring the temple," said Lucy. "What's it used for, if you don't mind my asking?"

"Uh, storage — chairs and cushions, that sort of thing."

"Can we see?" asked Lucy.

"Sorry, but no can do. Don't have the key."

"No matter," said Sue, giving Lucy a reproving glance. "We ought to be heading back to the manor."

"Good idea, good idea," he said, sputtering like a walrus, "but be careful of the ha-ha. Wouldn't want to tumble into a cow pat would you?"

"We'll be careful," said Lucy.

Gerald lumbered awkwardly down the steps, then turned to face them. "It's never a good idea to go looking for trouble," he said before marching off.

CHAPTER SIX

"What was that all about?" asked Lucy, pulling herself to her feet and finding the maneuver rather painful.

"He's obviously having an affair with the blonde," said Sue, "and doesn't want us to mention seeing them."

"Gerald? With that gorgeous girl?"

"Yes, Lucy. Older rich guy, ambitious young woman. It's a tale as old as time."

"Poor Poppy," said Lucy. "She seems so nice."

"Nice isn't any help at all when a man decides to stray," said Sue as they walked together along the path.

Lucy was silent for a while, then spoke up. "No wonder he was so defensive when I asked to see inside the folly."

"He's probably got a little love nest in there."

"How horrible. There are probably spiders." Lucy disliked dark, dank spaces. "It was obvious he had the keys, even though he said he didn't."

"You're a regular Sherlock Holmes." Sue stepped aside to let some visitors pass. "Shall we investigate the amazing maze?"

The way to the maze was clearly marked and took them past rolling lawns dotted with trees and bluebells. There was no attendant at the maze entrance, which was simply a gap in a tall wall of privet hedge.

Lucy hesitated. "What if we can't find our way out?"

"Don't be silly," said Sue. "How hard can it be?"

"At this point, I don't think I could do a connect-the-dots," said Lucy with a sigh.

"Well, I think we have to try it. What will the folks back home think?"

"How would they even know?" grumbled Lucy, following Sue as she stepped boldly into the maze.

At the first intersection, she insisted on turning right. "There's always a key to these things, and it's usually to keep turning the same way, so we'll go right."

"Why right?" asked Lucy.

"Why not?" replied Sue, confident as ever. Nevertheless, they followed the narrow mowed paths lined on either side with twelve-foot tall hedges and kept turning right at every intersection until they encountered the same statue of a cupid that they'd seen before.

"Uh-oh," said Lucy. "I'm afraid we're just going in circles."

"Maybe there's two of these little guys," said Sue.

"I doubt it, Sue, and I'm really tired," said Lucy, pulling her cell phone out of her pocket. "I think we should call for help."

"Not yet," protested Sue. "Let's try going left."

"Which way is left?" asked Lucy.

"I don't know," admitted Sue. "I thought I had a good sense of direction, but I'm all turned around."

"That settles it," said Lucy. "I'm calling."

Perry took the call with some amusement and promised to send someone to lead them out.

True to his word, it was only a matter of minutes before a gardener showed up. He was a good-looking, muscular young man with sun-bleached blond hair, and was wearing an unbuttoned plaid shirt over a tight wife-beater shirt and jeans.

"This is so embarrassing," said Sue, greeting him with a rueful smile.

"Not to worry," said the gardener. "It happens more than you might think."

"Is there a trick to it?" asked Sue, who was unable to resist twisting a bit of hair flirtatiously around her finger. "You found us very quickly."

"It's pretty simple, really. Do you want to go to the center of the maze, where there is a charming bit of sculpture clearly designed to promote a bit of dalliance or would you rather go directly to the exit?"

Lucy began, "It is getting rather late —"

"Oh, I think we want to see the naughty sculpture," interrupted Sue with a definite twinkle in her eye.

"Righto," he said, leading the way. "It's left, right, left and so on until you reach the center and then it's right, left, right until you come to the exit."

"That's rather a lot to keep straight," said Lucy, who was finding the narrow pathways rather claustrophobic. "I don't know what we'd do if you hadn't come to our rescue."

"I was double-digging a flower bed, so it's you who came to my rescue," said the young fellow.

"We really appreciate your help," said Sue. "By the way, what's your name?"

"Geoff. Just Geoff will do." He stepped aside with a flourish so they could enter the center of the maze. "Meet Diana, Goddess of the Hunt," he said, indicating the statue that was the centerpiece of the outdoor room.

It wasn't the nude sculpture that caught their attention, however, but the prone body of a young man lying at her feet.

"Oy! What's this?" exclaimed Geoff in a take charge voice. He strode across the neatly clipped grass and bent over the young man, shaking his shoulder.

Lucy stood next to Sue, trying to understand this unexpected and shocking situation. She studied the man on the ground, observing that he was young and was wearing tight jeans and a black T-shirt; he had a shaved head and his arms were covered with tattoos. She thought he must have passed out, perhaps from a diabetic coma or a drug overdose.

"Shall we go for help?" she asked before realizing the question was foolish.

Geoff pulled a cell phone from his pocket. "I think it may be too late." He raised the phone to his ear and spoke into it then turned to Lucy and Sue. "It seems you're going to have to stay and give a statement, so you might as well make yourselves comfortable," he said, indicating a stone bench some distance from the body.

"Is he dead?" asked Sue, who had begun to tremble.

Lucy took her hand and led her to the bench, where they both sat down.

"I'm afraid so," said Geoff. "I've called the office and they will call the authorities and arrange for the maze to be closed to visitors. I'm to stay with you until —" Hearing laughter he broke off and went to head off the visitors.

They could hear him explaining that there had been an accident and the maze would have to be closed to visitors today and then giving them directions to the exit.

"This is so horrible," said Sue, who was unable to take her eyes off the corpse.

Lucy wrapped an arm around her friend's shoulder and patted her hand in that automatic way people do when they're trying to offer comfort. All the while, she was wondering how this person came to die in the maze at a stately home.

"He doesn't look like your typical visitor," she said, turning to Geoff. "Does he work here?"

"Not that I know of. I've never seen him before."

"Do you think he had one of those heart problems you hear about? Everything's okay until you drop dead?" asked Sue.

"Maybe he got scared and stressed by being in the maze," said Lucy.

"No, I think it was a drug overdose," said Geoff. "There's a syringe on the ground, next to the body."

"But why would anybody pay ten pounds admission to shoot up in the Moreton Manor maze?" wondered Lucy. "It doesn't make sense."

"It's beyond me," said Geoff, looking up as two uniformed police officers arrived. They were both men, one was black and the other white, and they went straight to the body.

"Naloxone?" inquired one.

"Too late," said the other. "Better call for the medical examiner."

While the black officer busied himself with his radio, the white officer introduced himself as he withdrew a leather-covered notebook from his pocket. "I'm PC Floyd. That's my colleague PC Lahiri. Can you identify the victim?"

"Afraid not," said Geoff. "These ladies got lost in the maze, called for help, and I was sent to lead them out. I called the office as soon as we discovered the body."

"And when was that?"

"About ten minutes ago," said Geoff.

"I'll need your names and addresses," said PC Floyd, opening the notebook and making a notation. After he'd taken down their information, he fixed his eye on Geoff. "Are you sure you do not know the victim?"

"Never seen him before," said Geoff rather quickly.

"Absolutely not," said Sue.

"Same here," said Lucy as a fortyish woman in a white jumpsuit arrived, accompanied by Harold Quimby.

"Thanks for showing me the way," she said, dismissing him and turning to PC Lahiri. "So what's the story?"

"Unidentified corpse, discovered twenty minutes ago," he said.

Quimby was speaking with PC Floyd. "May I take these ladies back to the manor? They're guests of the earl and I'm sure this has been very upsetting for them."

"No problem," replied the officer.

"Will there be an investigation?" asked Quimby.

PC Floyd shook his head. "Most unlikely. We don't have the manpower to investigate every victim of an overdose and that's the truth. All we can do is identify him and notify his next of kin so they can claim the body."

"Well, if you have any questions you know where to find us," said Quimby, turning to Lucy and Sue. "I am so sorry about this. Let's get you back to the house. The kettle's on the hob for tea . . . or perhaps you'd like something stronger?"

"Something stronger," said Sue, whose voice was still shaky.

There was no tea nor cocktails on offer in the kitchen when they returned and found Perry standing over the stove, cooking up a thick vegetable stew. He did offer glasses of wine, however, and they settled themselves with their drinks on the comfy sofa, dislodging the dogs who rather grudgingly rearranged themselves on the rug in front of the fireplace. It being warm there was no fire, but the delicious scent of the ribollita filled the air.

"I am so sorry you had to be involved in this sordid episode," said Perry, replacing the lid on the casserole before joining them and seating himself next to Sue. "That's the problem with opening your home to the public — people don't always behave very well."

"I suppose not," said Sue. "Have you had many people dying on your doorstep?"

Perry gave a rueful smile. "Not really. A few through the years. Mostly quite elderly. They get carried away a bit in the garden and overdo. The distances can be quite deceiving."

"This fellow didn't seem like a typical

stately home visitor," said Lucy. "He was quite young and dressed in jeans and a T-shirt. He had tattoos. . . ."

"Who had tattoos?" Flora had wandered in from the garden. As usual, she was dressed in a long flowing dress. Combined with her unkempt, stringy hair she looked rather like Ophelia after she'd drowned herself in the pond.

"A young man who was found dead in the maze," said Perry. "Sue and Lucy actually found him."

"Along with a gardener named Geoff," said Lucy.

"Thank goodness Geoff was there," said Sue.

"Someone was found dead in the maze?" asked Flora, wide-eyed. "Who was it?"

"They don't know," said Perry.

"Well, what did he look like?" asked Flora.

"Young, shaved head, tattoos on his arms," said Lucy.

"They said it was an overdose," offered Sue, but Flora was already leaving the room. Only her heavy perfume lingered, leaving any sign that she had been there.

"Do you think she knows him?" asked Lucy. "Maybe he was a friend."

"I hope not. He doesn't sound like the sort of person Flora ought to be friends with," Perry said. Rising and crossing the room to the stove, he lifted the lid on the pot and checked the progress of the ribollita. "So, apart from finding a body, did you enjoy the tour?"

"Oh, yes," exclaimed Sue, eager to change the subject. "We have nothing like this in America. There are grand houses, of course, but they were built by robber barons in the nineteenth century. We have nothing with such a long history."

"Willoughby's quite the historian," said Perry. "He's working on revising the guidebook for us."

"He's certainly a stickler for accuracy," said Lucy, recalling the way the historian corrected poor Marjorie.

"Is that Willoughby you're talking about?" inquired Desi. He'd paused at the island to pour himself a glass of wine before seating himself on the second sofa.

"He can be a bit overbearing at times," said Perry, "but he's certainly a hard worker. And that guidebook was last revised when Gram and Gramps were living here."

"It must have been wonderful when you had the whole place," said Sue with a sigh.

"Wonderful and scary," said Perry. "When I was a kid, they had a butler, Chivers was his name, who absolutely terrified me. He even frightened Gram. 'Whatever you do,' she used to say in this very serious voice, 'please don't upset Chivers.' "

"That was before my time," said Desi. "I used to love coming here when I was a kid. Of course, things were rather falling apart by then. Gramps had died and Uncle Wilfred followed soon after. Money was running short and there were no servants to speak of anymore. Flo and I were city kids so we loved the freedom here, having all this space to run around and ride ponies." He paused and took a sip of wine. "Rainy days were the best, though. Then we'd go exploring in the far reaches of the house, going from room to room and opening drawers and finding all sorts of trash and sometimes, real treasures."

"That's right," said Perry. "Remember when you found that sixteenth century inventory? It had been used to wrap up some jelly glasses."

"So typical, using a priceless antique document to protect some worthless jelly glasses," said Desi with a chuckle. "And there was that fabulous Chinese porcelain — a monkey, I think it was — used as a doorstop."

"We're still trying to sort things out. I don't know what we'd do without our curator," said Poppy, arriving with an armful of papers and a thick wad of upholstery fabric samples, all of which she dropped on an armchair where they joined the cushions and dented silver ewer she'd previously put there. "What a day." She sighed as she sank into another chair. "I am so sorry you were involved in the recent unpleasantness," she said, speaking to Lucy and Sue. "All I can do is offer my sincere apologies and assure you that this sort of thing is the exception rather than the rule." She turned to her son and deftly changed the subject. "Is this that good cab you brought, Desi?"

"Yup. My friend Henri grows it at the family domaine."

Sue caught Lucy's eye and winked, as if to say, "Look at us! Hanging out with people who know people who own vineyards."

"Delicious," said Poppy, savoring a sip before joining her son on the sofa. She looked up as an attractive young woman dressed in the countrywoman's uniform of cashmere sweater and tweed skirt entered the room. "Oh, Winifred, let me introduce our friends from America," she said, naming Sue and Lucy. "Winifred Wynn is our curator and a gift from God."

"I don't know about that," said Winifred,

smiling. "I just came by to let you know that the art restorer from the National Gallery is coming tomorrow to check out the damage to the general."

"Thanks for the update." Poppy dismissed her by adding, "Have a good evening."

When Winifred was gone, Poppy took a big swallow of wine. "Tomorrow is going to be a busy day. Don't forget Aunt Millicent is coming, along with that dragon Harrison."

"Harrison is Aunt Millicent's lady's maid," said Perry. "She's almost as bad as Chivers."

"Worse, I think," said Poppy. "We could hide from Chivers, especially in his later years when he took to drinking Gramps' port. Harrison is relentless. She won't take no for an answer. Aunt wants to sleep in the countess's bedroom —"

"That's impossible," said Perry. "It has to remain open to the public."

"I know, but that doesn't seem to matter to Aunt."

Perry frowned. "She can have the Chinese room. It's closed anyway while the bed curtains are restored."

"She's not going to like that," said Desi. "Can't you offer some treat to placate the old thing?"

"Have some folks in for dinner? Let her play the grande dame," suggested Perry. "We could use the big dining room, if we timed it right. The house closes at six and we could eat at eight. That would give the staff time to clear away the ropes and carpet savers, and reset the table with the second-best china."

"That's a good idea. She detests eating here in the kitchen," said Poppy. "I'll invite the vicar and his wife. They're always available on short notice. We've got Lucy and Sue, and there's Willoughby and Winifred." Poppy counted people on her fingers. "I need one more man."

"Quimby!" exclaimed Perry.

"And we'll get a couple gardeners to play footmen for the night."

"Oh," chimed in Sue, "we met the nicest fellow today, by the name of Geoff. We got lost in the maze and he came to help us. When we found the body, he took over."

"Dishy Geoff," said Poppy, determined to steer clear of any topic as disagreeable as the discovery of a body. "Hearts were broken throughout the county when his engagement was announced. With a wedding coming, I'm sure he'll be glad for a bit of extra cash."

Lucy was struck by Poppy's smooth direction of the conversation and wondered if she was simply determined to limit the discussion to amusing topics or whether she knew more about the dead man than she wished to reveal. Certain that Flora had recognized the description of the young man, Lucy suspected that Perry thought so, too.

"Will we have to dress?" asked Desi.

"Dinner jacket will do," said Poppy, getting a groan from Desi.

"This will be a treat," said Sue. "Dressing up for a formal dinner at Moreton Manor."

Not so much, thought Lucy, biting her lip. She didn't have anything to wear, and she wasn't at all sure she wanted to stay with people who regarded a young man's death as nothing more than an awkward inconvenience.

"Do you have plans for tomorrow?" asked Perry. "I'm afraid I'm going to have to neglect you, as I'm rather involved with the exhibition.

"Never fear," said Sue. "Lucy and I are perfectly capable of amusing ourselves. In fact, I was thinking of exploring Oxford. It's not far, is it?"

"Not at all far, twenty minutes or so," said Poppy. "We can have someone drive you.

Just give a call when you're ready to come back."

"Great," said Lucy, who had noticed Perry placing a basket of bread on the kitchen island. "Shall I set the table?"

"I think I'll just set the grub here on the island, buffet style, if that's okay with everyone?"

"Fine with me," said Sue.

Desi was opening a cupboard and counting out plates. "Shall I call Flo?"

"She'll come if she wants to," said Poppy with a sigh. "It's better not to force the issue. At least, that's what the therapists tell me. Flora knows when we eat dinner." Poppy looked up as Gerald arrived, stomping his muddy feet on the doormat. "Did you have a rumbly in your tumbly, dear?"

Lucy was tempted to say he'd had a bit of a *tumbly* in the *rumbly,* but thought better of it and bit her tongue. Sue, however, caught her eye and gave a mischievous smile and Lucy found herself giggling.

"Something funny?" demanded Gerald, who had advanced to the island and was emptying the wine bottle into his glass.

"It's just the way you English people have with words," said Lucy. "I feel as if I'm in a Winnie the Pooh book."

"It's more like a fairy tale," said Sue.

"This beautiful house, the garden, the folly — it's all so magical."

Lucy stared into her wineglass where the surface of the wine reflected light from the downlights in the ceiling. Sue was right, she thought. Moreton Manor was like a castle in a fairy tale, and fairy tales were full of wicked witches, evil queens, nasty trolls, and big, bad wolves.

Gerald glared briefly at Sue, then downed half his glass of wine. "Is there any more of this plonk?" he demanded.

"It's not plonk," protested Desi. "It's 2013 cabernet from Henri Le Vec's vineyard in France. It's rather special. It's the wine the family reserves for itself."

"Well, whatever it is, it's all gone and we're going to need another bottle," said Gerald. "Are you going down to the cellar or shall I?"

"I'll go," said Desi, promptly disappearing through a door.

"I think we can start. Desi will be back in a minute," said Perry, setting the tureen on the island and handing a plate to Sue.

Lucy's mood improved as everyone gathered around the island and helped themselves to generous servings of Perry's delicious ribollita. The vegetables were fresh from the garden and bursting with flavor, the whole grain bread had a crunchy crust, and the wine was plentiful. Even the butter was marvelously flavorful, tasting of sunshine and sweet meadow grass.

"This isn't at all what I expected," said Sue. "I have to say it's a pleasant surprise."

"Did you expect *Downton Abbey*?" asked Poppy.

"I guess I did, a little bit," confessed Sue, who was fetching second helpings for herself.

Lucy watched in amazement. In all the years she had known her, she had rarely seen Sue finish her firsts, much less go back for seconds.

"Well, you'll get plenty of *Downton Abbey* tomorrow when Aunt Millicent arrives," said Desi.

"I didn't bring any dressy clothes," admitted Lucy, getting an eye roll from Sue. "Can you recommend any shops in Oxford?"

"I'm afraid I'm no help. I haven't bought anything from a shop in years. Most of my clothes were bought at agricultural fairs," admitted Poppy.

"We'll put that question to Flo," said Desi. "She's certain to have some ideas."

"Great," said Lucy, rising to help Poppy clear the table for dessert.

"Rhubarb and custard," said Perry. "I

hope you like rhubarb."

"Love it," declared Lucy, thinking of the huge plant in her garden at home. That led to thoughts of Bill and Patrick and the girls and she was suddenly stricken with a huge wave of sadness and longing for home.

"Coffee, Lucy?" asked Perry, sounding concerned.

"Better not," she said, quickly rallying. "Jet lag, you know."

"I don't think even coffee will keep me awake," said Sue, accepting a cup. But even she turned down a second cup when it was offered. "I think Lucy and I need an early night."

"Of course," said Poppy. "You've had a difficult day. We'll see you in the morning. Sleep well."

Lucy and Sue started up the stairs to their guest rooms, Sue pausing midway to give her nose a good blow. "Dogs," she said by way of explanation. "I think I'm allergic."

They had reached the first landing when an odd sound caught their attention. Lucy pushed open the doorway. Leaning into the corridor that contained the family's bedrooms, they clearly heard someone sobbing.

"That must be Flora," said Lucy. "I bet she's crying over the fellow in the maze."

"Do you think she knew him?" asked Sue.

"She seemed to recognize his description. She ran out of the room."

"The others didn't seem to know him," said Sue thoughtfully. "I guess he really wasn't the sort of fellow you'd bring home to meet the family."

"I guess this is the side of Moreton Manor that the day-trippers don't see."

"It's not all strawberries and cream."

"It's not even rhubarb and custard," said Lucy.

Chapter Seven

Once in her room, Lucy decided to call home. The discovery of the tattooed young man's body had upset her, and she couldn't erase the picture from her mind. Who was he? Why had he come to Moreton Manor? And most disturbing of all, what had caused him to turn to drugs? Such a waste of a young life troubled her, but she was also upset by the family's determination to ignore the situation. She'd heard the term *stiff upper lip* before, but she hadn't realized what it actually meant. She didn't know if they were also troubled by the discovery of the body and were repressing an emotional response or if they simply didn't care. Flora was the only one who seemed upset, and Lucy wasn't sure if that was because she had some sort of relationship with the young man or if her reaction was a symptom of her obviously fragile mental state.

Lucy felt anxious. Dark clouds were building in her mind and she knew she needed to touch base with those she loved; she needed to reassure herself that everyone at home was safe and things were going well. She wanted to hear Bill's voice and needed to know that he was there for her, even if they were separated by thousands of miles of ocean. But when she punched in his cell phone number, he didn't answer, so she tried the land line in the house and got Zoe.

"How's it going?" she asked her daughter, making a determined effort to lighten her voice. "Are you all ready for the prom?"

"I think so. It'll be okay if I do my hair myself, don't you think? And I got a tube of self-tanner. I don't want to spend the money for a professional spray tan."

Hearing this, Lucy was puzzled. "But you had the appointments. I left checks for you to use."

"I know, Mom, but we got the reply from Strethmore . . ." Zoe desperately wanted to attend Strethmore College, and she'd been accepted, but the financial aid package had not been very generous. The family had appealed the award, explaining the need for more funds, and the answer had apparently arrived.

"How much did they come up with?" asked Lucy.

"Ten thousand and Dad says it's not enough, so that's why I'm trying to save money."

Lucy was impressed by her daughter's reaction, but thought it was misguided. "Look, sweetie, skipping a salon appointment and a fake tan session isn't going to make much difference in the big picture. We'll figure it out when I get back."

"Well, Pop is meeting some guy, some friend of Toby's who's a financial planner. He says this guy has some ideas about maximizing investments or something."

Lucy thought of the modest balance that remained in the education fund that had been depleted by the older kids' college expenses and wondered what sort of investment could increase it substantially in the short time they had before it was needed for their youngest child. "Is this that Doug fellow?"

"I didn't get his name," said Zoe.

"Well listen, I think you should get your hair done and get the spray tan. You'll be even more gorgeous than you usually are and you'll have a wonderful time at the prom. I want to see lots of pictures."

"Okay, Mom," said Zoe, sounding pleased. "And how's your trip?"

"Well, it's not quite what I expected," said

Lucy, choosing her words carefully.

"Life's full of surprises, isn't it?" said Zoe.

"It sure is," said Lucy. "Take care, sweetie. I love you."

"Love you, too, Mom."

Poppy was already at the big table, studying a spread sheet while she ate her boiled egg and toast, when Lucy and Sue came into the kitchen early the next morning. She looked up and greeted them with a smile. "Coffee's ready, help yourselves to whatever you want," she invited with a nod at the various offerings awaiting them on the island. "By the way, I got a call from the police late last night and it seems they've identified the young man. He's from London and it's a bit of puzzle what he was doing here at Moreton, but they're satisfied his death was due to an accidental overdose. Case closed."

"Did they tell you his name?" asked Lucy, slipping a couple crumpets into the toaster.

"They did, but I forgot," said Poppy, turning over a page of the spreadsheet. "Maybe it was Eric something or other."

Sue filled her mug with coffee and joined Poppy at the table. Lucy soon followed with her coffee and crumpets. They all looked up in surprise when Flora arrived, as she habitually skipped breakfast. Whatever had reduced her to tears in the night seemed to have been resolved as she was clearly in a much calmer mood and even helped herself to a small bowl of yogurt topped with three strawberries.

When she politely inquired if Lucy and Sue had any plans for the day and learned they intended to go to Oxford, she quickly offered to drive them and give them a tour.

"Hope you don't mind going in the Mini," she said an hour or so later, leading the way to the stable yard where an assortment of vehicles were parked, including an ancient MiniCooper.

"Not at all," said Lucy, who knew that she would have to sit in the back because that was simply the way the universe was ordered. Not that she minded, but it would be nice if just once Sue would at least offer her the front seat.

The Mini had no suspension to speak of, and the three women bounced along down the drive and along country roads bounded by tall hedges. It was a lovely spring morning, warm and sunny and not at all like spring in coastal Maine, which was always a rather chilly affair due to breezes blowing in over the cool ocean water. There were lots of flowers in bloom, including bluebells, and the birds were tweeting and trilling to beat the band. It wasn't long at all before they spotted the "dreaming spires" of Oxford in the distance.

Flora knew her way around and drove confidently down the narrow streets and past numerous bicyclists, taking them right under the quaint Hertford Bridge. Supposedly inspired by the Bridge of Sighs in Venice, it extended over a narrow street and connected two buildings.

"Ooh, look!" exclaimed Lucy, "I've seen that on TV."

"In the Inspector Morse mysteries," said Flora. "They've managed to use the whole city in one episode or another. It's kind of a local industry."

"Things do seem very familiar," admitted Lucy, who was a fan of the original TV show as well as the recent spin-offs. "It's kind of like déjà vu."

Flora zipped around the famous Radcliffe Camera, with its unusual circular design, and past the ancient stone colleges, whose walls were often plastered with announcements for concerts, sales, and other events. She soon popped out on an extremely busy main street, explaining that the Botanic Garden and Magdalen Bridge were at one end, the Ashmolean Museum was at the other end, and there was shopping in between.

"Oh, let's go to the museum," begged Lucy, recalling the description in her guide book. "It has Guy Fawkes' lantern."

"And the Alfred Jewel," added Flora.

Sue was not enthused. "On one condition. We'll take a quick peek, eat an early lunch, and spend the rest of the day shopping."

"The Eagle and Child is a famous pub. Tolkien hung out there with his writer friends, the Inklings. It's quite near the museum," said Flora.

"We must go there so I can send pictures to Toby — he loves Tolkien — and then we can shop till we drop," said Lucy, surprising her friend. "I do need to buy something to wear to dinner tonight." She leaned forward in her seat. "Flora, are there any shops you would recommend? That aren't too expensive."

"I usually go to one of the resale places," admitted Flora. "You can even take the dress back after you're done with it. I like Secondhand Rose. It's next to Marks and Spencer. You can't miss it."

"Lucy!" protested Sue. "Why didn't you pack something?"

"I really don't have anything I thought

would do," admitted Lucy.

"Well, here we are," said Flora, suddenly taking a U-turn and pulling up in front of a very ancient gray stone church with a tall tower. "I'll let you two explore while I, well, I have a bunch of boring stuff that I can't put off," she said, adding an exaggerated eye roll. "I have to meet my tutor."

"Oh, sure," said Sue, somewhat hesitantly. Lucy figured that, like herself, Sue was surprised by this sudden dismissal, but didn't want to seem unappreciative of the trouble Flora had taken.

"If you want a ride back, meet me here at three," Flora said.

"Three it is. See you then," said Lucy, beginning the process of extricating herself from the tiny car. Then the two friends stood on the sidewalk and watched as Flora zoomed off.

"I wonder . . ." began Lucy.

"She's a student, Lucy," said Sue. "She has to meet her tutor. That's how they do it here. More like independent study when we were in college."

"Funny sort of tutorial," insisted Lucy. "There was no sign of a book or a notebook or a laptop in that car. And why does a little rich girl like Flora buy her clothes at a secondhand shop?"

"Vintage is all the rage with young people," said Sue. "Give it up, Lucy. You're not Inspector Morse. I don't know about you, but I can't say I'm very excited about this Guy Fawkes." She gave Lucy a serious look. "You may not know this, Lucy, but he was a very bad sort. He tried to blow up Parliament."

"I do know," said Lucy. "They remember him with bonfires every fifth of November on Guy Fawkes Day."

"Well," sniffed Sue, "there's no accounting for tastes. As for that Alfred Jewel, it's nothing at all you could wear. I saw a photo and it's really a very ugly lumpish sort of thing."

"I take it you don't want to visit the museum," said Lucy.

"No, and I don't care about the musty old pub either. Eagles and children don't go together very well." She looked longingly at a sign pointing to the Covered Market. "I want to go shopping."

"Okay," agreed Lucy. "On one condition. We visit the Botanic Garden."

"It seems rather far to walk," began Sue, only to be silenced with a look from Lucy. "Okay. Okay."

"Good," said Lucy, who really didn't mind skipping the museum. She was eager to find something to wear to the formal dinner and was grateful for Flora's advice.

Secondhand Rose was just where Flora had said it was, and Lucy found an affordable long black skirt and a creamy lace top that Sue pronounced acceptable.

After visiting most of the shops, which offered designs aimed at college-aged girls, even Sue admitted defeat. She was able to satisfy her need to spend at a Boots drugstore, where she found a tempting array of bath and beauty products not available in the US, so the morning was not a complete loss for her.

They grabbed a quick lunch at a noisy pub mainly patronized by students, where Lucy ordered a sandwich and Sue opted for a liquid lunch of Guinness stout.

"It's only got ninety calories and it's awfully good for you," she insisted, but Lucy wasn't convinced.

Thus fortified, they made their way toward the Magdalen Bridge and the Botanic Garden, which Lucy found extremely familiar.

"I swear, half of those Morse episodes are filmed here," she said as they strolled along a wide path that ran along the river. Eventually finding a bench, they sat down and took in the busy scene on the Cherwell River filled with boaters floating along in punts they'd rented from the boat hire on the other side of the Magdalen Bridge.

The sun was warm and they were both feeling tired after their long walk. It was quite delightful to simply sit and rest and soak up the sunshine. They dozed off.

Lucy woke with a start. Checking her watch, she found it was twenty to three. "Sue, Sue, wake up!" she cried, jumping to her feet.

"Wha', wha'? I wasn't sleeping," protested Sue.

"Never mind. We have to go. It's almost three."

"Flora will wait for us," said Sue, gathering her things together and strolling in the direction of the garden's gift shop.

"I'm not sure she will. She might think we've made other plans," said Lucy, more to herself than Sue.

Inside the shop, Lucy confronted the array of tempting garden merchandise and paused to examine a pair of rose gloves said to be thorn-proof.

Suddenly, it was Sue who was in a hurry. "Come, come, Lucy. You can get those at home, you know."

Lucy reluctantly replaced the gloves. "I know."

They exited the garden together, and Lucy insisted on taking a quick look at the famous Magdalen Bridge, which irritated Sue.

"I don't want to have to hire a taxi or rent a car to get back," she said.

"Look, it's not that far to the tower," said Lucy. "We have to cross the road anyway so we might as well do it here."

The road narrowed at the bridge, which was very much in use and carried a constant stream of traffic. They were able to dart between the slowed vehicles without too much trouble. Then they took a quick peek at the river below where people were lined up and waiting to rent punts. Turning around, they headed back up the busy High Street toward the agreed upon meeting place at the tower. Lucy looked back across the bridge for one last view of the river. It was then that she caught a glimpse of Flora on the opposite side of the bridge, standing and staring down at the river water below.

Something in the way she was standing and the way her attention was so fixed on the river worried Lucy. It was hard to believe the young woman who looked like a homeless person, with her shoulder blades clearly delineated beneath her oversized shirt and her unkempt hair, was a member of one of England's most aristocratic families. "Look!" she told Sue, pointing through the traffic toward Flora. "We have to get over there."

"Hold on, Lucy," cautioned Sue. "We don't want to embarrass her."

"She might do something . . . desperate," said Lucy, spotting a break in the traffic and dashing recklessly back across the roadway, getting a chorus of honks from angry drivers.

By the time she reached the sidewalk, she discovered Flora had moved on and was already some distance ahead of her, making her way toward the tower with her loose clothing flapping about her skeletal frame. Lucy continued along on the left side of the street, with Sue on the other, until she was able to safely cross over once again and join her.

"That was foolish, Lucy," chided Sue. "You could have been killed."

"There was just something in the way she was standing," said Lucy. "It scared me. I was afraid she'd jump or something."

Sue took her hand and squeezed it. "I know. I thought the same thing."

"She knew that boy — the one who died. I'm sure of it," said Lucy.

"Do you think she's doing drugs?" asked

Sue, thinking aloud. "It would explain a lot."

"In addition to not eating. She's definitely a troubled soul."

"Poor Poppy is worried about her."

"Maybe instead of worrying, she ought to do something," suggested Lucy.

"I'm sure she tries," said Sue. "It must be a terribly difficult situation."

They were both relieved when they reached the tower and saw Flora waiting for them. She greeted them with a big smile and politely asked if they'd enjoyed their day in town then led them through narrow, winding streets to the parking lot where she'd left the Mini. Once they were in the car, however, she fell silent and seemed preoccupied with her thoughts, actually sailing through a red light.

"Watch out!" exclaimed Sue as they swerved around an approaching van and nearly collided with a bicyclist who twisted her front wheel sharply, causing her bike to tip over. She saved herself by hopping along on one foot until she was able to right her bike and continue on her way while raising a middle finger and shaking it at Flora.

"You could have killed that poor girl," said Lucy, impressed by the cyclist's coordination.

"If I had, they'd probably give me a

medal," declared Flora angrily. "Everyone agrees these cyclists are a menace. They're always knocking over pedestrians."

Neither Lucy nor Sue responded and they made the return drive in an uncomfortable silence. Lucy wondered if Flora's outburst was due to embarrassment, but when she caught a glimpse of her expression in the rearview mirror she thought Flora looked terribly sad. When they finally arrived at the manor, Flora didn't bother to park the Mini in the garage but left it in the middle of the stable yard. She hopped out and ran into one of the connected outbuildings, abandoning them without a word.

"Well, that was interesting," said Lucy as they gathered their bags and got out of the car.

"You have to admit she had a point about those cyclists. We almost got run down a few times today."

"I know," agreed Lucy, "but that cyclist had the right-of-way and Flora wasn't paying attention. That girl's got something on her mind, and it's not good."

When they went inside, Sally told them they were just in time for the obligatory afternoon tea with Aunt Millicent and sent them upstairs to the family's private living room. Lucy had expected Aunt Millicent to be a tall and forbidding Maggie Smith type, so she was surprised when they joined Perry and Poppy in the attractively furnished room and were introduced to a very short, very stout woman whose georgette dress smelled of moth balls. Her black, frizzy hair was obviously dyed and was thinning on top. Her Florentine gold necklace was much too tight for her plump neck.

"Since you're Americans, you won't know the proper way to address me, so I better tell you," she said, helping herself to a piece of cake from the plate Perry was passing around. "I'm Lady Wickham, but," she added, as if conferring a special privilege, "you may call me Your Ladyship."

"It's lovely to meet you, Lady Wickham," said Sue, accepting a cup of tea from Poppy.

"I hope you had a pleasant journey," said Lucy, taking a seat among the plump pillows scattered on a Chesterfield sofa. "Did you come far?"

"Not far, but it certainly wasn't pleasant," said Lady Wickham. "Everyone drives so terribly fast these days."

"Flora gave us a lovely tour of Oxford," said Sue, sitting down next to Lucy.

"I hope you didn't have to ride in that ridiculous Mini," said Lady Wickham, raising her eyebrows.

"It was tons of fun," said Lucy. "We had a fine day."

"More cake, Aunt?" offered Perry.

"Oh, all right," said Lady Wickham, taking a second piece. "Of course this walnut cake is nothing like it used to be when I was a girl. Then, we thought we'd died and gone to heaven if there was Fullers walnut cake for tea."

"Fullers has been out of business for quite a while," said Poppy.

"Times change, and not for the better, I find," said Lady Wickham with a dismissive glance at the tea tray loaded with an abundant assortment of cakes, sandwiches, and scones, as well as Devonshire cream, butter, and various jams. "Take this marmalade, for instance. Store bought." She sighed. "We always used to make our own with Lyle's golden syrup."

"I find Cooper's does it better than I can," said Perry.

"And why are you doing the cooking?" demanded Lady Wickham. "Can't you afford a cook?"

"I enjoy it. It's simple as that," said Perry.

"And I suppose you enjoy accommodating your American guests in the servants' quarters instead of proper guest rooms, and putting me in that dreadful Chinese torture chamber with writhing dragons climbing all over the walls."

"Aunt," began Poppy in a deliberately soothing tone, "you know that wallpaper is quite special. Art students come here to study it."

"The countess's bedroom is a feature of the house tour," said Perry. "Our visitors expect to see it. That suite of furniture is quite remarkable."

"You wouldn't want to wake up in the morning with a crowd of people staring at you, would you?" asked Flora.

"Certainly not," declared Lady Wickham, plucking a couple sandwiches from the tea tray. "If it were up to me, Moreton Manor would remain a private home, like my very own Fairleigh."

"You're very fortunate to be able to maintain Fairleigh," said Perry. "We have to cope with roof repairs and death duties and all sorts of enormous expenses."

"We consider ourselves fortunate to be able to keep Moreton from rack and ruin, and to share it with our visitors," said Poppy, looking up as Winifred arrived, along with another woman. "And tonight we're eating in the dining room. It will be quite like old times."

"I'm sorry to interrupt," began Winifred.

"But Jane and I did want to have a word with you about the damaged painting."

Lady Wickham pounced on this bit of information. "Damage? What painting?"

"The general," said Perry. "He fell off the wall."

"My goodness! How could that happen?"

"An accident, Aunt," said Poppy. "Let me introduce Winifred Wynn our curator and her colleague Jane Sliptoe, who is here as a consultant from the National Gallery. She's here to examine the damage and help us plan a course of action."

"And since you're here, would you care for some tea?" offered Perry.

"I would love a cup," said Jane, who was dressed professionally in a crisp white shirt and black pantsuit. "Milk, no sugar."

"Just a slice of lemon for me," said Winifred.

Perry poured while the two women seated themselves.

Winifred accepted her cup, took a sip, and followed it with a deep breath, as if she were about to plunge into a deep pool. "Do you want the good news first or the bad?"

"Is the general done for?" asked Perry.

"No, no. The general can be fixed, and it won't be too expensive, either. A bit of glue ought to do it."

Poppy let out a great breath. "That is good news. What a relief."

"So what is the bad news?" asked Perry.

"Well," began Jane. "Winifred asked me to take a look around the gallery where you're having the hat show. She was particularly interested in several Italian paintings attributed to Veronese and Titian."

"Attributed?" asked Poppy suspiciously.

"Wrongly, I'm afraid," said Jane. "They're copies. The sort of thing a young nobleman would collect on a grand tour. Actually quite a good example of that sort of stuff. Very high quality . . ."

"But not originals," said Poppy with a sigh.

"I took a look 'round the chapel, too," said Winifred, setting her cup and saucer on the coffee table. "There's a very good gold reliquary in there. I suspect it's a Bonnanotte and quite a nice one."

"I could use it in the hat show," exclaimed Perry. "It would go terribly well with that bishop's miter."

"Or we could sell it to pay for those, um, other repairs," said Poppy.

"What repairs?" demanded Lady Wickham, her eyebrows shooting up.

"Oh dear. Just look at the time," said Perry, pointing to his watch.

"Yes!" exclaimed Poppy. "It is getting late and we have to dress for dinner."

That was the signal that afternoon tea was over. The others went their separate ways, but Lucy and Sue stayed to help Perry collect the cups and saucers and load them into the dishwasher before they went to their rooms to change into their finery for the formal dinner in the manor's grand dining room.

In general, Lucy was skeptical of enterprises that required new clothes, but when she caught a glimpse of herself in a mirror as she descended the magnificent staircase in the hall, she decided this was a lifestyle she could definitely get used to. She felt as if she were in a movie when she stepped into the salon she'd seen earlier on the tour with Maurice and accepted a glass of sherry from Dishy Geoff togged out in crisp white shirt and black jacket with tails. She paused for a moment, taking sips of sherry and admiring the spacious room, which felt rather like an enormous tent because the ceiling was draped with yards and yards of rich, red, paisley fabric. The parquet floor was dotted with Persian rugs and the furniture was largely French, with curved legs and plenty of gilding.

She looked for Sue, who had gone ahead, and found her standing in front of an embossed leather screen, talking with Perry. Poppy was helping her elderly aunt adjust her shawl, a process that seemed to be hopelessly complicated, and Gerald was in a corner with the leggy blonde she'd seen at the folly. She was wearing a strapless red number that showed a great deal of bosom that rose and fell with every breath.

"Lucy, I don't think you know Vickie Prior-Keyes," said Flora, grabbing her by the arm and dragging her across the room. She was dressed head to toe in black, which made her look rather like Morticia Addams . . . if Morticia had been on a starvation diet. "Vickie is a buddy of mine from school."

Gerald didn't seem particularly pleased by the interruption and neither did Vickie.

"Delighted, I'm sure," she said with an expression that belied her words. "Now, Flora, I've been telling your dad that heritage is a valuable tool for image makers, and you have heritage to spare."

"What do you mean?" asked Quimby, who had joined the group and was clearly enthralled by Vickie's décolletage.

"Corporate sponsors, of course," said Vickie.

"Corporate sponsors?" asked Poppy, taking her husband's arm in a possessive way. "Like who?"

"Anyone, really. Take the tea you serve in the café. Whatever it is."

"Twining's, I believe," said Poppy.

"Well, I would suggest approaching them to see if they will pay for the right to mention that in an ad — Twining's, the tea served at Moreton Manor."

"Rather weak tea, I think," said Poppy with a chuckle. "Since they've got a royal warrant."

"Well, perhaps that wasn't the best example," said Vickie, allowing her breasts to rise and fall rather dramatically. "It's the idea of the thing. Ketchup or mustard or carpet cleaner — there are numerous possibilities."

"In my day," declared Lady Wickham from the throne-like chair where she was holding court with Maurice and Winifred, "commerce was never discussed at the dinner table."

Maurice, ever the sycophant, was beaming with pleasure, apparently thrilled to be talking with a countess, but Winifred seemed to be looking for an escape route. It came in the form of a black man in a clerical collar, who was entering the room holding hands with a white woman.

"Exactly. We should save talk of business for tomorrow," said Poppy in the unusual position of agreeing with her aunt. "I do hope everyone knows everyone. Aunt, I don't know if you've met our new vicar, Robert Goodenough and his wife, Sarah."

Sarah, who had curly blond hair and was wearing a dazzling African print dress, gave everyone a big smile. "We're so pleased to be here."

"I suppose this is quite an improvement from Africa," said Lady Wickham. "What with that ebony virus and those Loko Harem terrorists."

"Actually, we're from Hoxton," said Robert with a smile.

"And it's *Ebola* virus and *Boko* Haram," said Flora, rolling her eyes.

"And the children?" inquired Poppy. "Are they settling in?"

"Very well," said Sarah. "They like their new school very much, and I've been enjoying the garden. I'm growing lettuce and all sorts of lovely vegetables."

"I love gardening," said Lucy. "Coming from chilly New England, I'm terribly jealous of your gentle English climate."

"You must come and see my garden," invited Sarah. "Are you free tomorrow? For high tea?"

"High tea. A workingman's meal," sniffed Lady Wickham. "Beans on toast, I suppose."

"I'll do you better than that," said Sarah with a tolerant smile toward Lady Wickham.

"I've heard such lovely things about your house, Your Ladyship," said Maurice as Dishy Geoff made another pass with the tray containing glasses of sherry. "Can you tell me about it?"

"It's nothing very fancy," said Lady Wickham, accepting a fresh glass. "Just a simple Georgian, but I do think that's the nicest sort of house."

"I quite agree," said Maurice. "Lovely proportions."

"And I do have some rather nice bits and pieces from my family," she continued.

"Do tell," urged Maurice, before savoring a sip of sherry.

"Well, this ring you see," she said, presenting him with a rather plump, unmanicured hand. "I'm told it's a rather good emerald."

Maurice took her hand and bent his head to take a better look. "It's magnificent. Such clarity."

"Don't swallow the damn thing," advised Gerald, draining his glass of sherry and reaching for another.

"Maurice is revising the manor's guidebook," said Poppy. "He's discovered a wealth of information —"

"Costing a damned fortune, too," grumbled Gerald.

"These old houses are so rich in history," said Sue.

"Well, of course. You have no history to speak of in America," said Lady Wickham.

"Our town was settled in the sixteen hundreds by people who left England," said Lucy, who was finding Her Ladyship's condescension rather irritating. "They must have been very unhappy to risk their lives on a treacherous sea voyage and to struggle in a new land."

"Probably thieves or pirates," sniffed Lady Wickham.

"Do tell us about your upcoming show, Desi," said Poppy, eager to change the subject.

"It's *Sleeping Beauty.* One of my favorites," said Desi.

"Are you the prince?" asked Sarah.

"Prince! That's a good one," scoffed Gerald. "He's a prancing priss."

Lady Wickham shrieked with laughter. "He's a prance, get it? Not a prince. A prance!"

The sudden noise startled Dishy Geoff and he dropped the tray full of empty glasses, smashing several of the precious crystal wine glasses.

"No matter," said Poppy, determinedly calm.

"I'm terribly sorry," said Geoff, stooping to gather up the broken bits.

"It wasn't his fault," said Desi, defending Geoff.

"I think we should go in to dinner," said Poppy.

Lucy turned to Sue, who was now standing beside her. "How many courses?" she asked, under her breath.

"Probably far too many," replied Sue.

CHAPTER EIGHT

Lucy groaned and rolled over in her sleep.

Someone was running a chain saw in her bedroom and another crazed lumberjack was driving a wood-splitting maul into her skull. She wanted to call for help, but her mouth was filled with cotton. She was gagged. This was bad, very bad indeed. She had to find a way to save herself! But that would require opening her eyes and she could tell . . . right through her closed eyelids . . . that the light was intensely bright. So bright that it would hurt.

The chainsaw noise stopped, which was a mercy, but was immediately replaced by the cheerful ringing tones of "Frère Jacques" — her cell phone's ring tone. If only she could answer it, she could call for help!

She woke with a start and lifted her head from the pillow. Immediately, she felt nauseous, so she let it fall back and groped the nightstand with one hand. Realizing her hands were mercifully not tied, she gave a grunt. She wasn't a captive after all.

Finding the phone, she held it in front of her face and peeped at it through slitted eyes, making out a familiar shape.

Bill! It was Bill calling. He would rescue her.

She swiped at the phone with a clumsy gesture and heard his voice. "Lucy! Lucy!!"

She wanted to speak, to tell him about the maul in her head, but her mouth was so dry that all she could manage was another groan.

"Are you all right?" he asked. "What's the matter?"

"Hung . . . hunggg . . ."

"You have a hangover?" he asked.

"Unnnh!" she replied.

"That's too bad, but all you need, sweetheart, is the hair of the dog. That'll cure you."

The very thought made her nauseous. She waited for the feeling to pass then ran a fuzzy tongue over her lips. "Unh," she replied.

"Well, since you're monosyllabic, I'll do the talking," said Bill, his voice brimming with enthusiasm and energy. "Remember that friend of Toby's, Doug Fitzpatrick? Well, I ran into him at the pub. I just got home, actually. I was headed to bed and then I remembered the time difference and figured you'd be up since you're such an early riser. This news is too good to keep. Anyway, we got talking, Doug and I, and he's building a deck and said he wasn't sure if he should use treated wood or mahogany or that AZEK stuff and I gave him some ideas. Anyway, it turns out that he's a financial planner and he said since I'd been so generous with my knowledge about decks, well he had a really good tip for me.

"We know that Zoe's four years at Strethmore will cost in the neighborhood of two hundred forty thousand bucks, and they're giving her ten a year so that brings it down to two hundred thou. There's seventy thousand left in the college fund and that's only enough to send her to the state university . . . which she really doesn't want to do. Anyway, this Doug told me he has this amazing opportunity that would double the seventy thousand in three months, so with a hundred and forty thousand, we'd only have to come up with fifteen thousand a year. We could use the home equity line for that, which is much smarter than taking out those education loans. The interest is much lower. So what do you think?"

"Mmmm," replied Lucy, who hadn't

really been listening after he started rattling off numbers.

"I know. You probably think it's too good to be true. That's what I thought at first, but Luce, you know, ever since I left Wall Street, I've missed wheeling and dealing and making real money. This is the sort of thing that the big guys, the insiders, do all the time. This is my chance to get back in the game."

The maul was still stuck in her head, but Lucy figured she could live with it. She let out a big sigh and sank into sleep, the phone slipping from her fingers.

When she woke up a couple hours later, she still had a headache, but it wasn't nearly as bad. She still felt horrible, but her mind was clear enough to recall the lavish formal dinner of the night before. How anyone could manage to consume eight courses accompanied by six different wines, followed by coffee and liqueurs was a mystery to her, but the rest of the company seemed to have no difficulty.

Her Ladyship, for one, had chomped her way through every course, leaving nary a crumb on her plate. It was no surprise that Gerald drank heavily, but he wasn't the only one. Quimby had kept pace with him, and

Vickie and Sue hadn't been far behind. Even Robert Goodenough drank rather more than she would expect of a man of the cloth, but perhaps she was simply reflecting the Puritan attitudes that lingered in New England. She certainly felt a nagging sense of guilt and considered her headache was well deserved, but that didn't stop her from downing a couple Advil. She thought she might have actually spoken to Bill on the phone, but she wasn't sure, and resolved to call him later when she felt a bit better.

Lucy assumed Sue was sleeping off the effects of the booze. When she cracked open the door to Sue's room from the connecting bathroom, she found her bed was empty and neatly made. Returning to her own room, Lucy got dressed slowly and attempted to tidy up the clothes she'd tossed every which way the night before but found that bending down to gather the stockings and underwear strewn on the floor was really too painful. Maybe later, she decided, heading downstairs for some coffee.

Much to her surprise, Sue was already in the kitchen, looking remarkably perky as she sat at the scrubbed pine table with her mug of coffee. Perry was toasting up crumpets, which Poppy was buttering, and a woman Lucy had not seen before was getting in their way. She was tall and thin, with very short and badly cut hair, and was wearing an extremely plain gray dress topped with a faded black cardigan that did nothing for her pasty complexion. It was hard to guess her age, but Lucy thought she was probably younger than she looked, since it was clear she wasn't interested in her appearance. She moved surely and quickly, however, which probably meant she was in her early sixties.

"M'lady must have her tea," she was saying. "Where would I find a tray? And why is it taking the kettle so long to boil, may I ask?"

"We prefer coffee in the morning so the kettle's not on," said Perry. "You have to plug it in."

"What sort of house doesn't have a kettle on the boil in the morning, I ask you," fumed the woman, lifting the pot and finding it empty. She rolled her eyes dramatically before taking it over to the sink and filling it. "M'lady had a terrible night, you know. There's an awful pong in her room. It's very noticeable." She sniffed. "Not at all the sort of thing you expect in a grand house like this, but then again, I told her, things aren't what they used to be."

"Lucy," said Perry, "I don't think you've met Harrison, Aunt's, um, companion."

Lucy had seated herself beside Sue at the table and was trying hard not to look as awful as she felt.

Harrison tightened her lips and glared at Perry. "I am not a companion. I am a lady's maid."

"Probably the last of a noble breed," said Poppy. "Coffee, Lucy?"

Lucy managed a nod and a grateful smile.

"They ought to put her on the endangered list," cracked Perry with a mischievous grin.

"Enough of that," chided Harrison with a sniff. "I will need tea and a pot, a cup and saucer, cream and sugar, toast and silverware, a pot of jam."

"And you know exactly where to find all of those things since you've been here many times and know this kitchen as well as you know your own," said Poppy, filling a mug with coffee and bringing it over to Lucy.

"Humph," said Harrison, setting a small teapot on a tray with a thump. She continued collecting the items she needed for Lady Wickham's breakfast tray, constantly crossing Perry and Poppy and even tangling with the dogs. "Blasted beasts," she finally declared, kicking Churchy, who yelped before slouching off to his bed in the corner.

Poppy protested. "There's no need for that."

But she was speaking to Harrison's back as she disappeared through the doorway, bearing the breakfast tray. When she turned to push the swinging door open with her bottom, Lucy noticed a strange bulge in the sweater beneath one of her arms and wondered, fleetingly, if she had some sort of tumor.

"Awful woman," muttered Perry, setting a platter on the table. "Crumpets, anyone?"

"Yummy," declared Sue, eagerly reaching for a couple crumpets and surprising Lucy, who had never known her friend to actually eat breakfast.

"Maybe later," said Lucy with a sigh, staring into her coffee cup.

"Oh, dear," said Poppy in a sympathetic tone. "I think Lucy has a case of the Irish flu."

"Oh, dear. You're undoubtedly suffering the wrath of grapes," said Perry.

"My mother, who knew a thing or two about the horrors, used to rely on a Prairie Oyster. You take an egg and break it into a glass of beer," suggested Sue.

"I don't think so," said Lucy, feeling a surge of nausea. She rose quickly from the table and pointed in the direction of the downstairs loo, making it just in time to throw up in the toilet. She was horribly embarrassed and wanted nothing more than to slink back to bed, but neither Sue nor Perry and Poppy seemed to disapprove of her condition.

"What you need," said Perry in a bright tone, "is fresh air." He glanced to the windows where sunshine was streaming in. "It's a perfect day for a picnic in the bluebell woods. What say you all?"

"That would be delightful," said Sue. "Do you think you could manage a picnic, Lucy?"

"Actually," said Lucy, finding herself taking an interest in her coffee, "I'm feeling much better."

"Terrific," said Perry. "I will start packing the picnic basket."

"Hold on," protested Poppy. "It's all very well and good for you to go chasing after bluebells and butterflies and rainbows, but I have to meet with Quimby. He had the builders in yesterday and I suspect he has bad news for us."

"How can I help?" asked Perry, raising an eyebrow. "Do you want me to hold your hand?"

"That would be ever so nice," said Poppy.

"Quimby will be gentle, I'm sure," said

Perry, rising from the table and disappearing into a pantry, from which he returned carrying a vintage picnic basket.

"You're a rat," said Poppy with a smile.

"No, I'm more like Toad," said Perry. "I think that's why I've always loved *The Wind in the Willows.*"

"It's all right. You go and tear around the countryside, just like Toad. I'll make you pay when you come home."

"Speaking of paying," said Perry, staring into the open refrigerator. "I could have sworn we had a couple bottles of May wine in here."

"We do," said Poppy.

"No. We only have one."

"Perhaps Flora or Desi had a late-night party," suggested Poppy.

Or perhaps, thought Lucy, remembering the mysterious bulge under Harrison's arm, the lady's maid was planning an early-morning tipple.

Lucy felt much improved after drinking the coffee, so she headed back upstairs to tidy up the clothes still scattered on the floor. She didn't have much energy, though, and after gathering everything into a heap, she threw it onto the closet floor, sat down with her phone, and called Bill. The call went to voice mail, however, so she left a message for him to call her back. Then she brushed her teeth, grabbed her jacket, and went into Sue's room to see if her friend was ready.

Sue was studying her limited wardrobe and trying to decide whether to stay in the tailored slacks she'd worn to breakfast or to change into jeans.

Lucy knew it could take quite a while, so she decided to go on without her. When she reached the big family kitchen, she found the picnic basket sitting on a table, ready to go, but there was no sign of Perry or anyone else. She added her jacket to the pile of neatly folded blankets and, at a bit of a loss for something to do, decided to explore the main house. She had been wondering what the rooms that were not included on the tour were like, so she made her way through the underground tunnel to the manor. Reaching the utilitarian flight of stairs, she continued on up past the first floor with its enormous hall and followed the twists and turns of the staircase until she reached the next landing.

When she stepped through the doorway, she found herself in a wide, carpeted hall where the doorways to various rooms were interspersed with antique chests, tables, chairs, and lots of paintings. There were numerous bouquets of garden flowers, and the window at the end of the hallway was open, but the air was not fresh. Harrison was right; there was an undeniable stink in the air. Lucy, who lived in an antique house in the country was familiar with the smell and put it down to an animal that had died inside a wall. She knew from experience that the corpse of a tiny little house mouse could give off a fearful stench.

Fortunately, she also knew from experience that it didn't last long and in a day or two the smell would certainly be gone. She returned to the stairway and descended to the bottom, where she met Sally in the tunnel.

She was marching along, pushing an upright vacuum cleaner and muttering to herself. "Hares, hares, hares."

"Hares?" asked Lucy.

"It's the last day of April, so I'm saying *hares,*" she answered.

"Whatever for?" asked Lucy.

"Good luck. Between you and me, they could do with a bit of luck around here." She rolled her eyes. "D'you know there was a body in the maze? You'd think people would have the decency to die in their own backyards, wouldn't you? I don't know what the world's coming to, I tell you. So I'm doing what I can and tomorrow, the first of May, I'll say *rabbits.*"

"Well, with any luck that awful smell will be gone. Probably a mouse or something."

"Oh, yes," said Sally, grimacing. "Lady Wickham has been on about it, that's for sure. And that Harrison has probably gone through several cans of air freshener, which just makes everything smell worse." She paused, thinking. "Do you and your friend have any special plans for today? I was just wondering because I'd like to hoover those rooms."

"Perry is taking us on a picnic in the bluebell woods," Lucy said.

"Well, better wear your raincoat."

Lucy glanced out the window, where the sun was brightly shining. "Really?"

"This is England," said Sally. "It rains a lot."

"Thanks for the advice," said Lucy, holding the swinging door open so Sally could push the vacuum through and into the kitchen.

The picnic basket and other things, including her jacket, were gone so Lucy hurried on outside. The others were in the stable courtyard where Perry was loading the picnic things into the Land Rover and Sue was already sitting in the front passenger seat. Lucy climbed in the back, where Church and Monty greeted her happily, wagging their tails and smiling doggy smiles, regaling her with doggy breath.

"Don't mind them," said Perry, slamming the hatch shut and climbing behind the wheel.

"I don't," said Lucy, who really did as each dog had claimed a window, leaving her to make do in the middle of the seat.

"I just love dogs," said Sue, who had never owned a dog, or even a cat, in her life.

"I can't imagine life without at least one," said Perry. "The more the merrier. Right, Lucy?"

"I have a Lab," said Lucy, thinking of Libby back home in Maine. "She's getting old and sleeps a lot."

"These fellas are only a year old. They're brothers," said Perry. "They're rambunctious now but they'll calm down."

"They're lucky dogs, having all this," said Sue, indicating the manor's extensive grounds with a wave of her hand.

"They just get to enjoy it," said Perry. "They don't have to fret and worry about making payroll and keeping the house in good repair, like Poppy and I do. It's a real challenge and it seems to get harder every year."

Lucy was finding it hard to sympathize. For one thing, Monty and Churchy were jumping around in the backseat, walking all over her and occasionally smacking her with their powerful tails. When that happened, they seemed to realize apologies were due, which meant giving her a sloppy lick on the face.

Putting the annoying dogs aside and gazing out the car windows at the passing scene, she thought that Perry was very lucky indeed to live in such beautiful countryside. "Is all this part of the estate?"

"Oh, yes, we've got thousands of acres."

Amazing, she thought. Back home in Maine nobody but the timber companies owned thousands of acres; most of the land had been carved into small farms hundreds of years ago, and even those had been shrinking as bits were sold off for houses and shopping malls.

"Well, here we are," announced Perry, turning off the road onto a narrow track that wound through a sparse woodland where the ground was covered with a sea of blue flowers.

Lucy had never seen anything like it. There were hundreds, thousands of the blooms, and the color was so intense that it seemed to radiate blueness. The very air seemed to vibrate with it, like heat waves rising from an asphalt road on a hot summer day. A sweet fragrance filled the air.

"Wow," said Sue, taking it all in. "This is gorgeous."

Lucy was already out of the car, examining the plants, which she decided were like the wood hyacinths in her garden at home. Except that where those sort of popped up scattershot, and came in different colors, the bluebells had grown together in a mass, crowding out everything except the trees, creating an incredible expanse of vibrant blue.

"How do you do this?" asked Lucy, watching as the dogs bounded off through the flowers. "Did you plant them? Do you fertilize them? Cut them down after they bloom?"

"No," said Perry, opening the hatch. "They just grow like this. It's been this way for as long as I can remember." He handed Lucy a folded plaid blanket. "We usually set the picnic out under that big old beech tree," he said, with a nod. "Just follow the path."

When she reached the spot Perry had indicated, Lucy found the vast tree with its elephantine gray trunk had created a sheltering, tent-like environment beneath its massive branches, some of which grew downward, even meeting the ground. She and Sue spread out the blankets and cushions they had brought, making themselves comfortable while Perry got a portable CD player going with some soft rock. Sting was singing about golden fields of barley, and Lucy was humming along, thinking of azure fields of bluebells when Monty bounded up, proudly displaying something furry he had clamped in his mouth.

"Give!" ordered Perry and the dog very reluctantly dropped the furry object right in front of Lucy on the blanket.

"It's a baby bunny, and it's still alive," she exclaimed, eager to save the poor little thing. "We should take it to a vet."

"Don't be ridiculous," said Perry, scooping up the little creature and deftly snapping its neck before tossing it aside, where it disappeared beneath the bluebells. Both dogs chased after it as if it were a tennis ball.

Seeing Lucy's shocked expression, Perry offered an explanation. "Rabbits are pests. They cause a lot of damage."

"Even Peter got in trouble with Mr. McGregor," said Sue with a sad smile. "And Mrs. McGregor baked his father into a pie."

"We don't have pie. We have Cornish pasties and Scotch eggs and lovely strawberries, but first I think we should celebrate this beautiful day with a glass of May wine," said Perry, busying himself with a corkscrew.

Soon, the unfortunate baby bunny was forgotten as they sipped the sweet woodruff-flavored wine and nibbled on the delicious foods Perry had brought. Scenting the food, the dogs joined them, settling down on the blankets and falling asleep. They played a casual, hilarious game of Charades, and they laughed at Monty, who was continuing to chase rabbits in his dreams. Eventually they found themselves yawning and drifting off, lulled by the soothing music, the warm breezes, and the heady May wine.

They were wakened by a spring shower, proving Sally's prediction correct as they quickly gathered up the picnic things and ran to the car.

"Oh bugger!" exclaimed Perry. "I'm late! I'm supposed to meet some art students who are donating works for the show."

The dogs jumped in, settling on either side of Lucy as before, and they were off, bouncing down the unpaved track until they reached the road, then Perry drove much too fast on the twisting country roads. Lucy tried closing her eyes, afraid to see what might be coming round a corner, but that made her feel carsick. She concentrated instead on praying for their safe return to the manor, and her prayers were answered when Perry turned into the stable yard and braked.

The dogs were thrown off the seat, the jumbled picnic things crashed in the way back and Lucy and Sue were very glad they were wearing seatbelts. Perry hopped out of the car and hurried inside, calling his apologies to them.

When they had gotten out of the car, and realized they and the dogs were still in one piece, Sue announced she was in need of an allergy pill. "Maybe it's the dogs, maybe the flowers, but I'm feeling miserable," she said, giving her nose a good blow.

"Go on," said Lucy, "I'll take the picnic basket back to the kitchen."

When she and the dogs arrived in the kitchen, they found Poppy sitting at the scrubbed pine table, looking rather dejected.

"What's the matter?" asked Lucy.

Poppy drained her mug of tea, set it back down on the table, and refilled it from a brown crockery pot. She stared into the mug for rather a long time before speaking. "Quimby says the dry rot is everywhere," she said, dabbing at her eyes with a tissue. "He says they have to check the roof, too, as water must have gotten in somehow. We just had the roof done a couple years ago." She sighed. "It's going to cost millions, maybe billions. I don't know how we're going to afford it."

"I'm sure you'll find a way," said Lucy. It was the sort of thing you were supposed to say in such circumstances. She was unpacking the picnic basket, storing the leftovers in the refrigerator and putting the dirty crockery in the dishwasher.

"It's all the general's fault," muttered Poppy. "He had no business falling off that wall. There's Aunt Millicent's horrible smell and now this! It's really too much."

"But this is the end of the trouble," said Lucy, closing the dishwasher door. "Trouble comes in threes and you've had three catastrophes: the general, the dry rot, and the body in the maze. Now you're done with trouble."

Poppy stared at her. "I hope you're right, but somehow I have a feeling that the worst is yet to come."

Chapter Nine

"So, Lucy, are you feeling better and enjoying yourself?" asked Sue. The two friends were walking along a footpath that led through the estate to the village where they were going to have high tea at the vicarage with the Goodenoughs.

"I am. I really am," said Lucy, realizing with surprise that it was true. The black mood that had dogged her for so long was definitely losing its grip. "Everything here is so different, it's like being on another planet."

"I'm glad the change is doing you good," said Sue.

"How about you?" asked Lucy. "Are you having a good time?"

"I am, mostly, but I have to say I'm glad we're getting out this evening. There seems to be quite a gloomy atmosphere at the manor, and it makes me feel guilty about enjoying myself."

"Poppy does seem to take things rather hard," said Lucy. "And they really have had a run of bad luck."

"Well, being married to Gerald would make anyone gloomy," observed Sue.

"And then there's Aunt Millicent —"

"And the awful Harrison!" exclaimed Sue, finishing Lucy's sentence.

"Let's not think about any of that," said Lucy as they reached a vantage point from which to view the village and paused to admire the handful of thatched stone cottages clustered around the ancient stone church. The vicarage was a newer addition, built of red brick in neo-Gothic style with pointy windows and set in a large garden.

Lucy and Sue continued to follow the path, which descended gently and brought them to the vicarage garden gate. Two little boys, twins about eight years old, were chasing a soccer ball around the lawn. One gave the ball a ferocious kick and sent it soaring right over Lucy and Sue's heads and out of the garden. Lucy chased it a little ways down the path and retrieved it, bringing it back and handing it to one of the boys as she and Sue entered the garden. He took it and ran off, only to be stopped by his mother, Sarah.

"Matthew! What do you say to our visitors?"

The little boy stopped in his tracks and turned to face them, a puzzled expression on his round brown face. Lucy thought he looked quite adorable dressed in a school uniform of navy blue shorts with a white shirt that had come untucked. A loosened striped necktie hung around his open collar.

After a moment's thought he said, "Very pleased to meet you."

Lucy and Sue smiled, but Sarah was not pleased. "I think you forgot to thank Lucy for fetching your ball."

"Oh, that's right," said Matthew. "Thank you very much."

"You're very welcome," said Lucy.

"And Mark, I think you also have something to say, since you are the one who almost hit our friends with the ball."

"I'm very sorry," said Mark, whose high socks had slipped down to his ankles. "I didn't mean for the ball to go so high."

"No matter," said Sue. "No one was hurt."

"Well, back to your game, boys. I want to show our guests my Bible garden," said Sarah, leading the way through a hedge. "We haven't been here long, so it's just starting," she explained, waving a hand at a neatly organized flower bed. "There are over one hundred twenty-five plants mentioned in the Bible. I used box for an edging. It's mentioned in Isaiah."

"I see roses from the Song of Solomon," said Lucy, naming one of the few Biblical references she was familiar with.

"That's right," said Sarah with an approving nod. "I know you mentioned that you love to garden, but are you also a person of faith?"

Sue found this question extremely amusing and Lucy was forced to make a confession.

"I spend a lot more time in my garden than in church," she admitted, "and I mostly grow vegetables."

"What's this plant?" asked Sue, pointing to a handsome specimen with oval, rather bumpy leaves.

"That's sage. It's mentioned in Exodus."

"I didn't know you could grow it," said Sue. "Mine always came in jars."

"It's easy," said Lucy. "You can keep it in a pot in the kitchen."

"You could add parsley and basil and you'd have a little kitchen herb garden," said Sarah. "That's what I did when we lived in London and I had to content myself with house plants. It's been such a joy to me to have a real garden."

"The house in Hoxton was full of plants," said Robert, joining them and giving his wife a kiss on the cheek. "Sarah can make anything grow" — he beamed with pride — "even those two little rapscallions."

"Well, come on, everyone. I think I hear the kettle singing."

"Matthew, Mark! Tea!" called Robert, and the boys came running.

The kitchen table was already set with blue and white dishes in a flowery pattern arranged on a red and white striped oilcloth. Sarah busied herself filling a big brown teapot while Robert supervised the boys, making sure they actually washed their hands.

"Sometimes they just rinse them and dry them on the towel," said Sarah. "They're always mystified that I can tell. I say it's my super mother sense."

"But it's just the dirt they leave on the towel," said Lucy, taking a seat.

"Exactly," said Sarah, placing a large salad topped with ham and hard boiled eggs in the middle of the table, and adding a basket of bread. "I hope you don't mind a simple supper."

"It looks delicious," said Sue.

"And a welcome change from that enormous formal dinner last night," added Lucy.

Robert and the boys soon joined them and, after bowing their heads for a quick grace, they all tucked in to the lovely salad. Lucy found herself exclaiming over the lettuce and the early peas, which came from the Goodenoughs' garden, as well as the crusty bread from the village bakery and the sweet butter from the estate farm.

"The eggs came from there, too," said Robert.

"Just some of the advantages of living in the country," said Sarah. "And there's rhubarb custard for dessert."

"Rhubarb!" exclaimed Lucy. "My favorite."

When they had finished eating, Sarah set the boys to clearing the table, and Robert suggested they might like a tour of the church. He led the way, taking them in through a side door. "It's quite old. Parts date from the thirteenth century, or so I'm told," he said proudly.

Lucy and Sue followed as he led them past stained glass windows and around carved inscriptions in the stone floor that marked tombs. Numerous brasses were hung on the walls, mostly memorializing fallen soldiers from the British Empire's numerous wars. A single candle burned behind the altar, which was covered with a white cloth embroidered with gold thread.

"I've heard that church attendance has been dropping steadily in Europe," said Lucy. "Is that the case here?"

"Not if I can help it," said Robert with a hearty chuckle. "I can't do it alone, of course, but there is a solid core of members who are working hard to keep the church a vital part of the community. We have evensong on Sunday afternoons. We have musical programs, speakers, yoga classes, all sorts of activities. Sarah also does a lot, especially with the mums and babies."

"It's very peaceful," said Sue, and Lucy realized it was true. There wasn't a sound to be heard, except the twilight twittering of the birds.

"I think I could stay here forever," Sue added, surprising Lucy.

Robert nodded his head. "Things can be a bit complicated up at the manor."

"They have so many problems," said Sue. "They've discovered dry rot, for one thing. I guess it's going to be terribly expensive."

"It is," said Robert. "They had some here, before my time. Some of the older members told me about it. It was a crisis for the congregation."

"You see the photos of these beautiful old

country houses and they seem like something out of a fairy tale," said Lucy. "But the reality is quite different."

"Robert, you mustn't keep these ladies cooped up in this musty old church," said Sarah, joining them. "It's lovely outside, and I have a bottle of dandelion wine."

"What about the boys?" asked Robert as they stepped through the doorway.

"They're doing their school work," said Sarah. "They'll be busy for quite a while."

After they'd settled themselves in chairs on the lawn and been provided with glasses of homemade wine, the conversation drifted once again to the manor and the people who lived there.

"I was saying to Robert that life in a grand house like the manor seems enviable, but I really prefer a simpler lifestyle," said Lucy.

"I really admire Poppy and Perry for undertaking the work of maintaining the manor," said Robert. "It's a national treasure. It's part of our country's heritage and it should be preserved."

"If you ask me," said Sarah, "I think they're struggling to maintain a way of life that really wasn't very nice and is pretty much over and done with. I marvel at it sometimes, the way people will happily spend their hard-earned money to see these monstrous houses that were built on the backs of their ancestors. Where do they think the wealth came from? It came from mills and mines and railways, and from conquered people in the so-called Empire, from oppressed and overworked people who had no choice but to please their masters if they wished to survive."

"We decided that the visitors see themselves as the lord and lady for the day, not as the scullery maid or footman," said Sue.

"I think you're right," said Robert. "And in their vision, the lord and lady lead fairy-tale lives, with no problems at all."

"Unlike Poppy and Perry, who seem beset by trouble," said Sue, who was on her third glass of wine. "And it's not just the manor. They have family troubles, too. Gerald doesn't approve of Desi and Flora is wasting away."

"I think we can all agree that wealth and status do not guarantee happiness," said Robert. "In fact, sometimes I think it's quite the opposite. Some of the happiest people I know are quite content with very little. They trust in the Lord."

"Ah, Robert," sighed Sarah. "He loves the parables — the widow's mite, the loaves and fishes, the lilies of the field."

"And that we should not judge lest we be

judged," said Robert.

"That's all very well and good, Robert," said Sarah, "but don't we have a responsibility to stand up against injustice and demand what's right? If Poppy and Gerald and their sort had their way, there would still be fox hunting. And children like ours wouldn't stand a chance of getting into a good grammar school, much less university."

"I have to admit I was a bit shocked today," said Lucy, "when the dogs brought Perry a baby rabbit and he just snapped its neck and tossed it aside. And then there was the poor young fellow who overdosed in the maze. . . ."

"We heard about that," said Robert. "Any idea who he was?"

"Poppy said the police told her his name but she forgot it," said Lucy, a note of outrage in her voice. "She thought it might have been Eric something."

"Well, I'm not surprised," said Sarah, giving her husband a look. "It's typical, cold-blooded country squire behavior. They simply turn a blind eye to anything disagreeable."

"I will be sure to pray for the poor young man's soul on Sunday," promised Robert.

"I think you should pray for the dogs to behave themselves," said Sarah with a smile.

"They are awful and nobody even tries to control them. Perry and Poppy wouldn't think of leashing them. I can't tell you how many times I've had to shoo them out of my garden." Sarah paused. "They dug up my hollyhocks, you know."

"It's worth your life to move one off a sofa," said Sue.

"Now, now," said Robert. "I think you're forgetting all the good that they do. The manor employs hundreds of people. It's the biggest employer in the county."

"Robert can always find something good to say about everyone," said Sarah. "Even when we lived in Hoxton, not the fashionable south side but the north where there were some pretty desperate characters, he would insist that we should love our neighbors. That's a tall order when the neighbors are drug dealers and pimps, mind you."

"I'll say," said Lucy. "I found it impossible to love my neighbor when he ran a leaf blower for three hours on a Sunday afternoon."

"Well, some things are inexcusable," said Robert with a smile. "I firmly believe that God considers leaf blowers to be instruments of the devil."

Believing it was always preferable to leave on a light note, and not wishing to walk home in the dark, Sue and Lucy thanked their hosts for a lovely evening and headed back to the manor. Dusk was falling but it was still light enough to see without difficulty, although the trees and bushes were merely dark shapes — here a row of evergreens pruned into neat cones, there a massive century-old beech tree. An owl swooped over them in soundless flight, and bats flapped this way and that, darting after insect meals.

"Sarah told me that they have bats in the vicarage, and they can't do anything about it because they're protected," said Sue. "They have to leave an attic window open for them."

"You know," mused Lucy as they approached the manor, "you think a country like Britain is pretty much the same as the US except they speak with funny accents, but that's not true. It's very different, isn't it? I mean, you couldn't expect Americans to tolerate bats in their attics, much less leave windows open for them."

"You can say that again," said Sue as the door leading to the stable yard flew open and Vickie tottered out on her ridiculously high heels and fell at their feet.

"Oh, my," exclaimed Lucy, falling to her knees and cradling the fallen woman's head.

She was sprawled on her back, legs and arms spread wide, and her giggles were interspersed with hiccups. "Are you all right?"

"She's more than all right," said Gerald, stepping through the door. "She's blotto. Stinking drunk."

"What should we do with her?" asked Sue. "We can't leave her here."

"Come on, dearie," said Gerald, grabbing her by her hands. "Upsy-daisy."

Lucy and Sue each took a shoulder and together the three managed to get Vickie on her feet, then Gerald took over, wrapping his arm around her waist and supporting her as they made their way to the kitchen door. There, Poppy took one long, cool look at the situation and immediately left the room.

"I guess I'll be sleeping in my dressing room tonight," grumbled Gerald as he deposited Vickie in a big armchair.

She giggled a few more times, then passed out.

"We can't leave her like this," said Sue. "Someone should stay with her."

"Well, it can't be me," said Gerald. "I'm in enough trouble as it is."

"I guess it's us," said Lucy. "I'll go up and get some blankets and pillows."

When she returned with the bedding, Vickie was snoring loudly. Lucy and Sue quickly made up beds on the sofas for themselves, then took turns climbing back upstairs to wash up and change into pajamas. Once she was tucked in, Lucy found the sofa quite comfortable, but wasn't really able to sleep. She feared Vickie would be sick and there was the possibility she could choke on her vomit. Sue didn't seem to share Lucy's anxiety; she fell asleep as soon as her head hit the pillow. Lucy dozed off from time to time, only to waken with a start then be reassured by Vickie's regular snores.

Soon after the grandfather clock chimed four times, she did finally fall asleep, only to be wakened around six by Harrison.

"My word," the maid was exclaiming, "this is a pretty kettle of fish." She was standing with arms akimbo, surveying the unusual scene. After she'd taken it all in, she sniffed. "Don't tell me that dreadful pong is over here now."

"Not that I know of," said Lucy. "We were worried about her" — she nodded toward Vickie slumped in the chair with a blanket balled up in her lap. "She was a bit under the weather."

"Humph," said Harrison. "It's none of my

affair. I've got to get her ladyship her morning tea." She filled the kettle from the sink, then set it on the Aga with a clatter. "Her ladyship didn't get a wink last night, the smell was that bad."

Lucy stood up, considered folding up her bedding and decided instead to head upstairs to the bathroom for a much-needed pee. She certainly didn't want to waste the climb, however, so she gathered up the sheets and blanket and pillow in her arms. After she'd completed her original mission, she remade the stripped bed, then washed up and dressed, before going back downstairs to make some coffee.

Her curiosity got the better of her while she waited for the coffee to be ready. She decided to investigate and made her way through the underground tunnel to the manor house and up the stairs to the landing. When she opened the door to the hallway, a noticeable stench greeted her. It wasn't as strong as the smell Harrison had described so she proceeded down the hallway, discovering the offensive odor grew stronger with every step. When she reached the midpoint, she found she really couldn't go on. The evil stench was so overpowering she feared she would vomit. She turned and fled back to the fresher air in the stairway.

Definitely not a mouse, she decided, but something much larger.

Chapter Ten

When Lucy returned to the kitchen, the coffee pot was full of aromatic, freshly brewed coffee and there was no trace of the previous night's events. Vickie was gone, as was the bedding Sue had used. Sue herself was dressed and made up to her usual perfection. Perry was setting out boxes of cereal and bowls, along with fresh strawberries and a pitcher of milk.

"Help yourselves, ladies," he said, inviting them to partake. "I've got to run. I've got to put the finishing touches on the hat exhibit." He paused and wrinkled his nose. "But first I've got to deal with the pong. It's become quite atrocious and we've had to close the manor to the public."

"It sure is. I got a whiff and it made me feel quite sick," said Lucy.

"What is it with you?" asked Sue, who was filling her mug. "Have you got a tummy bug?"

"I don't think so," said Lucy, who was eying the strawberries. "I'm okay now. I'm even hungry."

"It's enough to make anyone sick," said Perry. "I have got to get rid of it before tomorrow. Poppy thinks we can get away with one day without attracting unwanted attention, but if we have to close it for longer, we'll end up on the evening news." He was standing at the island, sipping coffee from a mug. "Speaking of pleasanter things, I was working with the art students yesterday, you know, and I've got to say, even though I shouldn't, that the hat show is really quite fantastic."

"I can't wait to see it," said Sue.

"Well, do drop in anytime and tell me what you think," said Perry, stashing his mug in the dishwasher. "I would really appreciate your input, as they say."

"Okay," said Sue, who was filling her mug. "I'll go take a look."

"As for me, 'it is a far, far better thing that I do . . .' " he said, quoting Dickens and wrapping a handkerchief across his face, bandit-style. " 'All in the valley of death rode the six hundred,' " he continued, moving on to Tennyson and grabbing an umbrella from the stand. For dramatic effect, he flourished it like a sword.

"Such a fuss," said Sue, smiling indulgently.

"It is truly dreadful," he said, loosening the handkerchief and letting it hang around his neck. "I don't blame Aunt for complaining, but I've looked and looked in her room and can't find anything."

"Perhaps there's a secret chamber," said Sue.

"I rather doubt it, since nobody's ever mentioned one and it would be rather an attraction if we had one. We don't even have a ghost, which a lot of our visitors find disappointing. They simply love the idea of Katherine Howard's ghost shrieking her innocence at Hampton Court, apparently wandering about with her head tucked under her arm. I've asked Willoughby to do some research, but he hasn't come up with anything along those lines." He sighed and replaced the handkerchief over his nose. " 'Into the jaws of death, Into the mouth of hell,' " he declared, marching out of the room.

Sue had only coffee for breakfast, but Lucy was used to eating a hearty breakfast so she busied herself filling her bowl with several Weetabix biscuits, topped them with a couple scoops of luscious berries, and drowned it all in deliciously rich double cream.

"That cream is twice as rich as heavy cream," said Sue, watching with a raised eyebrow.

"Tastes like it, too," said Lucy, licking her spoon.

"A minute on the lips, a year on the hips," Sue added, then left to view the exhibit, taking her coffee mug with her.

Finding herself alone in the kitchen and noticing the sunlight flooding through the windows, Lucy decided to take her breakfast out to the terrace. She seated herself at a glass-topped table, savoring both her delicious breakfast and the incredible beauty of the manor house. She gazed at the ancient stone building while she ate, taking note of the intricate stone carvings and marveling at the work of the medieval stone carvers and masons who'd created them. There were gargoyles and pointy little turrets topped with graceful finials, and each window had an elaborately worked casing with rosettes at each corner. The stair tower, she decided, was especially fine with its neat oriel windows which rose in a spiral fashion, winding around the tower. A lacy band of carved stonework emphasized the unusual window placement, and ended at a huge round clock face with carved roman numerals and single massive black iron hand. The clock, a sixteenth century masterpiece, was still keeping time and ringing out the hours. It was no wonder that the stair tower had been chosen as a symbol to represent the manor and appeared on the admission tickets, most of the gift shop merchandise like mugs and tea towels, as well as all the promotional material.

As she studied the beautiful stair tower, she found something was bothering her. Something wasn't quite right, but she couldn't figure it out. In her mind, she climbed the stairs, retracing the climb she'd made on that first day when Willoughby gave her and Sue a tour. They'd progressed up the spiraling flights of shallow steps, designed, Willoughby had said, so that ladies in long skirts could glide gracefully up and down. The oriel windows followed the line of the stairs, set aslant, and offering impressionistic views of the estate park through wavy old glass. Each landing offered a window seat in case the climber should grow tired and need a rest . . . or perhaps a perch for a quick dalliance.

She was still gazing at the elaborate staircase and spooning up the last bit of strawberries and cream when Sue appeared.

She was carrying her jacket and tote bag on her arm and was ready to go out for the day.

"Don't tell me you're still eating?" she exclaimed. "Our driver is here and times a-wasting."

"No problem," said Lucy, remembering that she and Sue had planned to spend the day touring Windsor Castle. "I'll just take the breakfast things in and grab my bag. I won't be a moment."

Hurrying into the kitchen, she was happy to see that Sally was at the sink loading the dishwasher. "I've got a few more for you," Lucy said, handing off the tray. Then she bounded up the stairs, pausing in her room only to grab her bag and a light jacket, and to slap on some lipstick. She dashed down, quick as a bunny, and met Sue on the terrace.

They had a different driver, a young fellow they hadn't met before. "I'm Justin Quimby," he said, introducing himself. He looked like a younger version of Harold, albeit with sun-bleached hair and a muscular build.

"Are you related to Harold?" asked Sue.

"I'm his son," he said, opening the car doors for them.

"And you work here, too?" asked Lucy, as

Sue grabbed the front passenger seat and she climbed in the back.

"Only part-time. I'm at university."

"Which university?" asked Sue as he got behind the wheel of the Land Rover.

"Cambridge," he said, shifting into gear and taking off down the drive. He drove much faster than his father.

"And what are you studying?" asked Lucy.

"Physics."

"Oh," said Lucy, realizing she'd gone as far as she could on that line of conversation. "And what do you do for fun?"

"I'm kind of a keen climber," he admitted, swerving to avoid a bus full of day-trippers.

"Mountains?" asked Sue. "Like Mount Everest?"

"No, that sort of thing isn't for me. All that packing and planning. I like to go freestyle, without equipment. I see something interesting and I climb it. Most of my climbs are about twenty or thirty minutes."

"What can you climb in twenty minutes?" asked Lucy.

"Oh, say, church towers, cliffs, all sorts of things."

"Isn't it dangerous?" asked Sue.

"Especially if you don't use ropes and stuff," added Lucy.

"Well, that's the point, isn't it?" asked Justin, zooming onto the highway between two large trucks.

"We'd actually prefer to get to Windsor in one piece," said Lucy as Justin wove his way through traffic, seizing the tiniest openings to pass slower cars and trucks.

"Relax, Lucy. Justin is a very good driver," said Sue, giving him her most flirtatious smile.

"It's my tummy again," said Lucy, who never got carsick or seasick or airsick, but would say anything to get Justin to drive more carefully. "I'm feeling . . ."

Justin, she was happy to see, took the hint and eased up on the gas.

Sue, however, wasn't pleased. "You shouldn't have eaten such a rich breakfast," she said, admonishing Lucy.

"I know that now," said Lucy, relaxing her hold on the grab bar. Her fingers were quite stiff, she realized, massaging them briefly until Justin made another sharp swerve around a poky van and she had to hang on for dear life.

They made it to Windsor, much to Lucy's amazement, and Justin dropped them off at the entrance to the castle, arranging to meet them at the train station at four o'clock. After paying the hefty entrance fee, they entered the walled castle enclosure and were amazed at the size of the complex, which included numerous buildings around the old round tower. They dutifully trooped through amazing rooms, including the magnificent banquet hall that had been restored after a devastating fire.

Sue was impressed by Henry VIII's enormous suit of armor, which she said with a meaningful glance in Lucy's direction, was an excellent example of the effect of an untamed appetite. Lucy preferred the Queen's Dolls House, a replica of Buckingham Palace that had been made as a present for Queen Mary and featured tiny versions of the castle's contents contributed by British manufacturers. Saint George's Chapel, where Henry VIII and his favorite wife, Jane Seymour, were buried was the last stop on the tour.

"It's a fine example of perpendicular architecture," said Sue, reading from the guide. She looked up at the lofty ceiling and added, "I guess that means it's quite tall."

"It's spooky," said Lucy, gazing at the stone tablets marking the royal graves. "Henry VIII was a terrible man. If you ask me, six wives is five too many."

"I guess being able to have and do whatever you want, including having your wives beheaded, probably isn't good for your character. And if that suit of armor is an accurate indication, he must have been a glutton," said Sue, adding a little moue of distaste.

She pointed to the little balcony in one corner. It hung beneath the ceiling and was completely enclosed with wood paneling except for a small window. "That's called the queen's closet. It's where the queen and her ladies sat, able to watch without being watched."

Lucy gazed at the odd little feature, imagining what it was like to be a queen in the sixteenth century and concluding that despite her humble status, she was much better off as an ordinary middle-class woman in the twenty-first century.

"On to the gift shop," declared Sue, snapping the guidebook shut.

Lucy dutifully followed her friend to the shop, where she wondered if her friends at home would really appreciate Windsor Castle refrigerator magnets. She was browsing through the assorted wares when she spotted some lovely tapestry pillows she found hard to resist. She was wondering what she could sacrifice in order to fit the pillows in her small carry-on suitcase when one of the sales clerks caught her eye.

"You can just buy the covers," she said with a smile.

Lucy picked up one of the pillows, which was done in rich reds and blues, and realized it was exactly like a pillow she'd seen at the manor. There were actually three of them in a row on the window seat in the second-floor landing — one each beneath a narrow lancet window.

That was it, she realized. The second landing had three windows but the other landings in the staircase had four. And now that she came to think of it, that second-floor landing was smaller than the ground floor landing and the one above it.

"Do you want to eat here? I'm sure there's a café somewhere," said Sue, studying her guidebook.

"Not really. As a matter of fact, I'd like to go back to the manor. There's something I want to check out."

Sue did not like that idea at all. "Don't be silly, Lucy. This is probably our one time to be in Windsor and the book says the town is worth exploring — lots of shops and restaurants. There's also Eton College and you know you want to see that. Besides, we arranged for Justin to pick us up at four. I'm sure he has other responsibilities to attend to."

"I'm really not all that keen," confessed Lucy. "These old buildings are all starting to look alike to me. We could call him and ask if it would be convenient . . ."

Sue placed a hand on Lucy's forehead, checking to see if she had a fever. "That doesn't sound like you at all, Mrs. Can't Miss a Museum. And besides, these English people are so polite that he'd never admit it wasn't convenient to pick us up early."

"I know. You're right, but I've been thinking about the manor and I think I know where your secret chamber is located."

"It was just a notion," said Sue as they walked down the hill to the town. "Perry says there's no secret chamber. Besides, I'm awfully hungry, I had only coffee for breakfast. I want to eat something."

This was such an unusual admission from Sue that Lucy decided her exploration of the staircase could wait a few hours. Besides, she told herself, Sue was probably right and the secret chamber would turn out to be a bathroom or a closet added when the manor was modernized. She was hungry, too, and she had to admit that the town was charming, with ancient buildings lining narrow winding streets, and there were plenty of restaurants to choose from. They settled on a sleek, modern café that featured soups and salads, then continued exploring the town after they'd eaten. Following the path of least resistance, they strolled downhill toward the River Thames, where they paused on a bridge to admire a handsome flock of swans. Then they found themselves at Eton College, the famous establishment prep school, where they spotted a couple students in their distinctive uniforms with long black jackets and waistcoats.

"We're probably looking at a future prime minister," said Sue.

"Which one?" asked Lucy.

"I'm sure it doesn't matter," said Sue with a naughty grin. "They look to me to be cut from the same cloth — privileged, upper class, spoiled rotten little one per centers."

Lucy was surprised by her friend's attitude. "Well, since when did you become a rabble-rouser?"

"I guess it's seeing all this stuff, not just here in Windsor Castle but even at Moreton. Accumulating all these things represents centuries of excess."

"But there's art and amazing examples of craftsmanship, and history, and beauty," said Lucy. "And you're a collector yourself. Your house is full of lovely things."

"Too full," said Sue with a righteous little nod. "I'm going to give most of it away when I get home. I'm going to become a minimalist."

"Good luck with that," said Lucy as they began the climb back up the hill. She thought they'd done enough sightseeing for the day and was eager to get back to the manor. "Shall we head to the train station? It's after three."

"Not yet," said Sue, spotting a shop sign. "It's a Barbour store. You know, those fabulous waxed jackets that Perry and Poppy and everybody wear. Let's check it out."

"So much for minimalism," said Lucy.

But Sue was true to her word. After she bought herself a classic Barbour barn coat, she made a point of dropping off her old DKNY jacket at a nearby Oxfam shop. Lucy was unable to resist the thrift shop prices there and bought some gently read Puffin books for Patrick. Only then, did they head to the train station for their ride to the manor.

They reached Moreton Manor just in time for a late tea.

"We don't usually bother with afternoon tea," said a rather harried Poppy, setting a plate of freshly baked scones on the kitchen table, "but Aunt Millicent insists."

"Well, I think it's a jolly good tradition," said Perry, biting into a chocolate digestive biscuit.

"I think it's a lot of bother," said Poppy as Lady Wickham sailed into the kitchen from the garden.

"What's a lot of bother?" asked Lady Wickham, settling her plump little self on a chair and accepting a cup of tea.

"Dead heading the tulips," said Perry, adroitly changing the subject.

"Well, I suppose that's the price you pay for all those fabulous blooms," said Lucy, gamely joining the conversation. "My flowers in Maine are never as lovely as yours."

"We English are known for our gardens," said her ladyship complacently. She took a sip of tea, then set her cup and saucer down on the table and tented her fingers. "But I have to say, Poppy, that something has to be done about the smell. It's really quite unbearable."

"I agree," said Gerald, entering from the tunnel connecting the family's quarters with the manor house. "It seems to be coming from behind a wall in her room, as far as I can tell." He paused to blow his nose. "After a bit, it kind of overcomes you and it's hard to tell if it's stronger in one area than another."

"Well, we have to get to the bottom of it. We can't keep the manor closed to guests indefinitely. In the meantime, Aunt, perhaps you should move up to the guest level here with us," said Poppy. "There's plenty of room up there."

"The servants' quarters!" exclaimed Lady Wickham. "Well, I never thought the day would come when my own relations would consign me to the servants' quarters."

"There are no servants now, Aunt," said Perry.

"Our rooms are really very lovely," said Sue.

"It was quite a job doing them up," said Gerald, pouring himself a cup of tea and sitting down heavily at the table. "Just getting the plumbing in was quite a challenge, I can tell you."

"I suppose you have to cut out little bits and pieces where you can," said Lucy, adding a dollop of jam to the Devonshire cream she'd spread on her scone. "Like you did in the stairway."

"What do you mean?" asked Gerald. "What stairway?"

"Why, on the landing in the stair tower. The one that only has three windows instead of four. I thought you must have added a bath in that space."

"No," said Poppy. "We have so many extra rooms, we just remodeled dressing rooms or even bedrooms. That's what we did in the old servant's quarters."

"My bath is on the other side of the room," said her ladyship. "It's away from the stair landing."

"Well, why are there only three windows?" asked Lucy. "All the other landings have four. And from the outside, you can see four windows."

"A priest's hole?" suggested Sue.

"Very well could be," said Perry, "but if so, it's lost in the mists of time. I have no idea how to get into it."

"But there's a window," said Poppy. "We could get in through the window."

"Too narrow," said Gerald, speaking through a mouthful of scone. "But we should look and see what's what."

"How do you propose to do that?" asked Perry. "It's at least thirty, maybe forty feet up. We don't have a ladder that big."

"What about those gizmos construction fellas have?" said Gerald. "Those trucks with the little buckets that go up. You know."

"I do know what you mean, and I don't happen to know any construction fellas," said Perry.

"Why not ask Justin Quimby to take a

look?" suggested Sue. "He was telling us he likes to climb things."

"Free climbing, he called it. It's his hobby," said Lucy.

A few disappointed visitors who'd been unable to tour the manor because of the smell, but had been given free passes to the garden, were just leaving when Justin arrived to take a look at the proposed climb up the stair tower.

"Looks pretty easy to me," he said, "so long as the stonework is sound."

"We-e-ll, maybe," said Perry, sounding dubious. "I wouldn't want to bet on it."

"It should be all right," said Gerald. "After all, it's been standing for eight hundred years."

"My point exactly," said Perry.

"Well, I'll give it a try," said Justin. "If it's no good, I won't continue. I'll just come down."

"We have plenty of rope. You could lower yourself from the top," urged Poppy.

"Too much trouble," said Justin, who was seated on the ground, changing out of his heavy work boots and putting on a pair of light and flexible rock climbing shoes. He stood up, flexed his fingers, and stretched out his arms, then grabbed a hold of a knob of stone on the tower and literally sprang off the ground and began working his way up the tower toward the window.

Word of Justin's attempted climb had spread quickly and the entire family and a number of employees had gathered in the stable yard to watch. Most were holding their breaths as they watched the daring feat. When Justin reached the relative safety of the window sill there was a collective sigh of relief.

"Well, what do you see?" demanded Gerald.

"I see . . . I see legs," said Justin, peering through the window. "Somebody's in there! There's a body on the floor!"

"Oooh," moaned Poppy, swaying on her feet before collapsing to the paving in a dead faint.

Chapter Eleven

"It must be some Romish priest, probably been in there for centuries," declared Lady Wickham, adding a disapproving sniff.

"I rather doubt that, considering the stink," said Gerald. He was bent over his wife and flapping a newspaper rather half-heartedly in an effort to give her more air.

Desi was on his knees, rubbing his mother's hands and urging her to come to.

Perry was already on the phone, calling the police. "I'm afraid we have a bit of a situation here at the manor," he was saying. "It seems there's a body stuffed inside a wall." There was a long pause, then he continued. "No, no, it's not an old body. It's pretty fresh. Well, not actually fresh. It's quite gone off, but definitely recent. Within the last week or so, I'd say."

Hearing this, Flora went quite ashen and Justin urged her to sit down on the paving and shoved her head between her knees.

"This is no place for you, m'lady," Harrison was saying, urging her elderly mistress to leave the scene.

Lady Wickham was having none of that, however, and was clearly enjoying this shocking new development. "Don't be silly, Harrison," she said in a snappish tone. "I've been through much worse than this. Remember that trouble with the Irish. You never knew when they were going to blow the Ritz to bits!"

"Well, I'll just get you a wrap," Harrison replied, hurrying off.

Sue was watching Lucy, who was watching everyone else. "C'mon, Lucy," she hissed, pulling her friend away from the group. "Stop staring. I know what you're thinking."

"No, you don't."

"You're thinking that if there's a body in a wall it didn't get there by itself, which means somebody put it there, and that somebody is probably a murderer."

"Well, that's pretty obvious, isn't it? And don't forget . . . this is the second body that's turned up in a week."

"And you're thinking there's a serial killer on the loose and you're looking at everybody here, wondering if one of them is a murderous psychopath."

"Don't be ridiculous," said Lucy. "I don't think that at all. I'm just fascinated by this human drama and the way everyone is reacting. Poor Poppy, for example. Do you think she's got a sensitive nature? Or perhaps all this has revived memories of some traumatic event?"

"I think it's the straw that broke the camel's back," murmured Sue. "I don't think she wants to deal with this on top of everything else."

"She certainly didn't expect to have a dead body on her hands, much less two," said Lucy.

"But I'm not so sure about Gerald," said Sue.

"Now who's looking for suspects!" exclaimed Lucy.

"Not I and not you," said Sue as the *woo-wah* of a police siren was heard in the distance. "We," she said, making eye contact with Lucy, "we are going to leave this to the police. Remember Paris? They considered us suspects and they took our passports. This time we are not going to get involved."

"Absolutely right," agreed Lucy as the police car rolled through the gate and drew to a halt in the stable yard.

Everyone turned and watched as a middle-aged man with graying temples and a stocky build got out of the passenger side and a rather plain young woman extricated herself from the driver side.

"DI George Hennessy," said the man, briefly flashing his identification. He was sporting a beautiful Harris tweed jacket and a crisply ironed shirt topped with a striped tie. "And Detective Sergeant Isabel Matthews," he continued "Of the Thames Valley Police."

Sgt. Matthews' straight dark hair was fastened in a skimpy ponytail and she was wearing black polyester slacks and a blazer jacket that almost but didn't quite match, over a roomy beige cotton turtleneck.

"You reported a body?" DI Hennessy arched an eyebrow, rather as if he thought people who reported bodies ought to have the courtesy to provide them in an obvious location.

"Yes," said Perry, stepping forward to introduce himself. "I'm Peregrine Pryce-West —"

"I know who you are," said Hennessy, cutting him off. "And don't think the fact that you're an earl will have any impact on this investigation whatsoever, your lordship."

"None whatsoever," added Sgt. Matthews, chiming in.

"Of course. I certainly don't expect any

sort of special treatment," said Perry. "Now the body, well, it's in a wall." He pointed up to the window in the stair tower. "It's behind that window, the second row up."

"Let's take a look-see," said Hennessy, indicating that Perry should lead the way.

"It's not that simple," said Perry. "The area behind the window has been walled off."

"There's no jib door, no bookcase that swings around if you tap three times?" asked Hennessy.

"Not that we know of," said Perry.

"Sounds like a job for the crime scene officers, sir," said Sgt. Matthews.

"You get on with that," said Hennessy, instructing the sergeant. "I'll get the lay of the land." He turned to Perry. "So who are all these folks?" he asked, indicating the small group of observers.

"Just family, staff, and two visitors from America," said Perry. "Shall I introduce you?"

"Sergeant Matthews will get everyone's details," said Hennessy. "How about giving me a look 'round, while we wait for the CSOs." He paused. "I understand you've got some long borders here designed by Gertrude Jekyll."

"Indeed we do," said Perry, sounding

relieved by the distraction. "And I think this is the best time to see them when the flowers are just beginning to bloom. Would you like to take a look?"

"Wouldn't mind," admitted the inspector.

The two strolled off, chatting amiably about various types of fertilizers and agreeing that aged horse manure was by far the best, while Sgt. Matthews got her notebook out and started jotting down names and addresses. She started with her ladyship.

"For your information, I am the Countess of Wickham," she said, emphasizing the word *countess.* She clearly would have preferred to look down her nose at the police officer, but since Sgt. Matthews was quite tall, she had to express her haughty attitude with her voice while looking up her nose.

Sgt. Matthews wasn't impressed. "I presume you have a name as well as a title?" she asked.

"Millicent Pryce-West," admitted the countess.

"And do you live here at the manor?" Matthews asked.

"Of course not," snapped her ladyship. "Everyone knows I live at Fairleigh in Hazelton. The house was in my husband's family, y'see."

"And is your husband here with you?"

"Don't be ridiculous. I am the Dowager Countess."

"So sorry," said Sgt. Matthews in the polite way normal in such circumstances.

"Well, don't be," replied Lady Wickham. "Wilfred was really rather horrid and it was quite a while ago."

"I see," said the sergeant.

"I doubt it, but it's no matter," said Lady Wickham. "Are you quite finished with me?"

"Almost," responded the officer, raising a cautionary finger. "I gather you're a guest here?"

"I'm a member of the family," the countess declared, raising her eyebrows. "Lord Wickham is my nephew."

Sgt. Matthews was beginning to run out of patience. "What I'm trying to establish is whether you will be staying on here for some time, or whether you'll be returning to Fairleigh. In other words, how can we contact you, if need be?"

"What need would there possibly be?" demanded the old woman. "And how would I know whether my niece and nephew will need me here or whether it would be better for me to go? And in that case I might very well visit a friend. I have many friends, you see, as well as numerous relations, and they all beg me to come and visit. I simply don't know what I'm going to do. As it happens, I've been evicted from the Chinese bedroom because of the smell and they want me to stay in one of the old servants' rooms. Can you imagine?"

The sergeant didn't seem too troubled by Lady Wickham's predicament. "Well," she said, closing her notebook, "in that case you had better stay here until Inspector Hennessy notifies you otherwise."

"Well, I never," said her ladyship, drawing herself up to her full five feet. "If you persist in this nonsense, I shall have to call my dear friend the commissioner."

Sgt. Matthews had moved on and was methodically moving from one person to another, jotting down their names and details. When she reached Sue and Lucy, and learned they were Americans, she warned them they might need to provide their passports.

"Will we have to surrender them?" asked Lucy, mindful of Sue's warning.

"That will depend on how the investigation develops. Inspector Hennessy will make that determination," Sgt. Matthews said. "As I've been telling everyone, no one is going anywhere unless the inspector gives permission."

"I understand," said Lucy, noticing that Perry and the inspector had returned just as a white police van arrived, delivering several officers who began suiting up in white crime scene overalls.

Perry led them inside, along with Sgt. Matthews and DI Hennessy, leaving everyone else standing in the stable yard.

Lucy felt rather deflated and suspected that the others did, too.

"Well," said Poppy, letting out a big sigh, "we have to keep body and soul together. Rather a lot of bodies and souls," she added as more police vehicles arrived and the officers began unloading numerous cases containing equipment. "I could use some help making tea and sandwiches."

In no time at all, with her usual efficiency, Poppy set everyone except Aunt Millicent to work in the kitchen. Her ladyship considered herself far above such mundane chores and withdrew to a sofa where she began reading the latest *Country Life* magazine.

Lucy and Sue were setting out cups and saucers on trays when Robert Goodenough arrived to offer priestly support, having heard there was trouble at the manor.

"That's putting it mildly," said Poppy. "We've got a body in the wall."

"How dreadful," said Robert.

"The police are talking about using jackhammers to get it out." She shook her head. "What a mess! Just think of the damage . . ."

"To the manor, of course," said Robert in a thoughtful tone, as if switching gears. "I had thought it might be a friend or relation, perhaps an employee."

"We have no idea who it is," said Poppy. "Nobody is missing, that's for certain. I rather do resent people coming and dying here at Moreton. One was bad enough, but two is excessive. I think it's most inconsiderate."

"Perhaps I should go and lend a hand. See if there's anything I can do," offered Robert.

"They're up there," said Poppy, indicating the manor house on the opposite side of the terrace. "You can cross through the tunnel and take the stairs up to the second landing. Tell them there's tea and sandwiches down here."

"Splendid," said Robert, gratified to have a mission. He marched off, only to return a few minutes later.

"Good news," he reported. "No jackhammers, at least not yet. They've gone to see Willoughby in the library. They're looking for old plans to the manor, hoping to find the entry point. It was Winifred's idea."

"God bless Winifred," said Poppy, breathing a sigh of relief

"Yes, indeed," said Robert, "and all His creatures here on earth."

"Perhaps I should cover the sandwiches and save them for later?" asked Poppy, offering a plate of assorted sandwiches. "We've got ploughman's, roast beef, and chicken. I don't want them to dry out."

"I can take them along to the library, if that's all right," offered Robert. "Research is hungry work."

Seizing the opportunity, Lucy grabbed a tray filled with mugs of tea and followed him. "They'll need something to drink," she said, trying to sound helpful.

"I've got the cream and sugar," said Sue, refusing to be left behind.

"It's a mission of mercy," said Robert, smiling as they left the kitchen and made their way to the library.

They found the inspector and Perry consulting with Willoughby and Winifred; all four were bent over a table filled with maps and various documents. Some were clearly ancient with ribbons and dangling wax seals, others were modern architectural renderings. The estate manager Quimby and several crime scene officers were standing slightly apart, ready to assist if needed.

"We've brought food and drink!" exclaimed Robert, holding the plate of sandwiches aloft as if presenting a suckling pig at a banquet.

"How thoughtful. Thank you," said Perry, absorbed in the plan he was studying and taking no interest in the refreshments.

There was an awkward moment as some of the officers eyed the food hungrily, not sure if they should partake. Willoughby settled the matter and broke the ice, declaring a cuppa was just the thing to clear the mind.

Lucy thought *cuppa* was an odd term for the librarian to use, but she remembered he was not to the manor born, and had attended what he called a bricks and mortar university and not Cambridge or Oxford.

"I'll have milk and two sugars," he told Sue, accepting a cup of tea and perching on a sofa with the mug in one hand and a sandwich in the other. Soon everyone was eating, except for Winifred and Perry, who continued to pore over the plans.

When Hennessy finished his tea, he came to a decision. "We'll have to open the wall," he said. "I know you don't want to damage the fabric of the manor, but it has to be done. We can't wait."

"If the body got in there, there must be some sort of opening," argued Winifred.

Perry turned to the historian. "Willoughby, you've been studying this building for months. Have you found any reference to walling off the window?"

"I'm afraid not," said Willoughby, moving on to his second sandwich.

"Then I guess we have no choice," said Perry with a sigh. "Poppy will be devastated."

The police officers trooped off to begin the process of dismantling the wall and uncovering the body. Perry went to inform Poppy, and Lucy and Sue began collecting empty tea mugs and crumpled napkins.

"I can't believe there's no record of such a significant alteration," said Winifred, furrowing her brow and searching through the pile of documents.

"I'm sure you're right, but I haven't found it yet," said Willoughby. "You know how it is with these places," he added with a shrug. "They've never had an organized, systematic scholarship — what we professionals would consider standard operating procedure. In times past, they wrote it all down and tucked it away in a chest or someplace they thought would keep important papers safe. Two or three generations later, somebody decided that old chest was an eyesore and banished it to the attic or a pantry. Think of that inventory they found at Burghley. Used to wrap china, wasn't it?"

"I suppose you're right," said Winifred. "And I imagine they'll find the secret entrance once they've got inside."

"Mystery solved," said Willoughby.

"Well, one mystery, anyway. There's still the question of the corpse's identity."

"Of course," said Willoughby, busy rolling up the documents and replacing them in their glass case.

Lucy and Sue departed with their loaded trays and returned to the kitchen. They found Lady Wickham dozing on the sofa, and Robert and Poppy sitting at the kitchen table. The vicar was doing his best to console Poppy.

"You must think me awful," said Poppy, wiping her eyes with a tissue. "After all, a person is more important than a building, right? Instead of worrying about the wall, I should be thinking of this poor corpse and the people he left behind."

"It's completely understandable," replied Robert, covering her hand with his. "The manor is part of your heritage. It's like a member of your family."

"You're so understanding," said Poppy,

giving Robert a long look before lowering her eyes.

As Lucy and Sue loaded the mugs into the dishwasher, they were aware of the demolition work taking place in the ancient building. Through the windows, they saw the crime scene officers moving back and forth, carrying equipment. They could even hear the faint whine of power tools grinding through the thick stone wall, as well as bangs and crashes, and occasional grunts and exclamations. A sudden cessation of noise indicated the barrier had been breached, which was followed by an ear-piercing shriek.

Lady Wickham started, suddenly awake, and raised her head. Robert and Poppy came to attention at the table. Lucy and Sue were frozen in place at the sink.

The silence was broken when Sgt. Matthews brought an ashen-faced Harrison into the kitchen. "We need some strong tea with lots of sugar. She's had a shock."

"Why, Harrison, I wondered where you'd got to," said Lady Wickham, looking up from her magazine.

"I am sorry, m'lady," said Harrison, quickly wiping her eyes and tucking the tissue into a pocket. "I was gathering up your things. We had to move you, of course, because of the work. Them taking down the wall, you see,"

"Very well," said her ladyship in a rare exhibit of cooperation.

"Well, to make a long story short, I saw the body and it gave me quite a turn," continued the lady's maid.

"Quite natural, I'm sure," said Lady Wickham.

"It was me son, Cyril, you see," said Harrison, waving away the cup of tea that Lucy had prepared for her.

"Your son?" inquired the elderly countess, whose face had gone quite white. Then she quickly added, "I had no idea you had a son."

"Oh, how awful!" exclaimed Poppy, full of sympathy.

"I'm so sorry!" added Sue.

"What a dreadful shock that must have been," said Lucy, proffering the tea once again.

"Do sit down," urged Poppy. She glanced at the vicar. "Perhaps a prayer?"

"No, no," insisted Harrison, waving them all away. "It's time I got her ladyship settled in her new room" — she paused and added with a disdainful sniff — "such as it is."

Poppy turned to Sgt. Matthews. "May Harrison take my aunt to her room?"

"Of course," replied the sergeant, writing in her notebook.

"I shouldn't think I need permission to move about in my nephew's house," snapped Lady Wickham, accepting a helping hand from Harrison to rise from the sofa. Leaning heavily on her maid's arm, she was led away from the kitchen.

"My goodness," said Poppy after they'd gone. "You'd think it was Aunt Millicent who lost her son, instead of the other way around."

"Grief takes people differently," said Robert. "Poor Harrison is most likely in denial, clinging to her routine duties as a way of avoiding the dreadful truth."

"That doesn't change the fact that Aunt Millicent is a monster," said Poppy, looking up as DI Hennessy entered the kitchen, followed by Perry and Quimby.

"We have made a preliminary identification of the body, one Cyril Harrison," said Hennessy. "Considering the identity of the victim and his relationship to a member of the household, not to mention the location of the body, I will require a complete list of employees and family members and will be conducting interviews over the next few days."

"We are prepared to offer every cooperation," said Poppy. "Will it be possible to keep the house open for the visitors?"

"What about the hat show?" asked Perry. "Can it open as scheduled?"

"If I may," began the vicar in a reproachful tone. "Might I suggest a prayer?"

Somewhat chastened, they all fell silent and bowed their heads.

"O God, we give you thanks and praise for your goodness and pray that you may give to the departed eternal rest and let light perpetual shine upon them, and most especially on Cyril."

They all joined in the final amen, but Lucy knew that while Cyril might or might not find perpetual light and eternal rest, there would certainly be no rest for those left behind at Moreton Manor.

Chapter Twelve

"Now, if you'll show me the way, I would like to offer some support to the lady's maid, the victim's mother," requested the vicar.

"Do you really think that's a good idea?" asked Desi. "She didn't seem to want any sympathy."

"I won't press the issue," replied Robert, "but I do want to let her know that the church is there for her if she should find a need for support and consolation."

"Well, it's your funeral," said Poppy with a sigh. "Aunt Millicent's been moved upstairs here in the family wing. Desi can show you the way."

They left and Poppy collapsed in a chair at the big kitchen table, her chin propped on one arm. "I suppose we ought to do something about dinner," she said with a distinct lack of enthusiasm.

"I don't think anyone's very hungry,"

volunteered Flora. "I know I'm not."

Lucy didn't like the way this was going, not one bit. She was starving, although somewhat ashamed to admit it. "Aunt Millicent will certainly expect something," she said in an effort to divert blame.

"There's an Indian take-out place in the village, isn't there?" suggested Sue. "Lucy and I could pick up some supper there."

"What a good idea," said Perry. "I haven't had Indian in ages."

"I simply adore chicken korma," volunteered Vickie, who had just arrived in the kitchen with Gerald. She seemed to have made a full recovery from last night's binge, although she had substituted a pair of nubby-soled flat driving shoes for the perilously high-heeled Louboutins.

"What about Lady Wickham? Will she be okay with Indian?" asked Lucy.

"Absolutely," said Desi, returning to the kitchen. "It reminds her of the glory days of the Raj."

"But only if we put it on a Crown Derby plate," said Poppy with a laugh that was verging on the hysterical.

"I'll go dust one off," said Perry, handing a set of keys to Sue. "You can take the Ford. That's probably the most familiar to you. Before you leave, you better check with the inspector and make sure it's all right."

"Maybe they'll want some food, too," said Sue.

When Sue and Lucy found the inspector in the stable yard, he was deep in conversation with a scene-of-crime officer and wasn't interested in Indian food. "No, no, none for us. We'll fend for ourselves, but thank you for asking."

"It's all right for us to leave the estate, then?" asked Sue.

"Just don't try to leave the country," he advised.

"Wouldn't dream of it," said Lucy, speaking more honestly than the inspector imagined. She was finding the whole situation absolutely fascinating, and her reporter's blood was up, keen to discover the story behind the murder. "Do you have any leads so far?"

"Early days, early days," said the inspector, dismissing them.

When they reached the garage, actually converted from part of the stable, they found Sgt. Matthews busy checking out the vehicles parked there. In addition to Perry's Ford Focus, there were several Land Rovers, Flora's Mini Cooper, and a sporty MG convertible.

"Quite a collection," said Lucy.

"Never ceases to amaze me," said Sgt. Matthews, "how some people have so much and others have so very little."

"We're supposed to take the Ford to go get Indian food," said Sue. "The inspector said it was all right."

"I'm just getting the registration information," said the sergeant. "Routine."

"Any leads so far?" inquired Lucy. "It seems like one of those locked room mysteries. Something Agatha Christie might write."

"I've seen some pretty weird stuff and this one is right up there," said Sgt. Matthews. "Did you happen to notice anything out of the usual in recent days?"

"Only the awful smell," said Sue.

"Well, there was the body in the maze," offered Lucy.

"The OD," said Sgt. Matthews with a nod.

"There might be a connection," said Lucy.

"Perhaps," admitted Sgt. Matthews. "We'll be looking into it."

"We're only visitors," continued Lucy, responding to the sergeant's dismissive tone, "but it does seem to me that there's quite a bit of tension in the household."

"How so?" asked the sergeant.

"I think it's just the unexpected arrival of Lady Wickham," said Sue, giving Lucy a warning look. "She's rather difficult and demanding."

"It's more than that," said Lucy, disregarding Sue. "Poppy and Gerald don't seem to be getting along, Flora's anorexic, Gerald disapproves of Desi being a dancer, and I think there may be money problems"

"Money problems?" asked Sgt. Matthews, somewhat incredulous.

"Poppy frets about money all the time. There's a lot of expense running a place like this and there's dry rot and paintings falling off the walls. Things are not as perfect as they seem," said Lucy.

"They never are," said Sue in a cautionary tone. "But Lucy's one of those glass-half-empty people. On the other hand, there's a lot of excitement about Perry's hat show. It's due to open in a few days and it's already generating quite a buzz."

"I don't suppose you knew the victim, this Cyril Harrison?" asked the sergeant.

"How could we?" replied Lucy. "We've only been here a few days."

"People get around," countered Sgt. Matthews. "I understand you live near Boston, which is quite popular with British travelers."

"Sorry," said Sue. "Never met the man — not here and not in the US."

"Perhaps you heard some mention of him here?" asked Sgt. Matthews. "Or Eric Starkey?"

"That's the man in the maze?" asked Lucy.

"Right."

"Not at all," said Sue. "I never heard either of those names until now."

"I don't think they even knew of Cyril," volunteered Lucy. "Even Lady Wickham seemed surprised to learn that her maid had a son." But even as she spoke, Lucy wondered if Lady Wickham had been telling the truth when she claimed she didn't know Harrison had a son.

"Now that doesn't surprise me," said the sergeant, "since the upper classes tend to think only of themselves." She paused, then shrugged. "Somebody knew Cyril, that's for sure, and you know what else? They didn't like him."

"For sure," said Sue, unlocking the door to the Ford. "We better get going. People are starving."

"Death has that effect on some people," said Sgt. Matthews with a dismissive wave.

Sue started the car and Lucy hopped in, feeling slightly disoriented to be sitting on the left-hand side as a passenger. "Can you do this? Drive on the wrong side of the road?"

"Not sure," said Sue, carefully backing the car out of the stable and driving toward the gateway. "We'll find out."

After Sue had successfully negotiated the gateway and was proceeding at a stately pace along the drive, Lucy spoke up. "You know Sergeant Matthews was questioning us, don't you? At first, I thought she was just chatting us up, being friendly, but then I realized that we're suspects, too."

"Was it when she asked you if you'd ever met Cyril in Boston?" asked Sue in a rather sarcastic tone.

"That was a definite clue," admitted Lucy, "but I think it has to be an inside job. Somebody here at the manor killed Cyril."

"I'm putting my money on Vickie," said Sue. "She's an outsider, and so was Cyril."

"You just don't like her," said Lucy.

"True, but you have to admit, she's the one who was most likely to have known Cyril. She's a party girl. She's a networker and could have run into him anywhere. I betcha she knew Eric. In fact, I wouldn't be surprised if her little binge last night was a reaction to his death."

"You might be on to something," admitted Lucy. "But what about Cyril? We don't know anything about him. Why do you think he was going to parties and networking?"

"I don't have a clue about Cyril, true, but I do think Vickie's the sort of girl who gets around, who isn't above a bit of slumming," said Sue, attempting to make a left turn onto the wrong side of the road and causing some other drivers to honk at them. "Oops," she said, correcting her course.

"Do you want me to drive?" suggested Lucy.

"No, no, I'm getting the hang of it," insisted Sue as the car strayed over the line toward the opposite lane. "Do you have a favorite suspect?" she asked, swerving back into the proper lane.

"Willoughby," said Lucy, keeping a nervous eye on the oncoming traffic.

"The librarian?" exclaimed Sue. "Mr. Milquetoast?"

"Appearances can be deceiving," said Lucy, "and he's the one most likely to know about the secret room."

"But he insisted he didn't know about it," insisted Sue.

"He could have been lying," said Lucy.

"A librarian wouldn't do that," said Sue. "Think of Miss Tilley back home."

"Willoughby is nothing like Miss Tilley," said Lucy, who was very fond of the elderly, retired librarian. "I can't help feeling there's something a bit off about him." She fell silent for a moment, studying a green field dotted with white sheep. "If it's not Willoughby, I think it's probably Gerald."

"There's more to Gerald than meets the eye," agreed Sue, signaling left and turning right at a stop sign, much to the surprise of an approaching driver. "I don't trust him."

"So we're agreed?" asked Lucy as Sue pulled into the parking area in front of the Indian restaurant.

"Agreed. Chicken korma, assorted curries, jasmine rice, samosas, and plenty of naan bread, right?"

Lucy chuckled at this abrupt change of subject. "Right."

It was getting on to eight o'clock when they returned with the take-out food and appetites had definitely improved in the interim. There was great interest as Lucy and Sue unpacked the food and set it out on the kitchen island. Poppy added a pile of plates and a handful of silverware, Flora produced a stack of paper napkins, and Gerald, after considerable thought, decided that a Riesling was the perfect wine to accompany Indian food.

"Grub's ready," declared Perry, inviting

everyone to partake.

Vickie was the first to grab a plate and was just about to add a dollop of chicken korma when Harrison sailed in, grabbed a plate and shoved her aside. "Her ladyship specially requested chicken korma," she said, scooping up spoonful after spoonful of the stuff until it was all gone, then topped it with a small mountain of jasmine rice.

She set the plate on a tray, then added a huge piece of naan bread, a wineglass, a few pieces of silverware and a napkin. Then, tucking one of the bottles of Riesling under her arm, she lifted the tray and carried it out of the kitchen.

"Well, I'll be gobsmacked," said Vickie. "She took every last bit of chicken korma."

"There wasn't all that much," said Sue. "They were running out at the Curry Palace and they gave us all they had."

"Well, I guess it's curry for me."

Soon everyone had filled their plates and settled at the big scrubbed pine table. There was little conversation as they all focused on eating.

It was Desi who finally said what they all were thinking. "Did we know that Harrison had a son?"

"I certainly didn't," said Poppy. "And we've known Aunt Millicent our whole lives.

She was our mother's favorite sister-in-law. And Harrison, too. She's been with Aunt forever. If we visited Fairleigh, she was there; if Aunt came to visit us, so did Harrison. They were — they are — like Siamese twins."

"But Cyril was never mentioned?" asked Lucy.

"Never," said Perry. "I mean, we used to call Harrison terrible names. The Miserable Maid. The Spiteful Spinster. The Woeful Wonder. Remember?"

"I still call her names," admitted Gerald. "To myself, o' course. Wicked Witchy Bitch comes to mind."

"Now I feel rather awful about it," said Poppy.

"I don't," said Gerald, refilling his glass. "The woman's awful — and ugly to boot."

"She's certainly devoted to Aunt," offered Flora.

"Apparently to the exclusion of her own son," said Sue.

"I wonder if he came here to do one of those birth mother reunion things," speculated Lucy. "I mean, maybe she'd put him out for adoption so she could keep working. Maybe that's why nobody knew about him."

"I doubt it very much," said Desi. "I suspect he was up to no good."

"Probably right," agreed Gerald. "Who would want the Wicked Witchy Bitch for a mother?"

A short rasping sound caught their attention and everyone turned round to see Harrison standing in the doorway, tray in hand. "I'm just after a bit of the Major Grey's for m'lady. She does like a little bit of chutney with her chicken korma," she said, approaching the table. "I do hope I'm not intruding."

"No, no," said Poppy, hopping up and plucking the jar of chutney off the table. "Take this. We have more in the pantry."

"And if you don't mind, her ladyship would appreciate another bit of that funny flat bread."

"The naan, of course," said Poppy, producing the last piece. "Anything else? Or will that be all?"

"That will be all," said Harrison, turning rather smartly on her heel and leaving.

Once the door had closed behind her Flora and Vickie exploded in nervous giggles, which earned them a disapproving look from Poppy. The others, however, were embarrassed and finished the meal in silence.

Lucy felt a sense of relief when she finally

got back to her room and closed the door, shutting out everyone and being by herself. *Me time* they called it in the magazines and she was finding that it was something she really needed. Maybe it was all those years spent satisfying the needs of Bill and the kids, not to mention the demands of her boss Ted, and even the constant calls for "something for the bake sale" or "just an hour or two" selling raffle tickets on Saturday morning at the IGA.

It was too early to go to bed, so she decided to settle herself on the chaise by the window for an hour or so with P.D. James's fascinating Inspector Dalgliesh, and was just opening the book when her cell phone rang. She was tempted to ignore it and let the call go to voice mail but then panicked, thinking something might be wrong at home.

"Is everything all right?" she asked, fearing the worst.

"More than all right, everything's great," said Bill. "I just want to double-check and make sure it's okay with you if I close out the college fund and invest the money with Doug Fitzpatrick."

"Who?" asked Lucy as alarm bells went off in her head. "What?"

"Don't tell me you don't remember," said

Bill. "I told you all about it the other day. He says he can double our money in three months."

Lucy didn't remember that conversation, but she did remember Zoe's concerns about the investment advisor her father was spending so much time with.

"That's crazy, Bill," said Lucy. "There's no investment on earth that yields that sort of return."

"Now that's where you're wrong, Lucy. When I was on Wall Street, I saw some amazing deals go down, but I was never in on them. It was all insider stuff. Now I've got a chance to be on the inside."

"It sounds to me that you're letting your emotions cloud your good sense," said Lucy.

"You're a fine one to say that," snapped Bill. "I watched you wallow in a cloud of negativity all winter, and frankly, I'm worried that you're sinking into depression again. You're definitely drinking too much. That was quite a hangover you had."

"I am not depressed and that hangover was a one-time thing, after a big dinner," countered Lucy, who had a dim recollection of talking to Bill on the phone when she was hungover. "I just think that if something seems too good to be true, it probably is."

"See! That's what I would call negative thinking. You need to snap out of it and think positively."

Lucy couldn't believe what she was hearing. "Bill, I'm not depressed, honest," she said, deciding to take a different approach, "and I know how much you want to make it possible for Zoe to go to the college of her choice. For all I know, maybe this is the deal of the century. I'm no financial wizard; I can't even balance the checkbook. All I ask is that you check this guy out, and take a real close look at this deal. If it's as good as it seems, if you're really convinced we won't lose it all, then I guess we should do it."

"Aw, Lucy, I knew you'd come around," crowed Bill.

"Promise you'll at least call Toby, see if he remembers this guy," said Lucy with a sinking feeling.

"Good idea. I'd like to check in with him anyway. I haven't heard from them lately."

Lucy had a sudden vision of avalanches, tidal waves, and earthquakes; she saw the entire state of Alaska drifting off from Canada and floating in an iceberg strewn sea. It was nonsense, all nonsense, she decided, firmly banishing the nightmarish images. "No news is good news."

"That's my Lucy," said Bill, ending the call.

The tense atmosphere didn't improve much the next morning as Sue and Lucy discovered when they came down for breakfast.

"The police have set up an incident room in the stable and they're going to be interviewing us all," said Perry, "so don't plan on going anywhere today."

"They want to interview us?" asked Sue, pouring herself a cup of coffee.

"Hennessey said everyone, so I assume that includes you and Lucy."

"At least they've set up in the stable," said Poppy, emerging from the pantry with a box of Weetabix. "They're letting us open to the public, but the scene-of-crime people will be working on the hidey-hole. They still haven't figured out how the killer got Cyril's body in there."

An awful thought occurred to Lucy. "You don't think he was alive? That someone locked him in there and left him to die?"

Poppy and Perry exchanged glances.

"I suppose anything is possible," said Perry with a grimace.

"They're doing an autopsy, of course," said Poppy. "I guess we'll know more then."

"Right now, they're not telling us anything."

"Police procedure," said Lucy, who'd found official silence extremely frustrating as a reporter in Tinker's Cove. "They don't give out information because it helps them in the investigation."

"Aha," said Perry with a smile. "The one who says the victim was wearing blue nail polish is obviously the murderer."

"Right," said Lucy, pouring a generous helping of cream on her Weetabix.

After helping clear up the breakfast dishes, Lucy and Sue found themselves alone in the kitchen and settled themselves on the sofas with the dogs. Sue leafed through the well-thumbed pile of *Country Life* magazines, while Lucy curled up with her mystery.

If only Inspector Hennessy was more like Dalgliesh, she thought, admitting to herself that while a sensitive nature was a definite plus for a fictional detective, it would probably be a detriment to a real life detective.

Gerald, fresh from his session with Hennessy, seemed to agree with her. "Bugger the blasted fella," he declared, marching into the kitchen and heading straight for the drinks tray, where he poured himself a couple fingers of whiskey.

"So the questioning didn't go well," offered Sue.

"Damned impertinent. Wanted to know, well, things that are none of his damned business."

"Was there a drift to the questions?" asked Lucy. "Could you tell if he's got a theory about the murder?"

"Damned if I could tell what the fella's thinking," said Gerald, draining the crystal tumbler. "Fella didn't seem to know a thing about life in the country, that's for certain. Didn't know this time o' year you've got to keep an eye on the sheep." He set the empty glass on the counter next to the sink, grabbed a stout walking stick that was propped by the door, and marched out, apparently intending to keep an eye on the sheep.

"I thought he was keeping an eye on Vickie," said Sue after he'd gone.

Flora wandered in soon after her father had gone, opened the refrigerator door, and stood there for quite a while, staring at the contents.

"You remind me of my girls back in Maine," said Lucy. "They do the same thing, hoping the yogurt and mini carrots will morph into chocolate."

"I'm not really hungry," said Flora, plucking a strawberry from the bowl sitting on the kitchen island. "Just bored, I guess."

"And stressed, I imagine," said Lucy, noticing the blue shadows under Flora's eyes, and her twitchy fingers.

Flora bit into the strawberry and chewed thoughtfully. "I don't have anything to hide."

"Of course not," said Sue. "Still, it's not nice to be questioned by the police."

"It certainly isn't," said Poppy, arriving with a trug full of freshly cut flowers. She set the trug on the counter and produced a large vase from a cabinet, then began filling it with water. "I know I shouldn't say this, but murder is terribly inconvenient. I wish they would just solve the darn thing and move on."

"Are visitors staying away now that news of the murder is out?" asked Sue.

"Quite the contrary," said Perry, hurrying in. "They're coming in droves, attracted by the gruesome crime. So many, in fact, that we're running low on tickets. Do you know where they're stored, Pops?"

"Try the gift shop," advised Poppy, and Perry hurried off just as Vickie and Desi came in, faces flushed and dressed in riding clothes.

"Wonderful morning for a ride," said Desi, taking a bottle of orange juice out of the fridge and filling two glasses. "Mist on the moors and all that."

"It was beautiful!" exclaimed Vickie. "You are so lucky to have all this. Imagine riding for an hour at least and never leaving your land."

"It's not really all ours. It's . . . well, it's complicated," said Desi, draining his glass.

"Would you like a bit more?" offered Vickie, picking up the juice bottle and preparing to refill his glass.

"No, that was plenty," said Desi, holding up a hand as if to signal a stop. "Got to watch my weight, for the dancing you know."

"Oh, Desi, you're so fit and trim. You don't need to worry about that."

"Tell that to the ballet master," he said with a wink. "Now I understand I have a date with a copper."

"Perhaps later you can show me the folly?" suggested Vickie, cocking her head invitingly.

"Per'aps," said Desi, making a quick exit, much to the amusement of his mother.

Looking for elevenses, Winifred and Maurice arrived as Flora was leaving.

"I'll put on the kettle," offered Winifred,

"and, Maurice, why don't you see if you can find some biscuits." She turned to Lucy and Sue. "Will you be wanting tea, too? Poppy?"

"None for me," said Poppy, snipping the stem of a tulip and slipping it into the vase.

"No thanks," said Sue.

"Love some," said Lucy, eager to take advantage of the opportunity to question Willoughby, who she considered a prime suspect. "I'll get the mugs."

Soon she was sitting at the table with the two experts, nibbling on chocolate digestives and sipping tea. "Have the police figured out how poor Cyril got put in the secret room?" she asked, trying to keep her tone light and casual.

"If they have, they're not saying," said Willoughby, his mouth full of biscuit.

"I suppose you haven't found anything in those old plans?" asked Poppy.

"Not so far," said Willoughby with a shrug. "I did find plans for the memorial for that little girl — the one they pickled."

"Her portrait is in the east hall," offered Winifred. "If you'd care for a look, I'd be happy to show it to you."

"They pickled a little girl?" asked Sue, wide-eyed.

"She was dead. Died at sea," said Willoughby.

"Her father, the sixth earl, I believe, couldn't bear to have her buried at sea so he had them stuff her into a barrel of rum, just like they did to the General, old Horatio. It was the only way to preserve a body at the time. He brought her back home to the family burial plot," said Poppy. "A lot of visitors like to visit her grave. They leave little tokens."

"A touching story, I'm sure," said Harrison with a sniff. She was carrying a large plastic basket overflowing with dirty laundry. "I hope you don't mind if I use the washer? For milady's smalls?"

Poppy glanced at the huge basket and repressed a smile. "Not at all," she said, stripping the leaves off a lilac branch.

CHAPTER THIRTEEN

"So, how did it go?" asked Lucy when Sue emerged from her interview with DI Hennessy. Lucy was sitting on the terrace outside the family room, trying to enjoy the sunshine and abundant vines that clambered up the lichen-spotted stone wall of the manor, but finding instead that her mind kept returning to the murder.

"Okay, I guess," said Sue, seating herself on a teak garden bench. "There really wasn't much I could tell them." She paused. "Well, that's not exactly true. I could tell Sergeant Izzy quite a bit about how she could improve her appearance." She examined her fingernails, which were painted with pale pink polish. "Honestly, polyester should be banned, done away with. It's a crime against humanity."

"It is practical for a working woman," said Lucy.

"It's ugly," said Sue. "The sergeant has

great bone structure. She just needs a little touch of concealer and bronzer, a bit of mascara, and a slick of lip gloss. It would only take a few minutes in the morning and she'd look so much better." Sue paused for emphasis as if she was going to deliver earthshaking news. "I actually don't mind the ponytail. It works for her."

"I'm sure she'd be thrilled to know that you approve," said Lucy in a sarcastic tone.

Sue sighed and looked around, planting her hands on her thighs. "So what can we do today? We can't go anywhere until they interview you, right?"

"Right," said Lucy, watching with interest as Lady Wickham stepped through the French doors and crossed the terrace on her way to the stable for her interview.

As her voluminous skirts billowed around her, it was rather like watching a clipper ship in full sail. She was accompanied by Harrison, of course, who bobbed along behind her like an oversized dinghy attached to the mother ship.

"This ought to be interesting," said Lucy, rising from her chair and intending to follow the pair through the gate in the wall that led to the adjacent stable yard.

"What do you think you're doing?" asked Sue.

"Stretching my legs," said Lucy innocently. "We can't leave. There's nothing to do so I'm going to take a bit of exercise and walk about."

"You're hoping to eavesdrop, that's what you're doing," said Sue.

"Nonsense!" declared Lucy. "I would never do such a thing."

"I think I'll take a bit of exercise myself," said Sue, getting up.

"Good idea," said Lucy, smiling. "It will do you good."

As Lucy had expected, the dowager countess was not at all hesitant about making known her displeasure at the situation. Her strident voice could be clearly heard through the open window and was booming through the walled courtyard.

"This is outrageous!" she announced in ringing tones. "My father was a marquess. I was married to an earl. I am a member of one of England's most venerable noble families. We date back to 1066 I'll have you know, and I am not accustomed to being treated as if I were some common person of no account."

Sue and Lucy could not hear Sgt. Hennessy's reply, but they could figure it out from Lady Wickham's next remark.

"There is no question of Harrison leaving

my side! I might well find this trying situation too much due to my delicate condition. I might even faint and would need my maid's assistance with my smelling salts."

This argument apparently did not sway the inspector, as Harrison promptly emerged from the stable, clutching an ancient, cracked leather handbag. "Oh, shame on you!" she scolded, waving a knobby finger at Lucy and Sue. "Eavesdropping, were you?"

Taking a page from Lady Wickham's book, Sue pulled herself up to her full height and glared at the lady's maid. "How dare you say such a thing!"

"We're simply getting a bit of exercise," said Lucy.

"Don't be getting all hoity-toity with me," replied Harrison, narrowing her eyes. "I know quality when I see it and you're not it." Having delivered that sally, she marched off, her back ramrod straight beneath her black dress, shiny from being ironed too much.

"Well, I guess she told us," said Lucy as the open window of the interview room was slammed down, cutting off her ladyship's further remarks.

"Is Harrison for real?" asked Sue, musing aloud as they returned to the seating area on the terrace. "The woman lost her son, but she doesn't seem the least bit troubled by it, not to say moved or distressed."

"Maybe they were estranged. Perhaps she didn't even know him," said Lucy. "A lot of girls who found themselves pregnant gave their babies up for adoption. Sometimes they never even saw them."

"I know and thank goodness those days are over," said Sue. "Rachel would probably say that Harrison is compensating for her loss by substituting Lady Wickham for the child she lost."

"She's devoted to the countess. The horrid old woman is everything to her," said Lucy.

"Well, I don't approve," declared Sue. "It's twisted and unnatural."

"What's unnatural?" asked Perry, who was crossing the terrace, car keys in hand.

"We just encountered Harrison," explained Sue, "and were struck that she doesn't seem to be at all grief-stricken by her son's death."

Perry smiled and shrugged. "She's always been a bit of a puzzle," he said in a dismissive tone that seemed to Lucy to be yet another example of upper-class disdain for those who served them. "I'm headed into the village to the printers. Care to join me for a pub lunch?"

"Thanks, but I'm waiting to be interviewed," said Lucy. "Sue can go, though."

"Are you sure you don't mind?" asked Sue. "I hate to desert you."

"Go," said Lucy. "I'll be fine."

"Well, if you're sure . . ."

"I'm sure," said Lucy as Sgt. Matthews appeared in the stable yard gate, beckoning her.

Giving Sue and Perry a little wave, Lucy followed the sergeant into the borrowed interview room.

She found the inspector sitting at a card table with legs that folded away for storage. He was surrounded by shelves loaded with miscellaneous crockery, dusty old saddles piled on sawhorses, and cracked leather bridles and riding whips hanging from hooks.

"Do sit down," he said, indicating an aged Windsor chair that was missing a few of the spindles from its back.

"Thank you," said Lucy, seating herself and discovering the chair wobbled a bit on the uneven flagstone flooring.

"For the record, will you please confirm that you are Lucy Stone from Tinker's Cove, Maine in the USA and that you are a houseguest here at the manor."

"That's right. I came with my friend, Sue Finch, for the hat show."

"You have a shared interest in hats?" asked the inspector.

"Not really. I just came along for the trip."

"Have you any knowledge of the victim, Cyril Harrison?" he asked.

"None at all."

"And previous to your arrival at the manor, did you have any acquaintance with any of the other people here at the manor?"

"Only Perry, the earl. Sue met him in the cafeteria at the Victoria and Albert Museum a few years ago. I was introduced to him then."

"And what is your impression of the family at the manor?" the inspector asked, leaning back so his chair tilted on its rear legs and propping one argyle-socked ankle on the other knee as if settling in for a good old gossip.

"Oh, goodness, I don't know," said Lucy, unwilling to speak ill of her host family. "They seem pretty typical of any family, despite their wealth and titles."

"In what way?" persisted the inspector, leaning forward, which caused the chair to land with a thump.

"Just normal," said Lucy. "But I can't help wondering how that poor man got into that hidey-hole. Have they found the entrance? And what was he doing here, getting himself killed?"

"That is exactly what we are trying to discover, Mrs. Stone," said the inspector with an amused smile.

"I am a reporter back in Maine," said Lucy, finding the inspector's relaxed attitude encouraging. "I have covered the occasional serious crime. I've even helped solve a few."

"Well, I can assure you that the Thames Valley Police force is quite capable and will not require your assistance," he said, swiftly putting her down.

"I didn't mean to imply," she began, backtracking.

"Of course not," said the inspector. "But it would be wise for you to bear in mind that you are on unfamiliar territory here and we are dealing with a ruthless and cunning murderer." He paused, glancing around at the accumulated clutter that represented decades, if not centuries, of aristocratic country life, and leaned back once again in his chair, which creaked under the strain. "Mind you, these people are different from you and me, and it's best not to cross them. I'll be glad when this case is over and done." Then he seemed to collect himself and told her she could go. "Best be careful for the remainder of your stay," he said as she rose to leave.

Lucy didn't mind being left to her own devices while Sue lunched with Perry. She spent the rest of the morning admiring the manor's famous gardens, even chatting with a couple of gardeners about the famous fig tree that was two centuries old. Then she had a sandwich in the kitchen with Sally, who much to her disappointment had nothing at all to say about the family or the murder, preferring instead to dwell on the reproductive potential of the Duchess of Cambridge. "I reeelly don't think she'll go for a third, now that they've got an heir and a spare," she opined. "Especially since she has such dreadful morning sickness. Poor thing. Now I myself was never bothered much by that, but I did have dreadful swollen ankles with my fourth."

Fearing more obstetrical confessions from Sally, Lucy made her excuses and settled herself in her favorite teak chaise on the terrace where she planned to spend a quiet afternoon with the intriguing Inspector Dalgliesh, who always solved the murder.

Sue and Perry returned around three and Lucy joined them in a sneak peek at the hat show in the long gallery, which was almost ready for the gala opening.

"We're just waiting for a few last minute arrivals from the royals," said Perry, his eyes sparkling with excitement. "Camilla is sending the feather fascinator she wore at her wedding to Prince Charles, and we're also getting the toilet bowl hat Princess Beatrice wore at Wills and Kate's wedding. Bea doesn't own it anymore. She donated it to charity and it was auctioned off. I don't mind saying it was a bit of a struggle getting the name of the anonymous buyer and then tracking him down, but believe it or not, Poppy came to the rescue." He paused. "She can be quite persuasive when she wants to be. I think she promised to let the poor soul sleep in the Chinese bedroom after paying for the new curtains or something."

Lucy didn't share Sue's passion for fashion, but she had to admit the display of headgear was fascinating from a sociological perspective. It was amazing what people would put on their heads — anything from boxy Tudor headdresses that looked like cages for thought to Native American feather warbonnets. There was even a hideous, pleated, plastic rain hat that folded flat for storage in its own little plastic envelope, designed to be carried in a lady's purse, ready to protect her 1960s bouffant hairdo in case of a sudden shower. The exhibit was extremely well done, and many of the hats were shown with works of art that depicted similar designs.

"Did you curate this yourself?" asked Lucy, impressed by the broad knowledge and expertise needed to create such an exhibition.

"Well, I had a little help from Winifred," admitted Perry, "but I did most of it myself."

"It must have been an enormous amount of work," said Sue.

"Well, you know what they say about work. When you love what you're doing, it's not work at all. It was fun." He gave a wry smile. "I only hope the critics appreciate what I've done. They can be so cruel. They really savaged that Lucian Freud retrospective."

"Well, Lucian Freud is rather an acquired taste," said Sue, leaving Lucy to wonder who and what she was talking about.

"He's good enough for the Duchess of Devonshire. She's had him paint her several times, so he's good enough for me. But I say, enough of this idle chitchat. It must be time for cocktails." Perry checked his watch.

"Oh, well, rather early," he admitted, "but it must be six somewhere, right?"

When they arrived in the great room, they discovered other family members had the same thought. Gerald was wielding a corkscrew and opening a second bottle of wine, the first already having been emptied to fill his own glass, as well as those of Poppy, Desi, Vickie, and Flora.

"You must've heard the cork pop," teased Poppy.

"It's been a long day," said Perry, "beginning with my interview with Inspector Hennessy at the ridiculous hour of eight o'clock." He accepted a glass of wine from Gerald, sniffing it appreciatively. "I suppose the early hour was necessary," he admitted after swishing that first mouthful and swallowing. "They do say that crime never sleeps."

"Do you really think they'll ever solve it?" asked Vickie in a doubtful tone. "All they asked me was pretty much my name and address, and what I do for a living."

"And what exactly do you do, if I might ask?" asked Poppy in a rather snarky tone.

"She's a marketing consultant," snapped Gerald, glaring at his wife. "You know that perfectly well."

Poppy was not to be deterred. "I rather

thought she did something else," she insisted, giving Gerald a knowing look.

"Nonsense." Gerald drained his glass and promptly refilled it. "Stuff's rather thin, if you ask me. Goes down like water."

"I think we're all a bit on edge," said Desi in a soothing tone.

"Well, it's not at all pleasant having police in the house," declared Lady Wickham, sailing in and casting a rather disapproving eye on the group. "I believe it's teatime."

"I'll put the kettle on," said Poppy with a marked lack of enthusiasm.

"Oh, let me," said Lucy. "You must be exhausted."

"I am, rather," admitted Poppy. "I can't think why. I didn't really do much today."

"It's stress, Mummy," said Flora. "It wears you out."

"Nonsense," declared Lady Wickham, plunking herself down in the middle of a sofa and leaving no room for anyone else to sit. "When I was a girl, there was no such thing as stress and I do think that nowadays it's simply an excuse for all sorts of bad behavior. 'I would have replied to your invitation, but I was simply too stressed.' That sort of —" she dropped her thought, observing Quimby entering through the French doors.

"I'm sorry to interrupt," he began.

"Well, you should be," said the dowager. "You're intruding."

"I have something rather important to tell you," he said, looking at Poppy.

"Well, go on," said her ladyship, impatiently.

"It's bad news, I'm afraid." He paused a moment, allowing everyone to prepare themselves.

"Well, don't keep us hanging," ordered Lady Wickham. "If it's bad, it certainly won't improve with keeping. Best to tell it and get it over with."

"The police have taken the vicar in for questioning," he said as the kettle began to shriek and Poppy got up to make the tea.

"The vicar!" exclaimed Perry. "That's preposterous."

"I can't believe it," said Desi.

"Well, I think it's high time," declared her ladyship. "I always thought there was something suspicious about him."

"The only thing you found suspicious about him is his skin color," said Flora.

"I simply don't trust black people. It's as simple as that," said Lady Wickham, accepting a cup of tea from Poppy. After examining it she handed it back. "I do hate to be a bother, Poppy dear, but I do think this milk is a bit off."

"You're the one who's a bit off," continued Flora. "I can't believe you've decided Robert is a criminal simply because he's black."

"He hasn't been arrested or charged," said Quimby. "It's as they say . . . he's helping the police with their enquiries."

"I think we all know what that means," said Flora, implying something worse.

Poppy busied herself opening a fresh bottle of milk and fixing a second cup of tea for her aunt, but she gave her daughter a warning look. "The police have information that we don't have."

Flora reacted angrily. "You're just as bad as Aunt. Robert's been so good to us. It's as if he's a member of the family."

"Oh, heavens," moaned Lady Wickham. "Perish the thought."

"Well, I do not believe in deserting my friends," said Flora. "I'm going over to the vicarage to see Sarah. She must be beside herself with worry. She might even need someone to stay with the boys."

"And you're going to be the child-minder?" inquired Gerald. "That would be a first."

"Your father has a point," said Poppy. "Sarah doesn't need visitors now. You'd merely be a complication. I think you should stay home."

"Why must you all be so horrible?" demanded Flora, putting on her jacket. "I'm going, and if I'm not needed, I'll come home."

Lucy found that she agreed with Poppy, but for a different reason. She remembered the inspector's warning that a dangerous murderer was at large. "I don't think you should go," she said. "It might not be safe."

"I refuse to be afraid in my own back yard," declared Flora.

"Well, then," said Lucy, "I'll go with you. You shouldn't go alone."

"Oh, all right!" snapped Flora as Lucy grabbed one of the waxed jackets off its hook and followed her out the door.

Chapter Fourteen

Lucy felt extremely awkward, tagging along with Flora who didn't even deign to acknowledge her presence as she marched purposefully along the path to the vicarage.

"It's so pleasant here," said Lucy, hoping to strike up some sort of conversation. "And the garden is so lovely. You're very lucky to live in such a beautiful place."

"I guess," muttered Flora.

"I don't really know them, but the Goodenoughs seem to be such a lovely couple. This must be terrible for them," continued Lucy as they passed the maze. "Do you know them well?"

"Kind of," said Flora, keeping her head down, studying the path.

"When Sue and I had tea at the vicarage —" Lucy tripped on a root and nearly fell, but managed to save herself by executing a series of awkward maneuvers.

"Look," said Flora, turning to face her.

"I'm really fine on my own. I know every bump and twist on these paths. There's no need for you to come, too."

Lucy was not impressed by Flora's bravado. The girl looked so frail that it hardly seemed possible she could make it to the vicarage, much less fight off an attacker.

"There is a murderer on the loose," said Lucy, in her mother-knows-best tone of voice. "I don't think it's wise for anyone to be wandering about alone." She gave an uneasy glance in the direction of the afternoon sun covered with clouds. "Especially in the rain."

"I don't know how that man came to get himself killed and stuffed in that priest's hole," said Flora, "but I'm quite sure it has nothing to do with me."

"You can't be sure of that," said Lucy. "We don't know the killer's motive. For all we know, the killer could be some psychopath, some serial killer who simply enjoys killing people and hiding their bodies in unusual places."

Flora almost grinned, finding this amusing. "I suppose that sort of thing happens more in America. . . ."

"No, we go in more for mass shootings of innocent schoolchildren and police killing people they've arrested, especially if they're black," said Lucy, causing Flora to raise her eyebrows in surprise. "You Brits, on the other hand, are much more imaginative, what with your poisons, nooses, and lead pipes."

"Is that what this is to you?" asked Flora, challenging her. "A game of Cluedo?"

"Absolutely not," said Lucy. "I hate violence of any kind, and I also hate seeing an innocent man accused of a crime." She resumed walking. "Of course, we can't be sure that the police are wrong and that Robert is innocent."

"I'm sure," said Flora, falling into step beside her and surprising Lucy as she easily kept up with her brisk pace.

Lucy was struck by Flora's absolute faith in Robert's innocence, but couldn't share it. She was older and, if not wiser, more experienced, and knew that life was sometimes complicated. She could think of any number of reasons why Robert, or anyone, might commit murder and some of them — like self-defense — were completely justified.

When they arrived at the vicarage, the grassy yard was empty except for a soccer ball abandoned by the boys. The kitchen door, however, was ajar and they could see Sarah and the boys sitting at the table, eating their evening meal. Flora tapped on the door.

Sarah jumped up and invited them in. "We're just having tea. Will you join us?" She bit her lip, then added, "Since Robert's not here, there's plenty of food."

"He'll be back in no time, looking for his supper," said Flora in an encouraging tone.

"I wish I could believe that," said Sarah, collecting plates and mugs from the tall kitchen dresser and setting them on the table.

Lucy and Flora were soon tucking in to a delicious shepherd's pie, accompanied by a fresh garden salad and gallons of strong, hot tea. When they'd finished eating and the boys were dismissed to do their homework, Lucy and Flora helped clear the table.

"Do you have any idea why the police think Robert killed Cyril Harrison?" asked Lucy, spreading a piece of cling wrap over the remains of the shepherd's pie.

"Apart from the fact that he's the only black man in the county?" countered Sarah.

"They must have had a better reason than that," insisted Lucy, getting snorts from both Sarah and Flora. "Did he have a history with Cyril?"

"Years ago," admitted Sarah, "when he was a young curate, he was running a boys' and girls' club in Hoxton. He got in a dispute with Cyril over one of the kids, but that was years ago."

"What was it about?" asked Flora, scraping a plate into a container of food scraps intended for the compost heap.

"Wasn't that poor kid who died of an overdose in the maze from Hoxton?" asked Lucy. "Eric something or other?"

"Probably just a coincidence," said Sarah, "but I'm not surprised. Everything in Hoxton was about drugs. Cyril was trying to get one of the regular club boys to sell drugs to the others and Robert, well, I remember he was very upset about it."

"Did he threaten Cyril?" asked Lucy. "Did they fight?"

"I can't remember if it actually came to blows," said Sarah, who was bent over the dishwasher. "In most unchristian terms, he probably just told Cyril where to go."

"So Cyril was a drug dealer," said Lucy.

"Hardly what you'd expect of Harrison's child," said Flora. With a snap, she replaced the lid on the container of compostables.

"I wonder if the kid Eric had some connection to Cyril," mused Lucy.

"Oh, probably," said Sarah. "We like to think that drugs are an urban problem and a lower-class problem confined to council housing, but that's not the reality at all. Opioid addiction is everywhere and it's about time we started treating it like the disease it is, instead of criminalizing it."

Everywhere indeed, thought Lucy, wondering exactly what business had brought Cyril to Moreton Manor. Was it a desire to see his mother or was Eric one of his customers? Or both?

Their chores complete, the three women stood awkwardly in the kitchen. It was time for Lucy and Flora to leave and let Sarah get on with supervising the boys' homework, but they were reluctant to go.

"I'm not terribly worried about Robert," said Sarah in a reassuring tone.

"How so?" asked Lucy.

"Well, once they have established a time of death, it will be easy enough for him to produce an alibi. He is absolutely religious about writing everything down in his calendar, you see, and he's a very busy man." She smiled. "He hasn't had time to commit a murder!"

"That is good news," said Flora.

Lucy wasn't so sure, however. Her experience with criminal investigations had given her some insight into the way police operated, and she knew that a strong alibi was often seen as a red flag. Most people couldn't remember what they did the day before, and innocent people didn't bother to build alibis.

"Thanks for the dinner," said Lucy, remembering her manners. "If you need anything, don't hesitate to call."

"Right," added Flora, pausing at the door.

"Well," said Sarah, "you might mention Robert in your prayers."

Lucy wasn't normally given to praying, but Robert's situation was definitely on her mind as they walked back to the manor, reaching it just as the rain started.

Once in bed, she found it hard to get to sleep. She doubted very much that the police were interested in Robert simply because he was black and she wondered if his dealings with Cyril back in Hoxton had been as straightforward as Sarah had claimed. Lucy had found Robert to be a charming dinner companion, and she admired the warm and easy relationships he had with Sarah and the boys, but she also knew that people could change. Perhaps Robert had some secret that Cyril had threatened to reveal, a secret that could destroy the life he had created since leaving Hoxton. It was possible, she thought, as she finally drifted off.

■ ■ ■ ■

She woke up later than usual, and when she went downstairs to the great room she found Sue was just leaving, eager to see Camilla's feather fascinator that had finally been delivered. Left to her own devices, Lucy found there was just enough coffee left in the pot to fill her cup, which she took outside to the terrace. She was sitting in the sunshine, savoring the coffee and the fine day when two women came through the gate and seated themselves on the teak garden bench.

"It's quite nice here, isn't it, Madge?" commented the one with badly dyed hair cut in a mannish style. She was dressed in jeans and a sparkly top and was holding one of the maps of the manor given to visitors when they paid admission.

"I'm glad to get off my feet," said her companion, who was similarly dressed but had unwisely chosen to wear a pair of high-heeled boots. "I forgot how these boots pinch my bunion. It hurts something awful, it does."

Lucy was quite sure the two women were day-trippers who had no business being in the part of the garden reserved for the family, but she didn't know how to broach the subject. She wasn't even sure it was her responsibility and wondered if she should call someone.

The matter was decided for her when one of the women addressed her. "Pardon me," began Madge, "but could you tell me where you got that cuppa? I'm parched, I am."

Lucy glanced down at the mug in her hand, noting that it was decorated with the Moreton Manor logo. She realized the woman must think she was sitting in an outdoor café and decided she had to clarify the situation. "I'm afraid you've wandered into a —"

"Ooh, you're not from around here, are you?" interrupted Madge.

"I bet she's from America!" exclaimed her companion.

"I am," admitted Lucy. "I'm from Maine."

"That's near Boston, isn't it? I have a cousin who lives there. Perhaps you know Dennis Maitland? I think he lives in Marblehead."

"I'm afraid I don't," said Lucy. "And I have to tell you that you're actually trespassing on a private area. This garden is reserved for the family and their guests."

"You don't say," said Madge, raising her eyebrows. "It doesn't look like much, if you ask me. I'd expect toffs like them to have a nicer garden, wouldn't you?"

Her companion agreed. "I would. There's really nothing here but that sad climbing rose, and the furniture is pretty much past it."

"It's a shame, really, when you think how nice some of that plastic outdoor furniture is," continued Madge.

"And very reasonable, too," added the companion.

"Well, I guess they put most of their effort into the parts that are open to the public," said Lucy, getting to her feet. "The gate over there will take you back to the public area."

"And how did you come to be here, in this special private area?" asked Madge, narrowing her eyes.

"I'm a guest of the family," said Lucy, feeling rather annoyed at the women's persistence. "I haven't had my breakfast yet. So if you'll just move on . . ."

"Do tell," said the companion, who had gotten up from the bench and was standing next to Lucy. "What does the earl eat for breakfast?"

"If I was rich, I'd have a big fry-up every day," said Madge, who had also gotten up from the bench and was examining the developing buds on the climbing rose.

"I hate to disappoint you," said Lucy, "but it's mostly Weetabix and fruit."

"That's how these rich folk stay so thin, I expect," said the companion, wandering over to join Madge by the rose plant that was clambering up the side of the manor. "What are you looking at, Madge?"

"Aphids. Look here."

"Oooh, you're right."

"Better get the gardener on it right away, dear," said the companion, speaking to Lucy.

"I will," said Lucy, "but you really have to leave. Now. Or I will have to call someone."

"There's no need to get all shirty," said Madge, shifting her carry bag from one arm to the other.

"We're just being friendly, is all," said the companion, taking Madge's arm. "I guess we know where we's not wanted, don't we Madge?'

"Indeed we do," said Madge as the two made their way, in a maddeningly slow fashion, to the gate.

Once they'd finally gone through, Lucy considered latching it, but remembered that various family members and manor employees went through it all the time. There had to be a better way, she thought, considering the ease with which Madge and her friend had entered the private garden.

As she thought about it, Lucy realized the manor had virtually no security system at all. There were no keypads requiring insiders to enter a number code, there were no ID cards with magnetic strips or readers to scan them. The manor relied on the guides and other workers to keep a watchful eye on the visitors. If no one was looking, which seemed to be case this morning, anyone could just walk in and make themselves at home.

Lucy supposed that Cyril, as Harrison's son, had a legitimate reason for being in the manor, but what about his killer? Could it have been an intruder? Someone with absolutely no connection to the manor except the fact that Cyril happened to be there? It was possible but unlikely, she decided as she went inside in search of something to eat. Anybody could have killed Cyril, but that left the problem of the secret room. As upsetting as it was, she had to conclude that the murder was an inside job after all.

Chapter Fifteen

After she'd finished her bowl of Weetabix, Lucy went in search of Sue, figuring she was probably in the long gallery with Perry, making last minute adjustments to the hat show. As she expected, she found them oohing and ahhing over Camilla's feather fascinator.

"Such a smart choice for an older woman," Sue was saying as Perry fussed over the delicate assemblage of feathers. "Flowers would have looked silly and much too young."

"She could have gotten away with an orchid or two," said Perry, "but I agree with you. This was much more sophisticated." He set the hat on the stand awaiting it, which had an enlarged wedding photo of Prince Charles and the Duchess of Cornwall. "Camilla is a very sophisticated lady. Did you know her great-grandmother was Mrs. Keppel, who had a famous long-term affair with Edward VII? She was really a sort of official mistress . . . in the French style. His wife Queen Alexandra even invited her to be present at his death bed."

"I'm afraid I'm too much of a New England puritan to approve of such goings-on," said Lucy, joining them.

"Well, things have certainly become tamer for us nobs, now that we have to work for a living," said Perry, stepping back to admire the fascinator.

"Is it really true that the Edwardians were into wife swapping in a big way?" asked Sue. "I've heard there were little name plates on the guest room doors so adulterous couples could pair up at house parties."

"It's true," said Perry. "Those little brass card holders are still on the doors in the main wing. The day-trippers love them."

"I guess Lady Wickham, old as she is, wasn't around to flirt with Edward VII," said Lucy.

"No, but she was around in the swinging sixties, and there was quite a revival of naughtiness then," said Perry, with a knowing nod. "We have photographs of house parties she attended. There was a lot of nudity, lots of drugs and booze. Rock stars, too. Aunt was quite a looker and rumor has it she had a fling with the Mad Boy."

"The Mad Boy?" asked Sue, eyebrows raised.

"Robert Heber-Percy, but everyone called him the Mad Boy. He was famously bisexual." He paused, pursing his lips. "Came from a fine old family."

"Do you suppose they might have discovered the secret room then? During one of those house parties?" asked Lucy.

"Perhaps playing Sardines," suggested Perry with a smile. "You'd have to ask Aunt, but I wouldn't advise it. She doesn't like to be reminded of her youthful indiscretions, now that she's become such a self-righteous old thing."

"I guess it's not so unusual for people to become more conservative as they get older," said Sue. "Our friend Rachel majored in psychology and she'd have a term for it, I'm sure."

"Damned annoying, that's what I call it," said Perry. "Now, what do you think about the bishop's miter? Should we have it front on to show the embroidery or backwards so people can see the little dangly bits?"

Sue took a long look at the display, examining it this way and that, a process that Lucy found somewhat irritating. "Perhaps a mirror?" Sue finally suggested.

"That way we can have our cake and eat

it too!" exclaimed Perry, making a note on his ever-present clipboard.

Lucy decided that she would have to amuse herself since she really didn't share Perry and Sue's passion for millinery. "I'll see you guys at lunch?" she asked by way of a farewell.

"Mmm, yes," murmured Sue, tweaking a silk flower on a hat that had belonged to the Queen Mother.

Lucy was feeling rather sorry for herself as she left the long gallery and made her way along a dimly lighted corridor she hoped led back to the wing reserved for family and guests; she really didn't know what to do with herself. It was no wonder those Edwardians got up to so much mischief, she decided, concluding that there really wasn't much to do in these grand country houses, after all. She would have liked to take a walk in the garden, but a glance out a leaded casement window revealed a steady drizzle had begun to fall. Perhaps she could snag a book from the library and have a little chat with Willoughby, she thought, taking a turn down another long corridor she suspected might lead to the library.

She hadn't gone far when a door opened and out popped Harrison, carrying a rather heavy tray holding the extensive collection of crockery that had contained Lady Wickham's substantial breakfast. As she drew closer, she realized the lady's maid was crying and tears were running down her withered old cheeks.

"Let me take that," said Lucy, reaching for the tray. "Why don't you sit down for a moment," she urged, indicating one of the chairs that lined he corridor. "I'm sure I have a tissue in my pocket."

"No need," said Harrison with a heroic sniff. She was hanging on to the tray for dear life.

"You've had a terrible loss," said Lucy, her voice gentle. "There's no shame in grieving."

"I must get on," insisted Harrison.

"But Cyril was your son. Even if you weren't very close, that's how it is with sons." Lucy continued, thinking of her own Toby. "They make their own lives, of course, but we mothers still love them and they love us. Isn't that right?"

"I wouldn't know, madam," said Harrison, formal as ever. "And now if you don't mind, m'lady is waiting for a fresh pot of tea."

"Of course," said Lucy, stepping aside and letting the maid pass. She watched as the elderly servant made her way down the long hall, bearing the massive mahogany tray. Her back was ramrod straight. Strange, Lucy thought.

Realizing that Harrison was going to the kitchen, she decided to follow her. Unlike herself, Harrison knew her way around the manor.

"I hope you don't mind my following you," Lucy said, eager to explain her behavior. "It's just I'm always getting lost."

"Suit yourself," said Harrison, marching along.

It was quite a hike to the kitchen, and rather awkward, too, since Harrison did not indulge in small talk. Lucy respected her silence, finally concluding that it wasn't all that unreasonable. Harrison was obviously grieving, even if she didn't want to admit it. But Lucy suspected that silence and keeping her thoughts to herself was a form of self-defense for a servant like Harrison. When you were at another's beck and call, without even a home of your own, your only truly private space was your mind. It was no wonder Harrison didn't want to share her personal thoughts in idle chatter.

The kitchen was empty when they arrived, and Harrison got busy loading her ladyship's used breakfast crockery into the dishwasher. Then she set about making a fresh pot of tea, which Lucy hadn't realized was quite such a complicated process involving her ladyship's special loose tea leaves and much rinsing of the china pot with hot water until it was deemed to be the correct temperature. When she'd gone, Lucy fixed herself a mug of tea, using one of the tea bags everybody else used.

Cradling the warm mug in her hands, she settled herself in a huge, rather tattered wing chair arranged with its back to the room, and gazed out the French doors, admiring the sodden lilacs that hung heavily on their stems amid the shiny wet leaves. She was thinking that when she finished her tea she would borrow a pair of Wellies and brave the weather to continue her exploration of the garden, which she expected would be equally beautiful in the refreshing rain.

She was just finishing the last of her tea when Desi and Flora came in and was about to make her presence known when Flora spoke. "Desi, something weird's going on."

Intrigued, Lucy decided to indulge in a bit of eavesdropping.

"Besides a dead body in a secret chamber?" asked Desi.

Flora chuckled. "This isn't quite on that scale, but it's been bothering me."

"Go on," said Desi.

"Well, it's that little statue of Saint Roch and his dog, I just love the way the dog's ear is bent," she began.

"The ceramic one in the library? Is that the one you mean?"

"Yes. That's where it's always been, but it's not there now."

"It's probably been sent for a repair," said Desi. "Check with Winifred. She'd know."

"I did and she said it wasn't sent out or moved."

"Well, then ask Willoughby. The library is his domain, after all. He'd know."

"I don't like to ask. It might make him uncomfortable." She paused. "He might think I'm accusing him of breaking it and hiding it or perhaps even stealing it or —"

"Why would he think that?"

"I don't know. Maybe because I sort of think he might do something like that. I don't quite trust him."

"Why ever not?" asked Desi.

Lucy leaned forward, the better to hear Flora's answer. Unfortunately, that movement dislodged a needlework pillow, which fell to the floor with a thump.

Realizing she'd been discovered, she got to her feet and yawned. "Goodness," she declared, "I must have dozed off."

"It's the weather," said Desi. "Gray days like this make me quite sleepy. Nothing to do but curl up with a good book that I can pretend to read while I doze."

"Good idea," said Lucy, eager to make her escape, "but I think I'll get some fresh air." She excused herself and left hurriedly.

As she had planned, Lucy spent the morning in the garden, tramping along the paths in a pair of borrowed Wellies. As she'd expected, the rainfall had refreshed all the plants and the lawn was a vibrant emerald green. The leaves on the shrubs glistened with damp, and the various hues of the flowers had deepened. She especially admired the little pools of pink and magenta fallen petals beneath some flowering trees. She even climbed the hill to the folly to admire the view.

When she'd finally had enough, she returned to the great room where Poppy was arranging sandwiches on a large platter, which she set on the big scrubbed pine table with a thump. She sat down, a glum expression on her face. Perry and Sue were already sitting at the table, Desi and Flora were adding various condiments, and Gerald was helping himself to a bowl of soup from the pot on the stove.

"It's mulligatawny soup," said Poppy with a huge sigh.

"That will please Aunt no end," said Perry.

"When is the old girl leaving?" asked Gerald, seating himself beside his wife.

"No time soon, I'm afraid," said Poppy. "She announced this morning that her boiler has given up the ghost and has to be replaced. She says she's making arrangements to have it fixed but, according to her, it's practically impossible to find knowledgeable workmen these days."

"Workmen who'll work for ten shillings a week, you mean," said Gerald. "And who know how to fix an old coal burner that was the latest technology in 1910."

"Exactly," agreed Perry, pausing to take a bite of pickle. "Her place at Hazelton is practically falling down, and I suspect she's short of cash to keep it up."

"Nonsense," said Poppy. "The old bird is just cheap."

"Penny wise and pound foolish," said Desi, sitting down with a steaming bowl of soup. "If she fixed the place up, she could rent it and make a fortune."

"Rent Fairleigh? She'd never consider it," exclaimed Poppy.

"Just as well," said Flora. "If she rented it, we'd be stuck with her permanently — and horrible Harrison, too."

"Well," said Poppy with another big sigh, "it looks like they're going to be here for the foreseeable future, so we'll just have to make the best of it."

"You mean the worst of it," said Perry with a mischievous grin.

After lunch, Lucy and Sue agreed that it would be best if they cleared out for the afternoon and gave their hosts, amiable as they'd been, some time to themselves.

"Poor Poppy's been a rock," said Sue as they headed down the drive in the borrowed Ford, "but she's got an awful lot to deal with. There's the murder and the police investigation, Aunt Millicent who looks like she's going to be a permanent guest, which means she's also got to deal with Harrison, and on top of all that, there's the hat show."

"Don't forget the painting of the General and the dry rot," added Lucy.

"And people think it's easy being a lady with a big manor," said Sue. "So where shall we go? Any ideas?"

"I wouldn't mind checking out some antique shops," said Lucy. "I saw one mentioned in a magazine that's supposed to be around here. It's called The Jugged Hare."

"Do you know where it is?" asked Sue.

"I do. It's on Tinker's Lane —"

"Easy to remember," said Sue with a laugh.

"In a town called Riverdale, which is also easy for me to remember because my grandparents lived in that section of the Bronx."

"Well, it seems fated to be," said Sue. "Put it in the GPS."

Riverdale, it turned out, was actually some distance from the manor, but they had the entire afternoon to fill and enjoyed the drive along winding country roads, past green fields dotted with sheep, quaint thatched farmhouses, and through picturesque little towns.

Reaching Hazelton, Lucy had a sudden brain wave. "I think Lady Wickham's place is in Hazelton. What's it called? Fairmore?"

"Fairleigh," said Sue, pulling off to the side of the road and reaching for a map. She opened it and the two put their heads together, tracing their route. "Here it is," declared Sue with a stab of her finger. "And you're right. Fairleigh is just a bit farther along this road."

"Shall we check it out?" suggested Lucy.

"Absolutely," agreed Sue. "I must say, I'm burning with curiosity. From what she says, it's a fine example of Georgian architecture."

When they arrived at the gates to Fairleigh, they found them closed and locked, and any view of the house was blocked by an imposing stone wall. Driving on, however, they found the imposing stone wall soon became the ordinary wire fencing that enclosed most of the farms in the area. That fence was broken a bit farther on by a utilitarian gate that opened onto a dirt road.

"Shall we?" asked Sue with a nod at the gate.

"Not if it's locked," said Lucy. "If it's open, well, that's as good as an invitation, right?"

"Right," agreed Sue, pulling the Ford onto the verge and braking.

As it happened, the gate was unlocked and the two walked along the dirt road that ran between two large, empty pastures.

"No livestock," said Lucy. "Maybe she sells the hay."

Sue kicked at one of the many weeds growing in the dirt roadway. "I don't think this is used much."

"It doesn't seem like an active farm," said Lucy. "At the manor, tractors and trucks are always coming and going."

"How far should we go?" asked Sue as they began climbing a slight rise.

"Let's just check out that little woods,"

said Lucy.

As she guessed, a thin strip of woodland marked the edge of the lawn that surrounded the ancient house, and they could clearly see Lady Wickham's home. It was much smaller than Moreton, but still very large, and did have the classic Georgian proportions that her ladyship was so fond of.

"Rather spooky, isn't it?" said Sue.

The dreary weather didn't help, but it was obvious, even from a distance, that the house had seen better days. A large urn, one of a pair that sat on either side of the front door, had fallen from its base and was lying on its side. Brown, dying vines covered the walls, and clumps of grass sprouted in the drive. The place seemed deserted, and no watchman or groundskeeper approached to question their presence.

"No wonder Aunt Millicent is in no hurry to leave Moreton Manor," said Lucy.

"It looks to me as if her ladyship has come on hard times," said Sue as they made their way back to the car.

The Jugged Hare, it turned out, was practically just around the corner in a charming thatched cottage and the two friends enjoyed browsing amongst the bread tins, plate racks, Windsor chairs, and Toby jugs that were displayed for sale. Sue was contemplating buying a Nottingham lace panel when Lucy spotted a charming porcelain figurine of a ragged man accompanied by a little dog with an adorably bent ear that exactly matched the description Flora had given of the missing statuette.

"That's a very fine piece," the shopkeeper told her, noting her interest. "That's Saint Roch. He was driven away by folks because he was a leper. The little dog brought him bread, keeping him alive until he was miraculously healed."

"That's quite a story," said Lucy. "Do you have any idea how old it is?"

"That I can't say," admitted the shopkeeper. A balding man with a very red face, he was dressed in a faded brown cardigan sweater. "It's not from one of the English potteries, y'see. My guess is that it's French. But," he added, lowering his voice, "it's got excellent provenance. It comes from a fine lady, it does, and that's no lie."

"Really?" Lucy suspected she knew who the fine lady was and leaned a bit closer. "Can you tell me who?"

"Now that I can't. Sworn to secrecy. She's a bit short of the ready and is selling off a few bits and pieces." He paused. "If you're interested, I could do a bit better on the price."

Lucy turned the piece over and saw the price written on the little sticker was one hundred pounds. "That is a bit rich for my blood," she admitted, "but I do like the piece very much."

The shopkeeper took the statuette from her and checked the price, then went off to consult his records. "Eighty pounds?" he inquired when he returned from the back room.

"Sold," said Lucy.

Sue watched with amazement as her notoriously thrifty friend forked over four twenty pound notes.

Encouraged by the reduction in price, Sue attempted to bargain for the lace panel. "It's machine made," she said, offering half of the ticketed price of fifty pounds.

"Of course it is," retorted the shopkeeper, indignantly pulling himself up to his full five feet four inches. "That's what Nottingham lace is, and it's very popular these days. I sell a lot of it."

"Forty pounds?" offered Sue.

"Sold," said the shopkeeper.

When they were back in the car, Sue spoke up. "I didn't think china figurines were your thing, and certainly not at that price. It's pounds, not dollars, you know."

"I know," said Lucy, "but I have a hunch about this little guy."

"What sort of hunch?" asked Sue, unfolding the map.

"I think it might be a missing piece from the manor," said Lucy. "I heard Flora saying that a St. Roch figurine had mysteriously disappeared."

"And putting two and two together . . ." prompted Sue.

"Well, it wouldn't be the first time that an impoverished old lady found a way to supplement her meager income by stealing, would it? Maybe it isn't even her ladyship. Maybe it's Harrison."

"I think you're reaching," said Sue. "Harrison seems to be a pillar of respectability."

"It's true that she seems incorruptible, but I think it may simply be a façade. And you've got to admit, she'd do anything Lady Wickham asked her to do. She's insanely devoted to the old woman."

"I think it's more likely that Cyril is the thief," said Sue. "According to Sarah Goodenough, he was hardly a model citizen. Maybe he was at the manor to steal valuables and was discovered and that's why he got himself killed."

"By a member of the family?" asked Lucy,

incredulous.

"They're the ones most likely to know about the secret chamber, what with all those games of Sardines," said Sue, barely able to keep a straight face.

"Oh, you're teasing me!" exclaimed Lucy.

"Only to make a point," said Sue in a serious voice. "I think you may be getting too involved. Remember, we're guests and we have no business poking into the private affairs of Perry and his family. No family is perfect."

"Most families don't have dead bodies in their closets," said Lucy.

"Everyone has a skeleton or two, though," said Sue. "And they don't appreciate having their dirty laundry aired publicly, pardon my mixed metaphor."

Lucy smiled, imagining a couple dancing skeletons stuffing dirty clothes in a washing machine. "Well," she said, stroking the little figurine she was holding in her lap. "It will be interesting to see if this really is the missing statuette." And even more interesting, she thought to herself, would be seeing how the various members of the family reacted to her discovery.

Chapter Sixteen

The sun was coming out when they returned to the manor. The day's visitors were drifting along the path to the parking lot where their cars and busses awaited them. Aware that she and Sue attracted some curious glances as they drove through the gateway marked PRIVATE, Lucy couldn't help but feel a bit smug. She had never flown first class, she'd never had front-row seats at the theater, and she didn't have a platinum credit card so it was a rare treat to find herself on the VIP side of the rope.

Looking down at the package in her lap that contained the figurine the shopkeeper had wrapped with great care, she wondered what it was like to be one of the privileged few, like Perry and Poppy and the rest of their family. They came and went from grand houses that were filled with priceless treasures. Did they really take it all for granted? Or did they pause now and then in front of the Renoir painting or the Hepplewhite chair and thank the fates for their extraordinary good fortune?

When she and Sue entered the great room, it was clear that Poppy was not enjoying her exalted position. "We're going to have to go begging to English Heritage," she was saying to Gerald, waving a piece of paper. "There's no way we can afford a million and a half pounds. No way at all."

"It's got to be done," said Gerald, taking the paper from her and studying it. "If we don't stop the dry rot, it will wreck the whole place."

"Just thinking about the paperwork makes me weak," said Poppy, sinking into a chair.

"There is another way, you know," said Gerald. "That Vickie girl has some good ideas, and she's had some interest from Cadbury and Watney's."

"I'd rather fall on my knees in front of that stuck-up English Heritage examiner than use the manor to sell chocolate bars and beer," said Poppy with a sigh.

"Come on, Mum," said Flora, drifting into the room. "Maybe Watney's will brew a special ale for us. Moreton Manor IPA — drink as if you're to the manor born."

"Perish the thought," groaned Poppy, shaking her head. Smiling wanly, she addressed Sue and Lucy. "Sorry to burden you with our problems. How was your day?"

"Interesting," said Lucy, unwrapping the figurine. "I found this darling little piece in an antique shop. What do you think about it?"

"I think it looks a lot like one of ours," said Poppy, narrowing her eyes.

"It is!" exclaimed Flora, who had picked up the piece and was examining it closely. "See this little chip on the dog's ear? I'd know it anywhere."

"We must reimburse you," said Poppy. "Did you pay a lot for it?"

"Let it be my gift," said Lucy. "A thank you for your generous hospitality."

"Wherever did you find it?" asked Flora.

"In a shop called The Jugged Hare."

"That place near Aunt Millicent's house? In Hazelton?" asked Flora, exchanging a meaningful look with her mother.

"In Riverdale, I think," said Lucy, unwilling to admit she'd made the connection.

"You know what this means, don't you?" Flora posed the question rhetorically. "It proves what I've thought for some time . . . that things have been disappearing from the house. We need to get to the bottom of this."

The door opened and Harrison entered the kitchen, bearing her usual burden of a tray overloaded with crockery.

Flora continued. "Tomorrow, I'm going to enlist Winifred to check the inventory of the manor's contents, starting with the library."

Lucy watched in horror as Harrison seemed to lose her grip on the tray and various cups and saucers began sliding toward one end. She regained control at the last moment.

"Can I help you with that?" offered Lucy.

"No, thank you, madam," replied Harrison, adding her usual sniff. She set the tray down on the island and turned to Gerald. "Her ladyship asked me to request a dry sherry, if you have one."

"I think we can manage that," he replied, stepping over to the drinks tray and choosing a small stemmed glass.

"She would prefer to have a bottle in her room," said Harrison, busy filling the dishwasher. "She's not feeling up to coming down for meals just yet."

"Of course," said Gerald with an amused smile as he handed over a bottle of Tio Pepe.

Harrison set the bottle on the empty tray and carried it out of the room with an air of great solemnity that was broken as soon as the door closed behind her and everyone erupted into giggles.

"Shame on us all," said Poppy.

"If we didn't laugh, we'd cry," said Gerald, who was opening a bottle of wine. "Rose all right?" he asked, getting nods all round.

After dinner, when Lucy and Sue were climbing the stairs to their rooms, Lucy voiced a revised opinion of Gerald. "You know, at first I couldn't imagine what Poppy sees in Gerald. I even suspected he was carrying on with Vickie."

"If he isn't, I think he'd like to," said Sue. "He does seem sort of a stereotype — a Barbour-wearing, hard-drinking, tweedy snob."

"He is all that," agreed Lucy, "but we got a glimpse of the man beneath the bluster tonight. I suspect he behaves exactly the way Poppy expects him to, the way she thinks all husbands behave, and as a good wife, she turns a blind eye to his failings."

"I think you're right, but I still wouldn't want to find myself alone in a secluded spot with him," said Sue.

"Better safe than sorry, as my mother used to say."

Next morning, DI Hennessy and Sgt. Mathews were back at the manor for a second round of questioning. The police weren't saying much, but word spread quickly that

Robert was no longer a suspect. As Sarah had insisted, he had an unshakeable alibi. He'd been having dinner with the Bishop of Canterbury at the time of Cyril's death, determined to be between six o'clock and midnight on April 27.

DI Hennessy had nothing to say on the subject when he interviewed Lucy, however, and he wasn't very interested in her suspicions about Lady Wickham and Harrison.

"I overheard Flora saying a favorite figurine of hers was missing," said Lucy. "A little ceramic figure of Saint Roch with a little dog. You can imagine how surprised I was when I found a figurine matching her description in an antique shop practically around the corner from Fairleigh, which happens to be the home of Lady Wickham. The shopkeeper said it came from a titled lady who had come on hard times and was selling off some of her things. Except it wasn't Lady Wickham's to sell, after —"

"Actually, Mrs. Stone," the inspector interrupted, "all I really need from you is a statement of your whereabouts on the evening of April twenty-seventh."

"Of course," said Lucy, feeling rather put down. "That was the day we got here. We had dinner with the family and went to bed early. I was pretty wiped out with jet lag."

"You slept alone?" inquired the inspector.

"Of course. My husband is in Maine," responded Lucy. It was only after she'd spoken that she realized her virtue had left her without an alibi. "I certainly didn't spend the evening killing Cyril," she added. "I didn't even know him or anything about the secret room." She watched as the inspector wrote it all down in his notebook. "I gather you've figured out how the secret room works." She hoped he wouldn't be able to resist showing off a successful bit of investigation.

"Trap door. Neatly hidden under the floor and a rug. No sign it was there unless you knew."

"And I suppose whoever knew about it is the killer," said Lucy.

"Not necessarily, but so far nobody is admitting to knowing about it."

Lucy thought of Desi and Flora's youthful explorations of the manor. "Not even —" She stopped, thinking it better to not mention it.

"Yes?" coaxed Hennessy. "You were about to say . . ."

"Nothing, really," said Lucy, "except that with all the research and restoration that's gone on through the years, you'd think it would have been discovered."

"Exactly," said the inspector, leaning forward as if he was going to share a confidence. "I suspect some of the people I've interviewed here at the manor haven't been entirely forthcoming."

"I suppose that's par for the course," said Lucy, smiling.

"Sadly, it is," the inspector said, nodding. "The trick is figuring out who's lying and who's telling the truth."

"Well, I'm going to be helping Flora and Winifred with the inventory of the manor's contents and if anything interesting turns up, I'll let you know."

"That does put my mind at ease," said Hennessy, dismissing her with a wave.

It wasn't until she was outside, in the stable yard, that she realized he was being sarcastic. *Never mind,* she told herself. She hadn't exactly been impressed with his investigation so far, and prospects for a sudden breakthrough seemed slim. Most crimes were never solved and it looked as if that was going to be the case for Cyril's murder, too. Even if the police had someone in mind, it seemed doubtful they could make a case against the murderer. Time wasn't on their side, and neither was the fact that the crime had taken place in a manor owned by one of England's oldest aristocratic families.

The law was supposed to apply equally to all, but Lucy knew that was not always the case, not in England and not home in the US, either.

She caught up with Sue in the library where the little figurine of St. Roch was back in its proper place, and asked about her interview with Sgt. Matthews. "Did you tell her about the figurine and our suspicions of Lady Wickham and Harrison?"

"I did," said Sue, "and she seemed quite interested."

"Really? Hennessy just gave me the brush off when I told him."

"Well, that's the difference between men and women," said Sue with a smile. "Women are more open-minded."

"I think you mean they're more willing to think poorly of one another," said Lucy.

"That, too," agreed Sue as Winifred arrived, accompanied by Flora and Willoughby.

Winifred had come armed with copies of the manor's inventory, which she admitted was incomplete but was a starting point.

"You might find items that are not listed, so please jot them down. And if something is missing, we mustn't conclude that it's gone. It might just be in another room. Things do get moved, especially in the rooms that aren't on the tour." She paused. "I'm quite confident about the public rooms, but with over one hundred smaller rooms, it's very difficult to keep track of things."

"I think you will find that the library is in good order," said Willoughby, pursing his lips.

"Everything present and accounted for."

"Absolutely," agreed Winifred.

Looking around the huge room, however, Lucy wasn't convinced. Dotted here and there hung oil paintings and the walls were lined with shelves filled with hundreds of leather-bound volumes. A series of blue and white vases were arranged on top of the bookshelves, along with an occasional marble bust. The room also contained numerous couches and chairs, tables holding lamps and assorted bits of decorative china, as well as potted plants and vases of flowers. Even the floor was covered with numerous antique rugs laid over the wall-to-wall carpet. This room alone, she decided, must contain thousands of items and it seemed impossible that any one person could keep track of it all.

In fact, she realized, spotting a jib door that she would never have noticed if it hadn't been left ajar, the manor was full of back passages and hidden doors that made it quite easy for a person to move about without being discovered. She'd learned on her tour of the manor, that the grand master bedrooms once occupied by the earl and countess were connected by a discreet passage so the couple could meet privately without the entire household knowing whether they were spending the night together or not.

"Where does that door lead?" she asked Willoughby, pointing to the jib door.

"That's the little library. Gerald likes to sit there with his cigars and agricultural journals."

Winifred suggested they work in pairs, so Lucy and Sue were assigned to the hallway outside the library. Willoughby and Flora were given the job of checking the contents of the rooms along the hallway, which included a billiard room, a boot room, and several guest bedrooms. Winifred herself was doing a quick survey of the library and then planned to go on to Gerald's little hideaway.

The plan was for one member of the team to assess the various items in the assigned space and for the other to check them off on the printed inventory. Sue and Lucy were working their way down the corridor, with Lucy describing and Sue checking, when they heard a dreadful crash in the library. They rushed in and found Winifred on the floor where she'd landed after tumbling from a library ladder.

"Are you all right?" asked Lucy, bending over the fallen woman.

She was on her back, and one leg was twisted beneath her in an impossible position.

"My leg . . ." she began, then fell back with a groan.

"Don't try to move," said Sue, reaching for the phone. "I'm calling for help."

"We're here and you're going to be all right," said Lucy, taking Winifred's hand and holding tight.

Winifred was obviously in quite a bit of pain, her face was white and she was pressing her lips together. "I can't believe I was so careless," she whispered.

"That's how it is with accidents," said Lucy. "One minute everything is fine and the next you're flying through the air."

"The ladder just slid out from under me when I was reaching for the Thomas Aquinas."

Lucy glanced up at the ladder, which rolled on a track attached to the top of the bookshelf just below the row of vases. Sue, she noticed, was also eyeing the same spot with a curious expression on her face and the phone in her hand.

"Help should be here any minute," said Sue.

True to her word, Quimby rushed into the room and quickly took in the situation. "I was a medic in Afghanistan," he announced, taking over from Lucy. "I think I can make you a bit more comfortable until the ambulance gets here." He was already checking Winifred's pulse and examining her eyes. "Is there a blanket or any sort of cover around here?"

Lucy grabbed a paisley lying on the back of a sofa and he used it to cover Winifred.

"You're going to be fine," he said, looking into the stricken woman's eyes and holding her hands. "I know you're in pain, but you need to stay with me."

Winifred managed a little nod, but her eyes were closing.

"Hey, there," said Quimby in a sharp voice. "None of that. Rise and shine."

Her eyelids flew open.

"Tell me your middle name," he said.

"Guinevere," she whispered.

"So your folks liked old time names?"

"An aunt . . ." she said in a barely audible voice.

"So you were named after an aunt. I hope she was rich," said Quimby.

" 'Fraid not," said Winifred, her eyes closing again.

Fortunately, the ambulance crew arrived and quickly bundled her onto a stretcher and carried her off.

"That looked like a nasty break," said Quimby when they had gone. "She was going into shock."

"What happened?" asked Flora, who had noticed the commotion and come to see what was the matter.

"Winifred took a tumble from the ladder," explained Quimby. "She broke her leg."

"Oh, my God!" exclaimed Flora. "I have to tell Mummy!" She ran off just as Willoughby came in, looking rather put out.

"At this rate, we'll never get this inventory finished," he said, grumbling. "My time would be better spent on the guidebook. That's what I'm supposed to be doing."

"We've had an accident," said Quimby. "Winifred fell off —"

"I can't imagine what she was doing up there," said Willoughby, interrupting him. "She really had no business being there."

Lucy was surprised at Maurice's reaction and wondered if he simply wasn't interested in his colleague's mishap or if he was defending his turf. The library, after all, was his responsibility.

Quimby was studying the ladder's operation. "The fault doesn't seem to be with the ladder. It's perfectly sound."

"Of course it is," snapped Willoughby.

"She said it slipped right out from under her," said Lucy, joining him.

"Well, it shouldn't have. See here. It has a kind of braking mechanism. When a person stands on it, puts weight on it, it doesn't slide. As I said," insisted Willoughby, "everything in here is shipshape and present and accounted for . . . except for Flora, who was supposed to be helping me."

"Flora wasn't with you?" asked Lucy.

"Winifred probably reached too far and lost her balance," said Willoughby, ignoring Lucy's question and casting an eye at the ladder. "It's easy enough to do."

"I think I'd better find her ladyship and let her know that it was an accident, nothing more," said Quimby, taking his leave. "Flora can be a bit of an alarmist."

"That girl is little more than a nuisance," said Willoughby. "Since the inventory taking appears to be indefinitely postponed, I think I will go down to the chapel and check some dates on the tablets there. I believe I've found a significant discrepancy."

He also left, leaving Lucy and Sue alone in the vast library.

"Is it me or does Willoughby protest a bit too much?" asked Lucy. "If he was alone, which he admitted before realizing it was a mistake, he could have pushed the ladder out from under Winifred."

"You do have a suspicious mind. Why would he do that?" asked Sue, who was studying the vases with a puzzled expression. "I can't help but wonder . . . those vases look a bit modern to me."

Lucy looked up at the white Chinese vases that were decorated with blue designs. "I have to admit, I've seen similar ones in the Christmas Tree Shop," she said, naming a chain of popular discount gift shops back home.

"Me, too," said Sue, climbing the ladder to get a closer look.

"Do be careful," said Lucy, anxious for her friend.

"Quimby said the ladder is perfectly sound," insisted Sue, who was halfway up.

Lucy was hovering nervously at the base of the ladder, though what she thought she could do to prevent Sue from falling wasn't clear to her.

Reaching the top, Sue reached for the nearest vase with both hands and Lucy held her breath. "As I thought!" exclaimed Sue, a note of triumph in her voice as she made a half turn, still holding the very large vase and pointing to a label on its base. "Made in China."

"What do you think you're doing?" demanded Willoughby, making them both jump.

They hadn't noticed him returning to the room.

"This vase is not an antique," said Sue, looking down at him from her lofty perch.

"Of course it is," said Willoughby, reaching for the inventory and flipping through it. "Right here it says eleven Tang dynasty vases."

"I'm no expert on dynasties, but I'm pretty sure the Tangs, whoever they were, didn't use little sticky labels that say MADE IN CHINA," declared Sue, handing the vase down to Lucy, who passed it to Willoughby.

He adjusted his glasses, looked at the label, and sat down on a sofa with a thump. "I don't know anything about this," he said indignantly.

An odd thing to say, thought Lucy, considering that nobody had asked him.

Chapter Seventeen

Armed with one of the vases, Lucy and Sue hurried off to find Poppy.

She was in her office, a large, sunny room that overlooked the parterre garden on the east side of the manor. It was a charming room with flowery chintz curtains on the windows and many gilt-framed watercolors on the pale green walls. The mantel was filled with family photos and numerous engraved invitations, many beginning with the letters *HRH.* Poppy's large desk, however, was all business with a couple of computer screens, several phones, and piles of papers. A top-of-the-line copy machine stood nearby; the control panel rivaled that of a 747 jet.

"What is it now?" she asked when they entered. Rolling her eyes, she looked heavenward as if for divine intervention.

"We were helping with the inventory —" began Sue.

"Yes?"

"And I thought these vases looked a bit, well, inauthentic . . ."

"And?"

"They were made in China," announced Sue.

"Of course. They are antique Chinese vases, part of a noted family collection," said Poppy.

"Not these. These have little gold stick-on labels," said Lucy.

"Catalog numbers, surely."

"I'm afraid not," said Sue, tipping the vase bottom up so Poppy could see the offending label for herself.

Poppy half rose from her chair to check the label and, recognizing it as one she was quite familiar with and knowing an identical label was actually affixed to many items in the manor gift shop, she sank back into her chair with an enormous groan. "Oh, dear," she said, adding a big sigh. "Are they all like this?"

"I didn't check each one," admitted Sue, "but I suspect they are."

"I'd better call Perry," said Poppy, reaching for a phone. "We have to look into this."

Fifteen minutes later, Lucy and Sue, Perry and Poppy were in the library. Perry was aloft on the ladder, checking the vases one by one and concluding that even the ones missing the tiny little gold labels were indeed fakes. "They're much lighter than the antiques. When you get a good look up close there's no question that they're modern. There's no crackling, none of those little spots that the old ones have. These are too shiny by far, though I think there's been a halfhearted effort to scuff them up and make them look antique."

"How long do you think they've been up there?" asked Poppy, biting her lip.

"There's not much dust," said Perry, rubbing his thumb against his fingers, "so I don't think the switch was made too long ago."

"If Lady Wickham took the little St. Roch figure, perhaps she's been helping herself to other things, too," said Lucy.

"She's probably had Harrison doing the dirty work," said Sue.

"I've actually seen Harrison sneak out of the kitchen with bottles of wine hidden under her sweater," said Lucy.

"I don't know who she thinks she's fooling with that caper," said Perry, smiling. "She's been doing it for years. I actually felt a bit sorry for her when she had to ask Gerald for that sherry. She couldn't snitch it because he was standing in the way, which I suspect he may have been doing quite intentionally."

"You've never challenged her?" asked Lucy, somewhat incredulous.

"Of course not. All that subterfuge is quite unnecessary, but I suppose it gives the old crow a bit of a thrill," said Poppy.

"And what about the items from the manor? The figurine and the vases?"

"Well, we can't be sure it's Aunt," said Perry.

"And even if it is, well, I don't think we want to make an issue of it," said Poppy.

"But those vases must have been enormously valuable," said Lucy. "You said they were part of a famous collection."

"Surely they belong to the nation, to everyone," said Sue.

"They belong to the family," said Perry, correcting her. "And this is a family matter, which the family will deal with."

"Of course," said Sue, chagrined. "It's really none of my business."

"Oh, no. We're grateful," said Perry.

"Absolutely," agreed Poppy. "Much better to discover something like this ourselves, so we can handle it without a lot of fuss."

"And it's about time we realized how desperate poor old Aunt Millicent really is.

I certainly didn't have a clue," said Perry, seating himself in a rose-covered slipper chair.

"We don't know for sure that she's been taking things," said Poppy, sitting down in the matching chair.

"I guess we'll have to have a little talk with her," said Perry, "even though I doubt she'll admit to any wrongdoing."

"I wouldn't come right out and confront her," cautioned Poppy. "We'll explore some options. She could live here."

"Perish the thought," said Perry.

"Or perhaps an allowance of some sort," suggested Poppy.

"Maybe we can get her into a Grace and Favor apartment at Kensington or Hampton Court," said Perry. "I've always felt rather guilty, you know. Poor Wilfred had the title for only a couple weeks when he had that heart attack; he and Aunt Millicent hadn't even moved into the manor."

"Don't forget. Wilfred was shagging that call girl at the time," said Poppy.

"I suspect Dad didn't want the title any more than I do," said Perry. "I'm sure it meant more to Wilfred than to either of us."

"Certainly to Aunt Millicent," said Poppy with a chuckle.

Lucy and Sue shared a glance. It was obvious they'd been forgotten.

"We'll be off," said Sue as they began to leave the room.

"She is quite chummy with the Queen," Perry was saying as they closed the door behind them.

Climbing upstairs to their quarters, Lucy expressed her surprise at Perry and Poppy's reaction. "I certainly didn't expect them to be quite so forgiving."

"I don't know if that's what they are being," said Sue. "I think they simply want to keep yet another scandal in the family."

"I guess I can't expect them to turn her in to the police," said Lucy.

"Not hardly," said Sue. "What is that upper class mantra? Never apologize and never explain?"

"I thought it was 'mad, bad and dangerous to know'," said Lucy, as they reached the guest level. "I never thought I'd be saying this, but I'm looking forward to returning to my simple middle-class life in Maine."

"The thing that really puzzles me" — Sue followed Lucy into her room and seated herself on a chintz-covered nursing chair — "is why Harrison is keeping up this stiff upper lip nonsense. It's her son who was found in the secret chamber, after all. Even if they were estranged, there'd have to be some sort of blood tie, wouldn't there?"

Lucy picked up an emery board and perched on the cushioned stool that sat in front of a charming dressing table, a feature that she was determined to recreate in her bedroom when she returned home. "Maybe there is no blood tie," she said as she filed her nails. "Maybe Cyril was actually Lady Wickham's love child, kept secret all these years. She's the one who's been in seclusion since his death was discovered."

Sue stared at her friend. "I think you're out of your mind. Secret love child? That phrase does not come to mind when I think of Lady Wickham."

"She must have been young once. Perry said she was quite the girl back in the swinging sixties," said Lucy, holding out her hand and examining her nails. "And maybe Cyril was killed because he would have had a claim on the earldom. Did you think of that?"

"No, Lucy, that never occurred to me. Cyril was a thug — a drug dealer from a tough part of London."

"Stranger things have happened," insisted Lucy, starting to file the nails on her other hand. "There are all sorts of rules about these titles and estates. Most are entailed but some aren't. Perry doesn't have any children and it doesn't look like he will. When the earl on *Downton Abbey* only had daughters, the title went to Cousin Matthew. Maybe Cyril was a cousin and that's why Perry and Poppy don't want to pursue the matter with Lady Wickham."

"Or maybe they simply don't want to embarrass a sad old woman," said Sue.

"Do you think they knew she was stealing all along?" asked Lucy.

"I wouldn't be surprised if somebody knew," said Sue. "That ladder was pretty steady when I was on it. I think it's entirely possible that someone pushed it out from under Winifred, fearing that she was about to discover the switch. What with all these jib doors and secret chambers, an assailant could have popped out from anywhere."

"And disappeared just as quickly," said Lucy with a shudder. "This place is starting to seem more like Wolf Hall than Downton Abbey. You don't know who you can trust."

Sue wrapped her arms across her chest and rubbed her upper arms. "I know. It's a horrible feeling, isn't it? I feel like I have to keep looking over my shoulders."

"We can't go on like this," declared Lucy. "We have to get to the bottom of this mess, and Cyril is the key. Somebody killed him for a reason."

"We have to be very careful, Lucy," warned Sue. "We're dealing with a dangerous person."

"You're right," agreed Lucy, "but there is one person who was vetted by the police and cleared . . . and that person also knew Cyril."

"Robert Goodenough, the vicar," said Sue.

"Right," said Lucy, standing up and marching over to the wardrobe where she pulled out a jacket. "Let's pay him a visit."

"Not so fast," said Sue. "He's a busy man. We can't just march in and start asking questions. We need to make an appointment."

"Right," said Lucy, watching and waiting while Sue called the vicarage.

As it happened, Robert was away at a diocesan conference but the church secretary said he'd be available the following morning and the meeting was set.

"What do we do until then?" asked Lucy. "They can't continue taking inventory without Winifred."

"Well, I'm going to stretch out on that lovely chaise longue in my room with the latest British *Vogue,*" said Sue.

"I've got my jacket out, so I think I'll go for a walk," said Lucy. "I do my best thinking when I'm walking."

"Be sure to take a stick," said Sue. "Just in case."

"Good idea," said Lucy, remembering a well-stocked umbrella stand in the kitchen.

When she got there she found Harrison sitting at the scrubbed pine table enjoying a cuppa and a smoke. Seeing her, Harrison quickly stubbed out the cigarette in her saucer.

"No need for that," said Lucy. "It's none of my affair if you smoke."

"Lady Philippa doesn't like me to smoke indoors," said Harrison in a resentful tone. "Things used to be different, you know, when servants had their own place downstairs. There was up and there was down, and those that lived upstairs weren't welcome downstairs. That was for them that was in service, you see. It's all changed now."

"Back then you could smoke if you wanted to?" asked Lucy.

"Different houses had different rules, o' course, but the butler that used to be here, Chivers was his name. He enjoyed a cigarette himself and didn't mind if others did, too, so long as it didn't interfere with their work."

"I suppose that was some time ago," said

Lucy. "I thought that people stopped going into service after World War I."

"Some places stuck to the old ways longer," said Harrison, lighting up a fresh cigarette. She inhaled deeply, then continued. "The old earl, Poppy and Perry's grandfather, he lived to be quite old. He didn't like change so he kept the house staffed just as it was when he was a little boy. When he died there were a lot of old folks still working here, including Chivers. The old earl's first son, that was m'lady's husband and Perry's uncle, he would've kept the old folks on. Some said it was like going back in time, coming here. They had maids laying the fires every morning and bringing tea in bed to the married ladies. There were footmen at dinner. People knew their places, that was for sure. But," she added with a sniff, "everything changed when his lordship that was died and this crew came in."

"You miss those days?" asked Lucy.

"I like being in service. I always have. I suits her ladyship and she suits me."

"It must have been hard when you had a child," suggested Lucy.

"Not so bad. Her ladyship sent me off to my sister's when she realized I was up the spout. That's what we used to call it, y'see."

"A funny term," said Lucy.

"But she kept the job for me and I came back after little Cyril was born. My sister kept him, and maybe that was a bit of a mistake. I think she was much too soft on him. If I'd raised him, I dare say he might've turned out a bit better. I sent money, o' course, but I didn't know that her husband — Alf that was — well, he had some friends that were what you call bad company. Alf himself wasn't above helping himself to anything that fell off a truck. That's what he called it. You'd see they had a nice new set of furniture or my sister'd have a mink stole. Alf would say it fell off a truck, and he'd wink."

"Some things have gone missing here," began Lucy, aware that she was treading on thin ice. "Do you think Cyril could have had anything to do with that?"

Harrison took a final draw on her cigarette and stubbed it out, then rose and carried her cup and saucer to the sink. She dumped the butts in the trash and put the crockery in the dishwasher, then turned to Lucy. "Like I told the cops, I don't know what Cyril was up to. We wasn't close and that's the truth. I don't suppose I could've expected anything else, not with Doris raising him." She straightened her shoulders.

"Don't get me wrong. I don't have any regrets, not really. I suits her ladyship and she suits me. I wouldn't want it any other way."

Lucy couldn't put her conversation with Harrison out of her mind while she wandered through the garden. In this day and age, it seemed impossible that a person could have such antiquated views and be satisfied with such a limited life. She wondered if there was more to the relationship between Lady Wickham and Harrison than that of an employer and employee. Could the two be lovers? Was it some sort of dominant-submissive relationship? Perhaps even sadomasochistic? Lucy was thinking of calling her friend Rachel, the psychology major, when her ring tone went off and she pulled her cell phone out of her pocket.

It was Bill.

She took a moment to consider how amazing it was that this tiny bit of plastic and electronic circuitry could connect her to him across the vast Atlantic Ocean. "Hi!" she exclaimed, seating herself on a stone bench. "I'm glad you called. I've been missing you."

"So you haven't fallen for some duke or other?" he teased.

"No dukes, but there are some pretty hunky gardeners around here," she said, noticing Dishy Geoff bending over a flower bed. "Unfortunately, from what I've gathered, they're all married."

"Well so are you and don't forget it."

"No chance," said Lucy, missing her husband's embrace and the way his beard tickled the back of her neck. "How's everybody? Have you heard from Toby lately?"

"I Skyped with Patrick last night. He showed me a picture he drew in school. It was a picture of you."

"I wish I'd seen it," said Lucy, practically knocked off the bench by a wave of longing for her grandson.

"Toby said he tried to call you but the satellite was down and he hadn't got the time difference right, anyway. Something like that."

"Likely story," said Lucy, somewhat doubtful of her son's supposed efforts to contact her. "How are the girls?"

"Usual stuff. Elizabeth's sick of her job at the hotel and hates all men. Sarah's been working hard preparing to defend her senior thesis paper, and Zoe's decided to follow in her sister's footsteps at Winchester."

"She's given up on Strethmore?" asked Lucy, surprised by this turn of events. "It was her top choice. She must be disappointed."

"To tell the truth, I think she doesn't understand why a college with a billion dollar endowment doesn't care enough about having her attend that they won't cough up more financial aid. She's a smart girl. She knows we just don't have the money and she doesn't want to be burdened with enormous student loans."

"She must be disappointed. What about that investment scheme of yours?" asked Lucy, fearing that Bill had gone ahead and invested the money.

"Funny thing about that," said Bill. "I took your advice and checked with Toby about this guy, and it turned out Toby never heard of him. He wasn't a friend at all. He was just posing to win my confidence and probably steal our money. Doug Fitzpatrick was not who he claimed to be."

"Wow," said Lucy. "That was a good catch. Did you press charges?"

"I did check with the police chief, but he said there was no crime because I didn't lose any money. If I'd invested and the guy had absconded, then we'd have a case." He paused. "In any case, Fitzpatrick's gone. I tried calling his so-called office and the number was no longer in service."

"That was a close one," said Lucy. "I'm glad you decided to check him out with Toby."

"I came close to being a sucker. I admit it," said Bill in a rueful tone. "I was having coffee at Jake's with some of the guys one morning and Sid mentioned getting an e-mail claiming his nephew had been arrested in Mexico and couldn't get out of jail until he sent him five hundred dollars to pay a fine. When he checked with his sister, it turned out the kid was working as a lifeguard at their health club. It got me thinking, you know?"

"Good thinking," said Lucy.

"You can't believe everything people tell you," said Bill.

"Funny thing," said Lucy, remembering DI Hennessy's claim that he suspected people didn't always tell him the truth. "I heard somebody else say that very same thing."

"Well, I'm glad you'll be home soon," said Bill. "I miss you."

"And I miss you."

Chapter Eighteen

Robert and Sarah were sitting in the vicarage garden, drinking tea from large mugs, when Lucy and Sue arrived the next morning. It was unseasonably hot and the sun was very bright, but they had set up chairs in a shady spot.

"Elevenses," said Robert with a huge grin. "I can't seem to break the habit of drinking tea even when it's so warm, like today."

"Will you join us?" asked Sarah. "The water's still hot."

"Thanks," said Lucy, who would much rather have had a tall glass of iced tea.

"I have lemonade," said Sarah, sensing her hesitation.

"That would be lovely," cooed Sue.

"Make that two," said Lucy, fanning herself with her hands.

"Make yourselves comfortable," said Sarah, "I'll be back in a minute."

Lucy and Sue seated themselves carefully

in the rickety deck chairs, which were nothing more than strips of rather old, faded striped canvas slung on folding wooden frames. Lucy wasn't convinced the fabric was still strong enough to support her, and found it quite impossible to sit up straight as the chair's design required one to adopt a semi-prone position. Sue, she noticed, was having the same problem. When Sarah arrived with the tall glasses of lemonade, she discovered that she had to stretch her neck like a turtle in order to drink.

"I hope we're not keeping you from your work," said Sue.

"No problem," said Robert. "I was working on my sermon, but I wasn't getting very far."

"It must be quite a challenge coming up with something new every week," said Lucy.

"Coming up with ideas isn't the problem," said Robert. "It's trying to present them in ways that will be acceptable to the congregation."

"Folks around here are very old-fashioned," said Sarah.

"I suppose it's quite a change from your church in London," said Lucy, attempting to steer the conversation in that direction.

"The thing I don't understand," said Robert, "is why so many people around here insist on voting for the Conservative candidate when it's not in their best interest. Of course, the folks up at the manor want to keep taxes low and the Conservative line definitely benefits them. But when old Simpkins, who's worked at the ironmongers since he was ten years old and never made more than fifty pounds a week says he's going to vote Conservative, I just have to scratch my head."

"I was actually surprised to learn that Perry and Poppy are Conservatives," said Sue, pausing to attempt the neck-stretching exercise necessary for taking a sip of lemonade. "They seem so modern and progressive."

"Progressive when it benefits them, like getting government grants to fix the roof on the manor, but quite resentful when the tax bill comes," said Sarah.

"I have noticed that when the manor is in need of some repair or other, it's a valuable part of the nation's heritage that belongs to all the people," said Lucy, "but when something goes missing or a visitor wanders through the wrong door, it's suddenly their family heritage that's being threatened."

"Have there been incidents at the manor?" asked Sarah. "Has something been stolen?"

Lucy suddenly feared she might have said

too much and shook her head. "No. It was just something Poppy said . . . or maybe it was Flora. I'm not sure."

"And Lucy knows better than to gossip about her hosts," said Sue with a meaningful glance.

"I do. I'm ashamed of myself," said Lucy.

"If you are truly penitent and contrite, your sins will surely be forgiven," said Robert with a twinkle in his eye.

"I have to admit that we are terribly curious about Cyril and his mother, who doesn't seem at all distressed by her son's grisly end," said Sue. "I understand you knew them in Hoxton?"

"I never met Cyril's mother," confessed Robert, "but Hoxton was a very tough place and Cyril fit right in. It was rumored that his grandfather had links to the notorious Kray brothers. And his uncle — I understand his aunt and uncle brought him up, and, well, there's really no way to say it nicely — his uncle was a small-time crook. I'm afraid that by the time I met him, Cyril was rather fixed in his ways. He ran a couple prostitutes and sold drugs. He even tried to get one of the boys in the church youth group to sell for him."

"Robert told him to get lost and the next day Robert was attacked by a couple thugs.

That's the way things were in Hoxton," said Sarah.

"Harrison told me she blamed her sister and her brother-in-law for turning Cyril to a life of crime," said Lucy.

"She definitely has a point," said Robert, "but I find people do what they need to do to survive and in Hoxton, crime was one of the few viable options available to people."

"Harrison herself isn't exactly honest," said Lucy. "We've seen her steal bottles of wine."

Sue gave her another meaningful glance and hurried to explain. "It's really kind of a joke. Everybody knows about it. She's not fooling anyone."

"Maybe larceny is in the blood," said Sarah, "and maybe she chose a life in service as a way to stay on the straight and narrow, a way to escape her criminal family."

"She is certainly very devoted to Lady Wickham," said Lucy. "We even wondered if maybe Cyril was actually her ladyship's child."

"Born on a long vacation in Switzerland and passed off to a childless couple?" suggested Sarah with a smile. "Like in a novel? And since the earl is childless, the poor outcast finds himself the lord of the manor?"

"I know it sounds silly, but I imagine these things do happen," said Lucy. "Especially when you consider how much morals have changed in recent years. When Lady Wickham was a girl an unwed mother was a social outcast."

"Don't forget. It can work the other way around, you know," said Robert after draining his mug. "We don't know who Cyril's father was. There's a long tradition in this country of the young titled gentlemen interfering with the pretty little maids."

"Robert!" chided his wife with a smile. "Such thoughts! You ought to know better!"

"You mean I ought to know my place," he said, rising from his chair. "And I'm afraid that right now, the place I ought to be is at my desk working on my sermon." He paused. "I've got to say, you ladies have given me much to think about, and I thank you."

"It's we who should thank you," said Sue, struggling to rise from the sling chair and finally getting a hand from Robert.

"It's been lovely," said Lucy, also needing a hand to extract herself from the chair.

"I keep telling Robert we need new chairs, but he says these remind him of his childhood," said Sarah.

"My da used to bring them when we went

to Brighton. It was a summer ritual."

"It's nice to have happy childhood memories," said Lucy.

"Indeed," said Robert. "I don't think Cyril had a happy childhood."

"Not that an unhappy childhood excuses the bad choices he made," said Sarah.

"It doesn't excuse them, but perhaps it helps us understand," said Robert. "And to understand all is to forgive all."

"He's hopeless," said Sarah, watching as her husband walked across the lawn and back to the church. "Absolutely hopeless."

Lucy and Sue thanked Sarah for the tea and headed back to the manor, grateful for the trees that shaded the path.

"You know," began Lucy, "maybe we've got things wrong. We keep expecting Harrison to break down in grief over her son's death, but maybe she really is a cold-blooded monster. Maybe this faithful servant act is just that, an act."

"Lucy, you really do have a mind like a sewer," said Sue, clucking her tongue.

"I'm taking that as a compliment," said Lucy. "It's what makes me a good reporter, not accepting the first thing I hear as gospel truth."

"So you think Harrison is really some sort of Mrs. Danvers character who makes life a misery for her mistress?" She chuckled. "Somehow I don't see Lady Wickham as a gullible Rebecca."

"Appearances can be deceiving," said Lucy, carefully negotiating a stile. "Don't you think it's odd that Lady Wickham has been confined to her room for days? Maybe she's a prisoner, and Harrison brings up these huge trays of food and eats them herself right in front of her. The poor old thing might be fading away, denied sustenance by her cruel servant."

"Well," said Sue, after negotiating the stile herself, "since you're writing a far-fetched romance, maybe someone in the family is trying to do away with Lady Wickham and has enlisted Harrison to help, promising her a nice pension and a seaside cottage."

"It's a lovely thought," said Lucy, plucking a long piece of grass and pulling off the seed heads one by one, "but Poppy and Perry seemed truly upset about the old woman's situation. Why would they want to get rid of her?"

"Maybe it's not either of them. Maybe it's Desi or Flora or Gerald."

"But you still haven't come up with a motive. What would any of them possibly gain by knocking off the old bird?"

"She must know something!" exclaimed

Sue, seizing on the idea. "A terrible secret that will ruin everything. Like the old earl got Harrison pregnant and Cyril was his love child, who will inherit the title and the whole caboodle."

They stepped out of the shade and onto the huge lawn that surrounded the manor. It stood on a slight rise, dominating the landscape with its three pointy towers piercing the sky. As they looked, a dark cloud passed in front of the sun, casting the ancient castle in shadow, and it suddenly seemed quite a forbidding, even menacing, place.

"You know, there's supposed to be an oubliette in the basement somewhere," said Sue. "Perry told me. It's a hole in the ground where you lock up somebody you want to forget and leave them to die."

"I know what an oubliette is," said Lucy, shuddering at the idea. "I suppose there's been a lot of strife and bloodshed through the years, considering the family's long history. I took a course in English history in college and I can tell you, it wasn't pretty."

"I watched *The Tudors,*" said Sue as they began the long march across the lawn.

They trudged along under the hot sun, discovering that while the lawn looked to be a smooth expanse, it actually undulated and contained a few surprises, including a hidden copse of trees.

"Let's go that way," suggested Lucy. "It will get us out of the sun for a little bit, anyway."

"I could use a bit of a rest," admitted Sue. "These are new sandals and they're not quite broken in."

Lucy glanced down at the bejeweled flip-flops Sue was wearing and contrasted them with her sensible athletic shoes. "There's nothing to them. How can they hurt?"

"It's the part that goes between my toes," said Sue.

"Well, perhaps there's a bench in among those trees and we can sit a bit," said Lucy.

When they reached the wooded area, they discovered it held an ancient walled garden. They pushed open the gate. The garden was largely given over to weeds but did contain a lichen-stained stone bench.

"It's just like *The Secret Garden,*" said Lucy, sitting down beside Sue. "I loved that book when I was a girl."

"Maybe Flora will restore it," said Sue, who had removed one of the sandals and was rubbing the space between her big toe and its neighbor. "It would give her something to think about besides not eating."

"We can suggest it when we get back,"

said Lucy, watching as Sue began working on the other foot. "Do you have blisters?"

"Not yet, but I'm working on them," said Sue, waving away a mosquito.

"We'll be eaten alive if we stay here," said Lucy, slapping at one of the bloodsuckers that had landed on her arm. "Can you walk?"

"I'll go barefoot," said Sue, slipping her fingers through the straps of her sandals and standing up. "I don't think they have snakes here, do they?"

"Just watch where you step," advised Lucy, pulling open the gate and discovering Gerald on the other side.

"Oh!" she exclaimed. "You startled me!"

"What in damnation are you doing here?" he demanded, blocking the opening in the wall.

Looking over his shoulder, Lucy saw Vickie walking across the lawn toward the house.

"We were just resting a moment," said Sue, holding up her sandals. "My feet were killing me."

"Serves you right," declared Gerald, "wearing foolish things like that."

"We were just leaving," said Lucy, hoping that Gerald would take the hint and move aside so they could leave the walled garden.

"Leaving, that's what women are good at," said Gerald. "She's leaving, too." He cocked his head in Vickie's direction. "All your sort care about is money. No contracts, no Vickie. That's what she told me." He fumed and shook his walking stick right in front of Sue's face. "Can you believe it? After . . . well, everything I did for her. Damned ungrateful. No notion of fair play whatsoever." He humphed. "And they call yours *the fair sex.* Nothing fair about any of you!"

"It must be getting on to cocktail time," said Sue, glancing at her watch.

"Rather early, isn't it?" said Lucy, who knew it was only lunchtime.

Gerald was having none of that. "Must be five o'clock somewhere," he said, turning abruptly and marching off.

Lucy collapsed against the gateway. "Good thinking," she said, congratulating Sue. "I thought he was going to start whacking us with that stick of his."

"What do you suppose Vickie did?" mused Sue in a low voice as they followed him across the lawn.

"I think it's pretty obvious," replied Lucy. "I think he thought she was interested in him, but she was really only interested in closing some sort of sponsorship deal."

"Poppy was dead set against that, wasn't she?"

"So Poppy nixed his chances with Vickie," concluded Lucy. "I see rough waters ahead. How many more days till we go home?"

"Three, sweetie. Only three."

Lucy sighed. "Well, I've got to say, life here among the blue bloods isn't at all what I expected."

Chapter Nineteen

As Lucy and Sue drew closer to the manor, they heard the wail of a siren and quickened their pace, fearing some sort of accident or perhaps a fire. When they reached the drive, they saw an ambulance arrive with its siren blaring and lights flashing.

"Probably one of the visitors fell ill," said Sue. When the ambulance continued past the visitor's entrance where a handful of people turned to watch as it turned into the gate to the private stable yard, she changed her mind. "Do you think it's Lady Wickham? Maybe she isn't faking like we thought and is really sick. She could have had a heart attack or stroke."

"I have no idea," said Lucy, quickening her pace. "Accidents can happen to anyone. I hope it's not serious."

When they entered the private yard, however, they saw the EMTs were already carrying someone out on a stretcher and loading the blanket-covered person into the ambulance. Poppy was a step or two behind, clutching a sweater and her purse as she hurried to accompany the victim in the ambulance. In a matter of moments, the doors were slammed shut and the ambulance took off, slowly at first but picking up speed as soon as it cleared the gate in the stable yard wall.

Perry was standing in the doorway, watching anxiously as the ambulance departed. They hurried up to him.

"What happened?" asked Sue.

"Flora overdosed," he said, his face white.

Lucy was shocked, but not surprised. Realizing that Flora's addiction to drugs explained a lot about the girl's condition — and perhaps about Cyril's presence at the manor.

"How awful," said Sue.

"Will she be all right?" asked Lucy.

"I think it's really bad," said Perry. "Desi found her. He's pretty shaken up."

They followed Perry into the great room where Desi was slumped over the sink, filling a glass with water.

"Thank heaven you found her," Perry told him, wrapping his arm around his nephew's shoulders.

Desi carefully set the glass down on the

counter and embraced Perry; the two men clung together for a long moment.

Desi pulled away, shaking his head. "Thank God she's into vinyl. She got this old turntable. Unearthed it from the attic, I think. She insisted the sound was better, richer. She was really into it. When the record stuck and Nina Simone was singing the same phrase over and over, I went in her room to see what was going on and there she was, lying on the floor." He paused. "I've been around drugs enough to recognize an overdose. I only hope I was in time. I shouldn't have waited so long before checking on her."

"You can't blame yourself," said Lucy. "You did the right thing."

"I was so mad at her. I kept thinking she should get off her butt and fix the damn thing. It was driving me crazy," he said, staring at the glass of water.

"How long do you think she was out?" asked Perry.

"The LP was about halfway through when it stuck," answered Desi, finally picking up the glass and taking a long drink.

"So maybe fifteen minutes at the most?" said Sue, estimating the time.

"She might have started the record and then shot up afterwards," said Lucy. "It may have been only a few minutes."

"However long it was, it was too long," said Desi

Full of bluster, his father came into the room.

"What's this? Quimby tells me Flora's overdosed? They took her in an ambulance and Poppy went, too."

"And I'm going, too," said Desi, setting down the glass. "I can't stand waiting here."

"I'll drive," said Perry. "You're in no shape —"

"He's in no shape? What's that supposed to mean?" demanded Gerald, waving his walking stick in his son's face.

"Back off, Gerald," said Perry. "Desi found her. It's thanks to him that she's in the hospital."

"It's thanks to him that she's in this mess in the first place, you mean," thundered Gerald, practically nose to nose with Desi. "Where do you think she got the drugs? From this artsy-fartsy ballerina, that's who!" he yelled, stabbing his finger into Desi's chest. "Actors and dancers and rock and rollers, they're all dope fiends and you can't tell me any different. Anybody who reads the papers knows they're always overdosing."

Desi was shaking his head. "I knew . . .

no, I suspected she was using, but I didn't know for sure. And you're right. I have seen a lot of people, some of them friends, get in trouble with drugs, but I was not getting drugs for Flora. I've seen how much damage that stuff can do and I stay clear of it."

Gerald didn't seem convinced, but he was less agitated, merely clutching the walking stick and occasionally lifting it and then thumping it on the floor. "Damned foolish girl," he declared. "You'd think she'd know better."

"Mother shouldn't be alone at the hospital," said Desi. "Are you coming?"

Gerald considered the matter for a moment. "No. You and Perry go. I'll hold the fort here."

"There's bound to be press," said Perry as he and Desi crossed the room toward the doorway. "You'd better have some sort of statement ready."

"Damned nosey bastards!" thundered Gerald. "I'm not saying anything to anybody. It's none of their business."

"Righto," said Perry, giving them a curt little wave of farewell.

As soon as they left, Lucy turned to Gerald. "Is there something we can get you? Something we can do?"

"Sorry about all this," he replied, seemingly at a loss now that there was no one to yell at. "Nothing to do but to carry on, I suppose. I know what I'd like — a stiff whiskey. How about you girls?"

"I could use a glass of wine," said Sue, sliding on to a chair.

"I could, too," admitted Lucy as Gerald took a bottle of chardonnay out of the refrigerator.

They were an awkward little group, sitting together at the big scrubbed pine table with their drinks. After a few minutes of silence, Lucy got up and opened the refrigerator, thinking she could make some sort of meal. She found some frozen pizzas in the freezer and asked if anyone would like some.

"I hate to admit it," said Sue, "but I am starving."

The phone rang and Gerald answered it, listened a moment, and then slammed it back on its hook. "Damned impertinent," he fumed, draining his drink. Then he picked up his walking stick and put on his hat. "I'll eat at the pub," he said, marching out.

The phone continued to ring frequently while Lucy and Sue ate their pizzas. They always answered it, hoping for news of Flora, but the callers were all reporters. Their answer was always the same — "no comment" — which got them some rather rude replies.

Lucy was shocked to discover that journalists in England seemed to behave quite differently from their American colleagues.

"I wish we could turn the phone off," she said after a particularly nasty exchange.

"I'll answer and give them what-for," said Harrison, who had come into the kitchen to prepare Lady Wickham's dinner. "You folks don't need to be bothered with the likes of them."

"Are you sure?" asked Lucy, surprised at this turn of events.

"Never fear, I'm used to these nosy-parkers. They're always calling m'lady, you see," said Harrison, frying up a rather large steak.

"How is Lady Wickham?" asked Lucy. "I understand she hasn't been well lately."

Harrison's eyebrows shot up and she gave Lucy a sharp look. "That's none of your affair," she snapped as the phone rang once again. "And that's exactly what I'm going to tell these Fleet Street muckrakers!"

Lucy decided it would be best not to reveal the fact that she herself was a journalist, even though her muckraking was limited to a small coastal town in Maine, and suggested to Sue that they leave the great room and let Harrison get on with her duties. Although still light outside, they had the garden to themselves since the visitors were gone for the day, so they took a stroll around the formal parterre garden, then paused by the fountain to enjoy the quiet.

It didn't take long, however, for the mosquitoes to discover them and they decided to go inside.

"You know," said Sue as they approached the big house, "I think this is the lull before the storm. I bet all hell will break loose tomorrow."

Her words hardly seemed prophetic when Perry greeted them with a big smile the next morning. "Good news!" he announced as they arrived in the great room for breakfast. "Flora's going to be fine."

"That's wonderful," said Lucy, accepting the mug of coffee he'd poured for her.

"What a relief," said Sue, taking her mug over to the table and sitting down.

"She's going to have to stay in hospital for a day or two" — he paused before delivering the bad news — "which is just as well because the police are coming back to question everyone again."

"I suppose they want to know how she got the heroin," said Sue. "Why don't they just ask her?

"Doctors have forbidden it," said Perry with a knowing look that Lucy took to mean they had been heavily influenced by Flora's parents.

"Maybe there's a connection to Cyril," said Lucy in a speculative tone. "Maybe he was the dealer. Maybe Cyril was involved with the poor kid who overdosed in the maze . . ."

"I wouldn't be at all surprised if he was," said Perry, who was busy slicing bread and putting the pieces in the toaster. "We're all supposed to gather in the library at ten this morning, just like in an Agatha Christie mystery."

"And all will be revealed," said Lucy.

"I rather doubt it," said Perry, leaning against the counter and cradling a mug in his hands while waiting for the toast to brown. "Sergeant Izzy there isn't as sharp as Miss Marple and the inspector is certainly no Hercule Poirot."

Lucy did feel a bit like a character in a mystery novel when she and Sue went to the library at the appointed time and found everyone, including Lady Wickham, gathered there.

She was dressed in one of her usual

flower-printed chiffon dresses, her dyed hair had been touched up, and if she truly had been sick, it seemed she had certainly made a quick recovery. She was scolding Inspector Hennessy, telling him in no uncertain terms that he had no business telling her what to do.

"I am the daughter of a marquess and the wife of an earl and I do not intend to allow someone like you to poke and pry into my private life."

"Lady Wickham hasn't been well," said Harrison, aware that the inspector was not sympathetic to this line of argument. "It would be best if she could rest in her room until she is needed for questioning."

"My health is not the issue," declared Lady Wickham, contrary as ever. "What I mean is that I am quite obviously above suspicion and I do not wish to waste time in pointless conversation when I have better things to do."

"You are not above the law, even if you are a countess," began Hennessy, glaring at the old woman.

"We will be happy to accommodate your ladyship," said Sgt. Matthews, interrupting her boss. "We will speak with you only if we feel it necessary after we've completed all the interviews." She paused. "Will that be agreeable?"

"I suppose it will have to do," said Lady Wickham, attempting to look down her nose at the sergeant and failing, due to the young woman's superior height.

"Now, please take a seat with the others as the inspector wishes to speak to all of you together."

"I don't imagine we'll need to keep you long," said Hennessy, placing himself in front of the fireplace and facing the assembled group, who were seated on three sofas. Gerald and Poppy, as well as Lady Wickham, were all on the center sofa, opposite the fireplace. Harrison stood protectively behind her ladyship. Willoughby, Quimby, and Vickie were on the inspector's right, and Sue, Lucy, and Perry were on the left. Winifred, wearing an ankle cast, was standing to one side, along with Sgt. Matthews. Lucy thought it might be her imagination, but she sensed an air of nervous expectation.

"I'm taking the rather unusual step of speaking with you as a group," began Hennessy, "because I believe recent events have made clear the need for you to come together as a community and to cooperate with this investigation. A young woman has nearly died and some of you had knowledge that, had you shared with us, might have prevented this terrible situation."

He studied the group, making eye contact with each member, and didn't find much encouragement, so he continued. "This young woman, a lovely young woman, seemed to have everything going for her. A loving family. A privileged life. No money worries. Acceptance at a top university. An aristocratic pedigree. But for some reason she became involved with drugs to the point of becoming addicted."

This got a reaction as Poppy gave a little gasp.

Hennessy was quick to press the point. "You can play the denial game and pretend that this was simply a one-time thing and she made a near fatal mistake, but the facts do not support that theory. Whatever the reason, this lovely young woman became entangled in the world of drugs and some of you knew what was happening and did nothing."

"I knew," said Vickie, blurting out the words. "She was getting the heroin from Cyril, the dead guy. Sometimes the kid Eric made the delivery. He worked for Cyril."

Hearing this, Lucy turned to see Harrison's reaction, but the lady's maid remained stone-faced and apparently unmoved as

Vickie continued speaking.

"She even had me pawn some jewelry for her so she could pay him when she got in debt. She couldn't do without it, and when he died . . . well, she must've got some bad stuff off the street in Oxford. That's why she overdosed."

Lucy and Sue exchanged a long glance, wondering if Flora hadn't been meeting her tutor as she claimed on the day she drove them to Oxford, but had been buying drugs instead.

"What do you mean, got it in Oxford?" demanded Gerald. "She hasn't left the manor for days. You were in Oxford yesterday, though, weren't you? You were the one who got the bad drugs."

Vickie looked as if she'd been slapped in the face, and then her face crumpled and she burst into tears. "I did and I'm so sorry. I didn't know. How could I know? She was so desperate . . ."

"Finally, I think we're making some progress," said Hennessy. "In addition, it has come to my attention that a number of valuable items are missing from the manor. Isn't that so?" he continued, giving a nod to Winifred.

"Yes. I haven't had time to complete my inventory — I've had to work off an older and incomplete one — but a cursory examination reveals that numerous pieces are missing, mostly from rarely used rooms on the upper stories. These include a small Cezanne, conservatively estimated to be worth at least a million pounds at auction. A rough estimate of the total value is well over two million."

"Oh, my God," moaned Poppy. "We're ruined."

"It wasn't that stupid girl, was it?" demanded Gerald.

"No, I'm sure not," said Vickie, quick to defend Flora. "She was using her trust fund. She told me it was pretty much gone and that's why she had me pawn some jewelry for her."

"This is unbelievable," said Perry, shaking his head.

"Now I'll be speaking to each of you individually, and I want you to examine your consciences and your memories and tell me anything that you think might have any relevance at all. An operation of this scope couldn't take place without somebody noticing something . . ."

It was then that the door opened and the vicar burst in, his face alight with joy. "I have wonderful news," he began, then sensing the tense situation, switched gears. "Oh, my goodness, do forgive me. I was so happy to hear that Flora will be all right. That hasn't changed, has it?"

"No, no," said Hennessy. "The young lady will recover."

"Praise be to God," said the vicar. "And no thanks to me. I should have spoken up about Cyril. I gave him the benefit of the doubt, which I now realize was a mistake."

"Perhaps you'd like to share what you know," said Hennessy in an authoritative tone.

"Well," began the vicar with a sympathetic nod to Harrison, "Hoxton is a tough environment and Cyril did what most people do in that situation — he did what he had to in order to survive. He had a gang of sorts and they started out stealing handbags from old ladies and beating up anybody who wasn't properly British. It was all about the group, about a group being stronger than one person. As they got older, the gang became less important. Some of them had families, a few got sent to jail. Cyril, however, got involved in the drug scene, first using and then selling. I had a run-in with him when he tried to recruit boys from the church youth group and I'm sad to say he was successful with young Eric Starkey. I lost track of Cyril and I must admit it was quite a shock when I ran into him here . . . at the manor, of all places."

Hennessy nodded. "Somebody was so shocked that they killed him."

"But it wasn't me," said the vicar, stepping beside Harrison and taking her hand in his.

Much to Lucy's surprise, the lady's maid didn't snatch her hand away and tears came to her eyes, causing her to blink furiously. Robert then made the sign of the cross on her forehead and gave her a benediction. When he was finished and the amen was said, she quickly wiped her eyes and resumed her previous stone-faced expression.

"But what brought you here today?" asked Perry. "You said you had wonderful news."

"Oh, yes, I almost forgot," said Robert as the sparkle returned to his eyes. "When I was in Hoxton, I made the acquaintance of a prominent couple who became interested in my work with the young people there. I have stayed in touch with them through the years, and asked them if they would like to attend the opening of the hat show. I'm happy to say that Kate and Wills —

"Oh, my," gasped Lady Wickham, collapsing in a dead faint.

Chapter Twenty

All attention was focused on Lady Wickham, who did not regain consciousness for some time, despite Harrison's efforts. The lady's maid rebuffed all offers of help and continued to chafe the old woman's wrists and to wave an ancient vial of smelling salts under her nose, to no avail.

"I really think we have to call for an ambulance," Poppy finally said after some moments had passed. "Perhaps she's had a stroke or something."

"Shall I put in a call?" asked Sgt. Matthews, indicating her walkie-talkie. "I can have the EMTs here in minutes."

That seemed to do the trick. Lady Wickham's eyelids fluttered and she made a great show of regaining consciousness. "Dear me," she moaned. "What happened?"

"You just took a turn. Nothing to worry about m'lady," cooed Harrison. "It was the vicar's announcement that took you by surprise."

"Yes, it was quite a shock," Lady Wickham said, nodding. "Imagine, a black man like the vicar on intimate terms with the Duke and Duchess of Cambridge. I never would have dreamt such a thing was possible."

"Really, Aunt, this is the twenty-first century," said Perry. "The royals are well aware that Britain is changing."

"It's rather more than that," said the vicar, looking somewhat amused. "The prince is committed to carrying on his mother's good works."

"Dear me," moaned Lady Wickham, sinking back on to the pillowed back of the sofa. "Don't mention that dreadful hussy Diana to me."

"Well, it's great news, Vicar, and I for one am terribly grateful, not to mention pleased and excited," said Perry. "I have a great deal to do to prepare for a royal visit." He turned to the inspector. "Do you need me? Is it all right if I get on with things in the long gallery?"

"No problem at all," said the inspector, consulting his notebook. "I think we'd like to begin this morning with Maurice Willoughby." He raised his head and looked around the library expectantly, but there was no sign of the librarian.

"I wonder where he's got to?" said Quimby. "Shall I go look for him?"

"No need," said the inspector, giving Sgt. Matthews a meaningful glance, which resulted in her leaving the library. "I'll begin with you, Mr. Quimby."

"As for the rest of us?" asked Poppy. "I have quite a few things I need to attend to."

"Just don't leave the manor. I'm sure I'll be able to find you when I need to," said the inspector.

"Good," said Perry, taking Robert's arm. "Would you like to come along with me and give me the necessary contact information? I imagine I will have to talk to Kensington Palace."

"I don't have it with me. I was so eager to share the good news that I didn't think to bring it. I'll have to go back to the vicarage and text you," said Robert, casting a questioning look at the inspector.

The inspector gave him an approving nod, then indicated to Quimby that he should follow him to the adjoining little library that had been prepared for the interviews. The group gradually dispersed, going their separate ways.

"I think I'll go along to the long gallery

and help Perry," said Sue. "Do you want to come?"

Lucy, who was curious about Willoughby's disappearance, declined the invitation. She recalled Bill telling her that Doug Fitzpatrick wasn't the man he claimed to be and she had a similar suspicion about Willoughby. "I think I'll take another look at that perennial border," she said, telling a little white lie. "I want to take some photos so I don't forget how they got that fabulous look."

"Planning something similar back home?" asked Sue, raising an eyebrow.

"Not on quite the same scale," admitted Lucy with a shrug, "but I think I could borrow a few ideas."

When she got outside, however, she didn't head in the direction of the fabulous serpentine perennial border that was the envy of gardeners throughout the world, but instead followed the shady path through the woods to a cluster of cottages that housed various manor employees, including Willoughby. The cottages were joined in a row like townhouses, with walled gardens to the rear and a road in front where a few modest cars were parked. Lucy wasn't sure exactly which cottage was Willoughby's, but when she walked around back she peeked through an open gate and spotted a woman hanging wash on a clothesline.

Taking a closer look, she recognized Sally, the maid who took care of their rooms at the manor. “Hi!” she called. “It’s a great day for drying.”

“It is indeed,” said Sally, whose hair was blowing in the breeze. “I have a machine, but I like to dry my clothes on the line. They smell so nice when I bring them in.”

“Me, too,” said Lucy. “I like nothing better than to see my pretty sheets flapping in the breeze on a sunny day.”

“It’s the simple pleasures that are the best,” said Sally. “Sometimes I feel sorry for them that’s up at the manor. It’s all very grand, but they don’t get to enjoy the little things.” She pointed to a flowerpot that contained a lush geranium. “When you’ve got millions of plants, all flowering at once, you don’t really see them, do you? I’ve had this geranium for years and I bring it in every winter and put it out every summer. This plant and me are old friends.”

“I have some like that, too,” said Lucy. “I have my mother’s spider plant. It must be more than twenty years old, since she’s been gone for some time.”

“Oh, I am sorry,” said Sally.

“Thank you,” said Lucy. “You know, I’m

actually looking for Mr. Willoughby. He's wanted up at the manor, but I'm not sure which cottage is his."

"Mr. Willoughby hurried out some time ago. It looked like he was setting out on a hike. He had a backpack and a stick." She paused. "He gave me a big wave."

"Interesting," said Lucy. "Is this his day off?"

"Not usually. He has the weekends. A lot of folks who work at the manor are needed on the weekends because that's the busiest time with the most visitors, but he doesn't have anything to do with them, and I think they like to show the library sometimes, too. They have special behind the scenes tours on the weekends. That's what they call them, and they charge an extra ten pounds." She grinned. "That Poppy doesn't miss much. She's quite the businesswoman."

"Yes, indeed," said Lucy. "Well, I guess I'll be off. It's been nice talking to you."

"Same here," said Sally, lifting her empty laundry basket and carrying it inside.

Lucy walked along, wondering if Willoughby was going for a hike or a quick exit and wishing she could get a peek inside his cottage. She still wasn't sure which was his. She had noticed a few window curtains twitching as she passed, which she took to mean she was under observation.

The trip wasn't wasted, she decided, as she intended to tell Hennessy what Sally had told her about Willoughby's departure. The historian had always topped her list of suspects in the murder because he seemed the most likely person to know about the secret room, apart from the family. She was mindful of Bill's discovery that Doug Fitzpatrick was not the person he pretended to be, and remembered a couple incidents when Willoughby seemed to have let his mask, or rather his accent, slip. She doubted an educated librarian would ask for a *cuppa* tea, and she was pretty sure she'd heard a bit of a Cockney twang once or twice. Not that she was any expert on British accents, she admitted, thinking that perhaps she was being overly hasty in suspecting Willoughby.

There was also the fact of Flora's overdose, which rather changed the equation. She remembered Flora and Desi saying how they had enjoyed exploring the manor when they were kids, and it seemed likely that they might have discovered the secret room. She didn't think Flora could have succeeded in killing Cyril and hiding his body by herself, but she and Desi were close and he might have helped his sister. Or he might have discovered that Cyril was her supplier and decided to eliminate him.

These were the thoughts that occupied her mind as she walked along the path, intending to make good her avowed intention of studying the perennial border, when she heard angry male voices. Most probably a couple gardeners voicing some sort of disagreement, she thought, pausing to listen and recognizing Robert's deep bass voice.

Giving in to curiosity she crept closer, confident that a tall hedge would conceal her, and peered through a gap in the greenery to see who the vicar was arguing with. She wasn't all that surprised when she saw that it was Willoughby, and that her suspicions about him were correct.

"I know you, and you're no more Maurice Willoughby than I'm Saint Peter. You're Bert Winston, right? You were one of Cyril's boys back in Hoxton, weren't you? And you did time for it, too, as I recall. You were delivering a warning to a Pakistani kid, Khalid somebody, wasn't it? You beat him to a bloody pulp."

"Don't be daft," snapped Willoughby. "I don't know what you're talking about."

"You didn't go to Southampton or Reading or any university. You took some jailhouse courses and watched a few movies and you've been putting on a big act. I suppose you had plenty of time to practice a posh accent —" Robert's accusation ended rather suddenly with a series of thuds and grunts.

When Lucy rounded the hedge, she saw the two men engaged in a fistfight. She ducked back behind the hedge and reached for her cell phone, but the only number she could remember was Sue's. She began punching it in with trembling fingers but must have done something wrong because the darn thing didn't work.

The thuds and grunts had escalated and included groans. She knew she had to get help fast, before Willoughby killed Robert . . . or Robert killed Willoughby. Lucy had rarely seen men fight, except in movies and TV, and she found it terrifying. Somehow she had to stop it. The phone was hopeless so she decided the only thing to do was to intervene. She plucked up all her courage and ran around the hedge, yelling, "Stop it, stop it!" at the very moment Willoughby delivered a roundhouse punch that knocked out Robert.

She instinctively ran toward Robert, intending to help him, but Willoughby blocked her and she realized her danger. She turned to run and dashed for a gap in the hedge but soon discovered she had taken the wrong direction and was in the maze. She could hear him panting behind her as she ran, trying desperately to remember if it was three lefts and then all rights or the other way around. Finding herself completely confused, she ran blindly, taking each turn as it came and miraculously found the exit. She was almost there when she took a terrific blow to her back and fell flat on her face. Willoughby's enormous weight landed on her back. She tried to free herself, but his hands were around her neck. Struggling to breathe, she scratched at the hands in vain.

Suddenly, a dark shadow seemed to float through the air, only to land with a thud, and she was able to breathe again.

Scrambling to her feet, she saw Desi deliver a serious punch to Willoughby's jaw and he crumpled to the ground.

"What was that?" gasped Lucy, her hands at her neck.

"A grand jeté," said Desi. "I needed to cover a lot of ground, fast." He shrugged. "Nothing to it, really. I do that ballet jump all the time."

Willoughby regained consciousness just as several uniformed police officers arrived and took him into custody. Lucy, along with Robert and Desi, followed the group back to the manor where several official vehicles were parked. Inspector Hennessy informed Willoughby of the charges against him, namely theft and murder, and he was bundled into one of the vehicles and taken away. They were watching the car disappear down the drive when Harrison was brought out of the house in the custody of Sgt. Matthews and a uniformed police woman, followed by Poppy and Gerald, who both looked quite solemn. Hennessy had his charges ready — conspiracy to commit theft and interference with police.

"What's this all about?" demanded Desi.

"It seems that Harrison and Willoughby were in cahoots, stealing bits and pieces from the manor," said Poppy. "One of the dealers who'd been buying the pieces identified them."

"What about Aunt Millicent?" asked Desi. "Flora rather suspected she was part of the ring, perhaps even the head of it."

"If so, we do not have a case against Lady Wickham," said the inspector, getting into his car and giving the driver a nod.

"Interesting morning," said Gerald, adding a *humph* before marching off.

"Where's he going?" asked Lucy.

"To the barns," said Desi with a smile. "Whenever things get tough, Dad goes to check on the livestock."

Poppy wasn't about to seek solace with the livestock, however, and turned to Robert. "You knew Cyril was engaged in selling drugs and never thought to warn us?" she demanded. "How could you do that in good conscience? And you a vicar, too?"

"I saw him only briefly. He told me his mother worked here and convinced me he'd changed his ways." Robert gave a rueful smile. "Being a man of faith, I took him at his word."

"Well, it would have saved us a lot of grief and sadness," said Poppy.

"I know, and I regret it," said Robert. "I have to confess I am more ashamed of my failure to recognize your librarian, Willoughby. I knew him before as Bert Winston . . . when he was in the same gang as Cyril and Eric, but I didn't make the connection. I think I was dazzled by the grand setting and never tumbled to the fact that he wasn't who he pretended to be."

"When did you figure it out?" asked Lucy.

"It was when I came here. I ran into him in the hallway, and something he said when he greeted me got me thinking."

"What was it?" asked Poppy.

"He called me 'Rev' and it took me right back to Hoxton. That's what they called me there." He paused. "Nobody here has ever called me that."

"It certainly wouldn't occur to me," said Poppy. "But why did he kill Cyril? They were old pals, no?"

"They were, and that was a big problem for Willoughby. He'd created a new persona and would have been terrified that Cyril would expose him, revealing his true identity. In fact, knowing Cyril as I do, I imagine he threatened to do exactly that. He might have demanded a cut of the antiques operation or even tried to blackmail him, which would have pushed Willoughby into a corner. He may have felt that killing Cyril was his only option."

"I feel a bit sorry for Willoughby," said Desi. "He worked so hard trying to be upper class, when we're trying not to be."

"What do you mean trying?" asked Poppy. "I'm a worker bee these days and, as you can imagine, I have quite a lot to do."

"C'mon, Mum," said Desi, wrapping an arm around his mother's shoulders. "Call it a day. I'll take you into town and give you lunch at the Ritz. What do you say?"

"I'd be delighted, that's what I say," she replied, giving him a fond pat on the cheek.

"What about you?" Robert asked Lucy as they watched mother and son walk off together. "Are you all right?"

"I am. What about you? I think you better get some ice on that jaw of yours."

"I will. Good thing Sarah's out today. She'd be furious with me."

"Where is she?" asked Lucy.

"Shopping for a dress to wear to the gala opening," said Robert, before striding off in the direction of the vicarage.

Dressed in a gold silk sheath that left one shoulder bare, Sarah did her husband proud at the opening, but it was Lady Wickham who drew the most admiring glances. She was dressed in a black chiffon evening gown topped with a white fur stole and numerous pieces of diamond jewelry, including a magnificent necklace and an enormous tiara.

"It's the Mucklemore Jewel," said Perry in a waspish tone. "She refused to lend it to me for the show and now I know why."

But even Lady Wickham's glory dimmed when Dishy Geoff, dressed once again as a footman, rapped his stick on the floor and announced, "The Duke and Duchess of Cambridge."

The crowd parted as the Red Sea did for Moses, and everyone, including Lucy and Sue, bowed or curtsied. Even if protocol didn't require bows from Americans, they had discussed the matter in advance and decided that they should adopt the custom of the country they were visiting and had practiced curtseying in front of the mirror in Lucy's room.

Lady Wickham took it upon herself to welcome the royal couple, neatly cutting off Poppy and Gerald, as well as Perry, who were the proper hosts. She rushed forward, coming to an abrupt halt in front of Kate and Wills, plucked up the sides of her voluminous skirt and attempted a deep curtsey that went wrong, and tumbled down onto her knees.

The prince reached down politely and gave her a hand, helping her rise to her feet. "The hat show is called Heads Up! not bottoms up!"

Everyone laughed, even her ladyship.

Epilogue

"The captain has informed me," began the flight attendant's announcement, "that we are preparing for landing. At this time we ask you to turn off all electronic devices. Please return your seats to the upright position, replace the tray tables against the seat backs, and fasten your seatbelts."

"Already," said Sue with a smile, checking her cell phone for texts before turning it off. "The flight home always seems so much quicker."

"In this direction the clock is our friend," said Lucy. "It's only a little bit past six and we left at four, right?"

"Crazy," said Sue, peering out the window as they flew over Boston Harbor.

Lucy leaned back in her seat, mentally reviewing the purchases she'd made in the shops at Heathrow: a bottle of single malt scotch for Bill, Cath Kidston tote bags for her friends Pam and Rachel, Burberry cologne for Elizabeth and Zoe, and a Paddington bear for Patrick. It was that last thought of Patrick, far away in Alaska, that prompted a deep sigh.

"Didn't you have a good time in jolly old?" asked Sue, a note of concern in her voice as she gave Lucy's hand a squeeze.

Lucy was suddenly overcome with gratitude and affection for her best friend. "Oh, Sue, I can't thank you enough. This trip was wonderful. I feel so much better. It was just what I needed."

"I'm really glad you came," said Sue. "It was good to have a friend, considering everything that happened. I wouldn't have liked to be there on my own, what with the murder and everything."

"It was quite an adventure," said Lucy as the plane began to descend. "But now it's back to reality."

"It's good to be home, right?" prompted Sue.

"Oh, yeah, but I'm kind of nervous about it, too. I don't want to sink back into depression, you know?"

"I'm sure you won't," said Sue when the wheels of the jet hit the tarmac with a thud.

"I wish I could be as confident as you," admitted Lucy as the plane taxied to the gate.

It seemed to take a long time for the plane to empty, and there was some sort of problem with the baggage carousel that delayed the arrival of their bags, but Sue used the time to check her messages. She didn't seem to notice that the friendly beagle making the rounds of the baggage area with a Customs officer was taking an awful lot of interest in her bags. That meant a nervous delay at Customs as her case was x-rayed and her stash of Cadbury chocolate bars was discovered.

"The ones in the UK are better tasting. Everyone says so," she told the officer. "Would you like one?"

"Now that would be against regulations," he said with a smile as he handed her the suitcase with the chocolate bars inside. "Have a nice day."

"That was close," muttered Sue as they headed for the big double doors that opened to the ARRIVALS area. "I was afraid that they'd confiscate my Cadburys or maybe even arrest me for smuggling."

"I don't think you should have tried to bribe him," said Lucy as the doors slid open and revealed a crowd of people — lovers and families and friends waiting to greet their dear ones.

"Makes you wish someone was here for

us," said Lucy, who knew they had a long drive ahead back to Tinker's Cove.

"Hold on," said Sue, "I think I see —"

"Patrick!" screamed Lucy, spotting her grandson waiting for her along with his father Toby and grandfather Bill. People stood aside as she ran to embrace Patrick, who had grown so much and was quite the handsome five-year-old.

"I c-can't b-believe it!" she stammered. "What are you doing here?"

"We spent the day in Boston," explained Bill. "We went to the Aquarium and the Children's Museum, all the time following the plane's progress on the British Air website, and then Sue texted us about customs and gave us the green light so we skedaddled over here. I gotta tell you the traffic was brutal."

"No," she said, turning to Toby. "Why aren't you in Alaska?"

"The agency sent me to take a course at the university. It's eight weeks so I brought the family. The house is rented so we'll have to stay with you. In fact, Molly's there now. That's okay, right?"

Bill scratched his beard. "It's going to be awfully crowded. . . ."

Sue looked doubtful. "There'll be so much laundry, and think of the meals and the grocery bills. . . .”

Lucy, who was holding Patrick’s hand, stared at them in disbelief. Then seeing their suppressed smiles, she realized they were teasing. “Oh, you guys!” she exclaimed, rolling her eyes. “It’s going to be wonderful. A full house! I can’t wait to get home. Let’s go!”

ABOUT THE AUTHOR

Leslie Meier is the acclaimed author of the Lucy Stone mysteries and has also written stories for several Christmas anthologies and for *Ellery Queen's Mystery Magazine*. She lives in Harwich, Massachusetts, where she is currently at work on the next Lucy Stone mystery.

The employees of Thorndike Press hope you have enjoyed this Large Print book. All our Thorndike, Wheeler, and Kennebec Large Print titles are designed for easy reading, and all our books are made to last. Other Thorndike Press Large Print books are available at your library, through selected bookstores, or directly from us.

For information about titles, please call:

(800) 223-1244

or visit our Web site at:

http://gale.cengage.com/thorndike

To share your comments, please write:

Publisher
Thorndike Press
10 Water St., Suite 310
Waterville, ME 04901